MICHELLE PRAK

BARREN CAPE

**SIMON &
SCHUSTER**

New York · Amsterdam/Antwerp · London · Toronto · Sydney · New Delhi

BARREN CAPE
First published in Australia in 2025 by
Simon & Schuster (Australia) Pty Limited
Level 4, 32 York St, Sydney NSW 2000

10 9 8 7 6 5 4 3 2 1

New York Amsterdam/Antwerp London Toronto Sydney New Delhi
Visit our website at www.simonandschuster.com.au

A catalogue record for this
book is available from the
National Library of Australia

ISBN: 9781761428432

Cover design by Luke Causby/Blue Cork
Cover images by Sam Farallon and Peter Porter. Cover images modified with the
assistance of AI tools.
Map by Josie O'Malley
Typeset by Midland Typesetters, Australia
Printed and bound in Australia by Griffin Press

The paper this book is printed on is certified against the
Forest Stewardship Council® Standards. Griffin Press holds
chain of custody certification SCS-COC-001185. FSC®
promotes environmentally responsible, socially beneficial
and economically viable management of the world's forests.

To Sam and Able
I promise there will always be a home

MAC
FEBRUARY 2025

When the sun sank, the resort became a museum of dark shadow, and although the night remained warm, the wind gathered strength, scattering leaves and rushing through crevices. Far away, the security gates rattled and other random clinking rang over the empty construction site. My nerves were only slightly calmed by the pounding of the nearby waves, a reassuring white noise.

It was the perfect season for bare-cube living: a raging summer, impossible to be outdoors for more than two minutes without building up a sheen of sweat. The naked floor and walls of my new domain were cooling, and the ocean breeze streamed through the balcony. I paced the area out; it was about five by five metres. The ceiling was high, difficult to know how high, way taller than house ceilings. You might think concrete would be one bland colour, yet it was a variety of patterns and raking, similar to the flat patches of nearby sand. A natural work of art.

With such a blank canvas, I was initially stumped on how to set up. I had bought a cheap inflatable mattress at the hardware store and dropped it smack-bang in the centre of the space, the exact opposite of every other room I'd inhabited. I threw my sleeping bag on top. There was nothing ordinary about this, so why should the furniture arrangement be ordinary?

The lack of plumbing was a problem. There was a secondary room, earmarked for an en suite, with drainage holes and a pipe trailing one wall, but no toilet installed. There was a public toilet by the beach, but using that would mean wriggling under the fence again and taking the dim footpath parallel to shore. It was a long way and another opportunity for me to be spotted – though I still hadn't seen anyone else. Before I went to sleep, I crept into the corridor, feeling intensely defenceless, as if predatory neighbours would emerge. I'd checked every room on this fourth floor, but I hadn't scoured the entire site. Anyone could be lurking. My pulse sped as I descended the stairs, the light of my phone only amplifying the horror-movie vibes. The isolation and loneliness of the resort had attracted me here – now I was coming to terms with the implications. I was on my own and couldn't yell for help if anything went wrong. Sleeping here wasn't only illegal, it was risky.

Outside, I crouched by a thicket. I reminded myself it was perfectly natural to urinate in the great outdoors, although I couldn't bring myself to squat too close to the ground, terrified of creepy crawlies creeping you-know-where. After I was done, I ran upstairs. For a few heart-pounding seconds, I couldn't find my room. When I did, I closed the door and sat against it.

I wondered: was I a genius or a fool? If I was discovered, if this was reported to the police and became public, my friends, family and workmates would find out. It'd be devastating.

I imagined my humiliation; the confusion on people's faces. *What happened to Mac? Did you hear?*

Some might find this setup daunting. Nerve-wracking, foolish. Breaking and entering, and sleeping alone on the outskirts of the city. Yet for me, it was worth the risk. Worth it for the independence, the privacy and the quiet.

There was no landlord, no neighbours, no hosts, no creeps. Nobody I was forced to make small talk with. I was in charge.

There were also no locks on the doors. Instead, I jammed a rubber stopper under mine to help secure it. Did it mean my room was impenetrable? No, but what place truly was?

1

ERIKA
NOVEMBER 2024

Our landlord said she was selling, and gave Mac and me sixty days' notice. Not having our lease renewed was a shock and disappointment, but I tried to see the situation positively.

'We'll probably find an even better place – with neighbours who don't complain about our music so much,' I said.

That optimism turned out to be foolish. We were stunned by rental prices; when did they climb so high? We arrived at open inspections to find a herd of other applicants already queued. The streets were choked with cars, we squeezed past others through doorways.

'Was it this busy when you first went flat-hunting?' I asked.

'Nope,' Mac said. 'This is nuts.'

We stuck to two-bedroom flats within our price range. We'd hoped to remain near the city centre but were forced to the outer suburbs. A lot of the affordable flats were on noisy main roads, decades old, and in drab, multi-storey blocks. Mouldy tiles, dented doors, stained and rippled carpet.

'Let's go for it,' Mac said during one inspection.

I pulled a face. 'You reckon?' The flat was opposite three fast-food stores and the whole neighbourhood smelled like deep fryer.

'The clock is ticking.'

'Okay, babe, you fill out the form.'

Our application was declined. I was both insulted and relieved.

Next, we inspected a maisonette in the northern suburbs, sitting in a rabbit warren of treeless streets. Torn wire screens clung to the windows and topless toddlers watched us from the yard opposite. 'We could get another person for the third bedroom,' Mac said.

'It's a dump!' I said.

'We'll ask for a short lease, and meanwhile we'll keep searching for something better.'

'Okay, fine, whatever . . .'

We were unsuccessful again. The letting agent said the home went to an applicant who signed a two-year lease. Two years in that hellhole!

As moving day approached, we made reluctant temporary arrangements. I returned to my parents' house, not the only kid at home. Of my three older brothers, two were still in residence and showing no desire to move out. It's why my parents didn't oppose my return: what difference would another body make?

But I was deflated, feeling like a failure, schlepping my belongings up the driveway and back into my childhood home. Being there would put a dent in my dating life too, just when I was on the brink of asking Theo out. He was a DJ at Horizon, the city nightclub where I worked the bar part time, and an absolute gorgeous god.

Shortly after we said goodbye to the flat, I saw it listed on holiday letting sites. It'd been repainted and a new stove and flooring installed. Shining pot plants lined the balcony – where had they come from?

I sent the link to Mac and called her. 'That bitch,' I said. 'She lied to us.'

Mac groaned. 'Unbelievable.'

'She's asking for two hundred dollars a night!'

'No wonder she didn't want to renew . . .'

'Look at how she's spruced it up. When we lived there, it took *months* to fix the leaking tap. Hey, we should stay there for a couple of days under fake names and leave a zero-star review.'

'She's not getting another cent out of me.'

After we hung up, I stared at the images a while longer. Mac and I had shared the tiny flat for almost a year, one of the best periods of my life. I was nineteen, studying, and keen to leave home. Mac was twenty-three, had dropped out of uni, was working two jobs and desperately seeking someone to share the bills after her first flatmate left. We cooked for each other, watched shows together, shared chores without any major arguments. Our lives gelled.

At least I had fallback accommodation and a willing family. Mum even baked a 'Welcome Home' red velvet cake. I felt bad for Mac, because her homecoming would be very different.

2

MAC

Sandy blocked the doorway when I turned up. 'The spare room isn't ready.'

My mother knew I was coming, she'd had a week's warning.

'That's fine, we can get it ready now,' I said brightly.

'You seem to think it's going to take five minutes.'

'Don't move mountains for me, I just need the bed . . .'

She huffed and moved aside. Bags draped over my shoulders, I lumbered past. I didn't have a lot of belongings, especially as our flat had come fully furnished. I'd already stashed kitchenware and electrical things in Erika's parents' shed, and planned to keep my clothes here, at Sandy's two-bedroom unit.

I'd called my mother by her first name since early high school. I can't remember the exact day it began or why, although I suspect it was after one of our regular shouting matches. My older sister Georgia still called her 'Mum'.

This wasn't the house I'd grown up in; that was several suburbs away. Sandy downsized after Georgia and I left home, and had the end unit in a row of four. She'd moved further west, where thick powerlines dominated the skyline and the hooting of the Osborne train could be heard regularly. I glanced at the two framed photos on the wall. They both showed Georgia in cap and gown at her graduation ceremony, the first in our family to finish university. Months earlier, I'd given Sandy a photo of me winning two bodybuilding medals. I hadn't seen it since.

Sandy led the way, arms swinging, shoulders stiff. Neither of us wanted this, but thanks to my fruitless flat-hunting, I had little choice. She paused at the entry to the spare room. 'Don't touch anything.'

The blinds were down, the air warm as a sauna. I hadn't stepped into the room in ages. My old double bed, pushed beneath the window, took up much of the space, the mattress invisible under piles of clothing. Two wardrobes shared a corner, so stuffed with packages that they were impossible to close. A card table in the centre of the room was covered in Australia Post packaging, and cardboard boxes full of enamel earrings, chunky necklaces and gold bangles that weren't real gold were stacked on the carpet. Sandy made a living selling crap – sorry, *bargain merchandise* – on Facebook and eBay. When we were growing up, Sandy was a salesperson in department stores. She hated it, used to complain about being bossed by 'clueless brats twenty years younger than me'. As soon as she became an empty-nester, Sandy quit, purchased a laptop and became a Marketplace Professional. I assumed it'd be short term and wouldn't possibly pay a living wage, so I was surprised when she earned enough for holiday bus trips with her girlfriends. She was doing all right.

'I don't know where to start,' Sandy sighed, waiting for me to relent and say I'd go elsewhere.

Instead, I lowered my bags to the floor. 'Where can we move those clothes? Is there space in one of the wardrobes?'

'No! Don't mess with them, I've got them all sorted.'

'Where, then? C'mon, I have to use the bed.'

She ventured further in, not looking at me. 'This wouldn't happen if you had a boyfriend.'

'Seriously?'

'You could live with him.'

'What makes you think he'd be any better off than me? I don't need a boyfriend, I can take care of myself.'

'Doesn't seem like it.'

I drew a deep breath. 'I won't mess with the room, I promise. I'll barely touch a thing.'

That night, I slept on the edge of the bed with the clothes stacked like cotton corpses beside me. Sandy banged cupboard doors and clinked teaspoons until past midnight. I pulled headphones on and lay on my back, fighting the urge to scream. Georgia was lucky to be far away in London. We'd talked about me visiting one day.

Maybe that day would come sooner than expected.

I reached for my phone and visited a flight comparison website, skimming the UK deals. Flights weren't as expensive as I assumed they'd be, and I could nab a seat tomorrow if I was ready. Tomorrow! I was stunned, electrified at how easy it would be to leave this life behind. All you needed was no home, no career, no relationship bolting you down.

I FaceTimed Georgia, taking a gamble that she might be

available. The dial tone sang for a while before she appeared on screen.

'Hey you!' she beamed, still in uniform, hair escaping from her bun. She was a nurse; a Hammersmith hospital had eagerly snapped her up when she arrived.

'Do you have a sec to talk?'

'Yeah, I'm at home. What's up? Everything okay with Mum?'

I snorted. 'She's fine. I'm actually coming to you live from the spare room.'

'Jeez. Don't touch any of her merch.'

We laughed.

'I shouldn't tease, it's awesome that Mum's able to earn a quid,' Georgia said.

'Ha, you sound like a real Londoner.'

'I *am* a real Londoner.' She mock-pouted and I giggled.

'Speaking of London . . . I'm thinking of visiting.'

'Really? About time! When?'

'I'm not sure, I thought I'd float the idea past you first.'

'How long would you stay?'

'I'm not sure about that either, but if I'm ever going to travel, now's my chance. I could backpack through a few countries, then maybe stay and get a job . . .'

'I've been telling you to do that for ages.'

'I know, I know.' I rolled my eyes. 'I have to apply for a passport and a working visa. How long did it take for your visa to get approved?'

'Less than a month, but I was classified as a skilled worker. It might be different for you – no offence.'

I pinched my bottom lip between my fingers. 'Do you think I'll be able to get work over there?'

'With your experience in hospitality? Sure, not a problem.'

'Awesome, that's good to hear.'

'What does Mum think?'

'I haven't told her but she won't care, she'll be happy to see the back of me.'

'Don't be like that, Mac. She loves you.'

'If you say so . . .'

'I s'pose you'll wanna stay with me at first?'

I smiled sweetly. 'I'd love to, if that's all right.'

'Of course.'

'Oh, wait. What about gyms? I'll need to find one asap, I can't lapse—'

'Mac. There's more than eight million people in London. We have gyms.'

'Of course, I'm just so excited. Wish me luck with the visa and passport paperwork nightmare.'

'Good luck!'

After we ended the call, I leapt off the mattress and danced between Sandy's overflowing cartons. *Yes, yes, yes!* Georgia supported me. My impulsive, huge, audacious idea was looking more solid by the minute.

When I'd calmed, I began typing a list on my phone. There was a lot to organise if I wanted to leave the country.

Sandy was at her laptop when I entered the kitchen the next morning dressed in my gym gear.

'Morning,' I said. 'Did you sleep all right?'

She shook her head. 'No, I don't sleep well when other people are in the house.'

I bit back a reply. She was insufferable. Other people? I was her daughter.

She scraped her chair back and went to the sink. There was a planter box on the other side of the window, and I copped a view of her dying parsley and coriander. 'Are you having a proper breakfast or still starving yourself?'

'That was last year when I was preparing for the comp,' I said, 'and you know it's called shredding.' I dropped two slices of bread into the toaster, poured a big glass of milk and stared at Sandy as I gulped it down.

'I guess I'll have to think of something to cook for dinner then.' She folded her arms and shrank into herself like she was standing at a funeral.

'I'll cook tonight,' I offered.

'No, it's my kitchen, I know my way around. Anyway, I don't have your ingredients.'

'You don't even know what I'm making!'

'Mackenzie, please don't shout so early in the morning.'

I stretched past her and dumped the glass in the sink. 'I spoke to Georgia last night. We're making plans. I'm going to visit her, stay in England for a while, find work over there.'

Sandy gaped. 'When did this all come about?'

'I just told you – last night.'

'It's very rushed, what's the emergency?'

'Well, I've got nothing holding me here. When you think about it, it's the ideal time for me to travel.'

'What about your jobs, what are your bosses going to say?'

'They can replace me, easy.'

'Where will you live?'

'With Georgia, at first. Then I'll get my own place. Jeez, what's with the hundred and one questions?'

Sandy slapped her palms on the laminate benchtop. 'You're going to mess things up for Georgia!'

'*Excuse me?*'

'Don't rely on Georgia to rescue you. She's doing so well over there, why do you have to ruin everything?'

The toast popped, but the rest of the room was still and quiet. We glared at each other. Her T-shirt had slipped, revealing a beige bra strap.

'Is that what you think? I ruin everything?' I said.

She plucked her T-shirt into place. 'You should stay here, Mackenzie, get a real job. Don't go running off. You already wasted a year studying and racking up uni debt. You need a good income, then you'll get another flat.'

'I've got a good income!' I said. 'The problem isn't the amount of rent, especially when Erika and I band together. I've told you a hundred times, there aren't enough vacancies. Don't you follow the news? I'm not the only person that's affected – there's a national housing shortage.'

'You have to get in first, Mackenzie, be quick off the mark. Ring the agent directly, ask them to tell you when a vacancy is listed.'

'I've done all that!' I waved my arms.

'Well, you can't run off to London, it's not fair on Georgia. Leave her out of this.'

'Georgia wants to see me, she wants to help me. Unlike you. Why are you never on my side? When it comes to me, you're such a fucking bitch—'

Her chin jutted. 'Don't swear at me.'

'You make it fucking impossible not to.'

'I don't have to put up with your behaviour, this is my bloody house.'

'Oh, well, aren't *you* the lucky one? It's no wonder you live alone, nobody can stand you!'

I raced into the spare room, flinging the door so hard that it bounced back at me. I kicked it in frustration, threw my backpack onto the bed and shoved in clothes.

Whump!

My toiletries bag landed near my feet.

'Watch it!' I said.

'Don't forget your toothbrush,' Sandy hissed.

When I was packed, I hurried down the narrow corridor, not caring when my bags scuffed the walls. 'Thanks for all your support,' I called out.

'You're welcome!'

I reached the tiny porch and Sandy didn't waste a moment in latching the door behind me.

3

BREX

Flynn emptied a can of spag sauce into a pot and began heating it. It was his best meal. It was so damn delicious I wanted him to visit and cook it every night. I stood by the stove and watched the way his wrist bent as it stirred.

'Why are you standing so close?' he grumbled.

'I wanna see how you do it.'

'Again?'

I'd tried to make spag bog a couple of times, but stuffed it up. The sauce stuck to the pan and burned, and the pasta was chewy. Whenever Mum wasn't home, I usually made cereal or toast for me and my little brothers. Tonight, though, I sweet-talked my best friend Flynn into coming over. 'Mum's taken the boys to see their dad, the place is empty,' I told him. 'I've got ciggies and vodka.'

'Okay,' he said.

I didn't invite our other mate Cindi because I didn't want to share – Flynn, the meal, the contraband. I hopped onto the counter and lit a smoke. Took a drag, then passed it to him. 'Don't get ash in my dinner.'

'I won't.' He had a puff before passing it back. He was wearing his grey T-shirt, the one that highlights his eyes, though I haven't told him that. He got blond streaks in his hair last month, regretted it immediately – he's waiting for them to grow out. His thick brows look way dark in comparison. Flynn gives grumpy vibes but in reality he's very chill. He stirred the pasta while I stared at the boiling water in a trance. He'd brought all the ingredients with him because there was fuck-all food in the house, as usual.

There was knocking at the front door.

'Who's that?' Flynn said.

'Dunno . . .' I dropped the cigarette in the drain and shoved the packet into a drawer. 'Wait here.'

Shithead was standing grinning on the front porch in a camo tank top, black shorts and black thongs. My pulse exploded. I went to slam the door but his hand shot out to keep it open.

'Hello, sexy Brexy. I'm back in town, did ya miss me?'

I kept a shoulder against the wood. 'Mum's not here.'

'Where is she, how long will she be?'

'I dunno. You better leave.'

'Hang on, hang on, I came all this way, at least invite me in for a drink.'

'I'm not supposed to let people in.'

'Don't be like that, I'm family.' He shoved past and went to the kitchen. 'Hey, ya got a lover boy here.'

Flynn didn't nod or speak, just stood with the spoon in one hand.

Shithead opened the fridge. 'No beer?' Mum had some in an esky in the laundry but I wasn't going to tell him that. He grabbed the carton of milk and poured it into a glass; it only reached halfway before it ran out. He crushed the empty carton in one hand and tossed it at the bin in the corner. 'What's been happening around here? What have I missed?'

'Nothing.' I crossed my arms over my chest.

'What's for dinner?'

'It's not for you.'

'Rude.' He leaned against the bench, drumming his fingers, his eyes sweeping me from head to toe. 'So, what are you two lovebirds doing home alone?'

'We're not lovebirds,' I said.

He jerked his bald head at Flynn. 'Does ya mum know he's here?'

'Does she know *you're* here?'

Shithead dropped his smile. 'Easy does it, don't get smart with me.' He walked out. A second later, we heard the TV.

Flynn looked at me. 'I thought you said they'd broken up. Didn't he go to Melbourne?'

'Mum promised, said he'd never come back.'

'What are you gonna do?'

'Dunno. Can't stay here.'

We stood by the stove, Flynn stirring the sauce, then the pasta, while I twisted my fingers together. We could hear Shithead talking on his phone. Then he yelled out: 'Ya mum says they won't be home for a couple of hours and you've gotta feed me.'

'Fuck off,' I muttered.

'Oi, I'm talking to ya!'

'All right, we heard ya!'

Flynn pulled out a string of pasta and tested it between his teeth. He had huge buckies, he hated them but I thought they were cute. I fetched three bowls from the shelves while Flynn strained the pasta over the sink. Steam rose as he doled everything out.

'Don't give him much,' I whispered.

'I wasn't going to,' he said.

After Flynn had put the last dollop onto Shithead's serve, I leaned and spat into it. We fell about silently laughing, tears streaming down my cheeks.

When I recovered, I yelled: 'It's ready!'

'Well, bring it here then, I'm a guest,' Shithead shouted.

Flynn added more spit. I nearly lost it, but pulled myself together enough to carry the food into the lounge. There was a motor race on the telly, the air smelled of chemicals and there was a glass pipe resting in the ashtray. He didn't even try to hide it.

'Here.' I held out the bowl with a fork stuck in it.

'Cheers.' He took it from me and began shovelling it in. 'Hey, how old are you anyway? Fifteen, sixteen?'

'I don't have to tell *you*.'

'Well, you've gotta be a certain age to have a boyfriend.'

'Are you deaf? I said he's not my boyfriend!'

He laughed and wiped sauce from his chin.

Flynn was waiting with our bowls. 'You all right?'

'Yeah.'

We sat on my bed watching YouTube, the pasta bowls on our laps. After a bit, we heard a crash in the kitchen as something landed in the sink, then Shithead opened the door without knocking and stuck his ugly head in.

'Hey!' I yelled.

'You two still got your clothes on?' he said. 'Pity.'

'Piss off.' My cheeks burned.

He laughed. I thought everything would be chill when he walked away, but then death metal began pumping from the lounge. I put my bowl on the floor; I wasn't hungry anymore.

'You know . . . you can come stay at my place tonight,' Flynn said.

'Thanks,' I said, 'that'd be good.'

4

MAC

I threw my bags onto the passenger seat and drove, trying not to let my anger provoke me into speeding. Staying with Sandy wasn't exactly my preference, but when it came to family, I had no other realistic options. Dad lived in Bali with his second wife, where they ran a dog shelter. It wasn't something I'd ever expected him to do – and I suppose he hadn't figured it in his life plan, either. But he met Anita on holiday and fell in love with her kindness and her determination. Dad showed me the place via FaceTime. The dogs were all sorts of breeds, colours and sizes, and they barged their way to the phone camera, tails wagging. 'You've done good,' I told him.

'You should join us!' he said.

But I didn't want to intrude on Dad's adventure or be a third wheel. 'I'll visit one day,' I promised.

Now the irony wasn't lost on me: my father sheltered dogs, while his youngest daughter didn't have her own fixed address.

Nan, my one surviving grandparent, was in a nursing home. It'd taken Dad months of paperwork and frustrating phone calls to secure the place for her. Nan had a tidy en suite, floral curtains, a small flatscreen at the foot of her bed. There was something achingly sweet and magnetic about her setup, and I hoped I'd have my own sanctuary when I got to her age.

And then there was Georgia, also overseas. My successful, reliable sister. In Sandy's eyes, I was a fuckup in comparison. I had no qualifications, having dropped out of my marketing degree after one semester. And now I didn't have a place to live, one of the most basic of all requirements for adulthood.

I gritted my teeth. I'd be at the gym soon, and could channel my frustration there. Five days a week, I lifted weights. I wouldn't give up on that, no matter what was happening in my life. I actually had Georgia to thank for this passion. She'd briefly dated a weightlifter, and I'd asked him a bunch of questions and he recommended I try a strength camp. I fell in love with it immediately: the steady, slow craft of it; the satisfying muscle-burn. The gym eventually became my part-time workplace and I counted myself super lucky to cadge the job after one year lifting weights there and becoming friendly with staff.

My second job was at a popular café called Clover's, named after its owner, a former reality TV chef. I hadn't mentioned the termination of my lease at either job because I didn't want worried questions or colleagues feeling sorry for me.

If my UK plans came to fruition, I'd have to give my resignation to two employers. The thought made my stomach twinge; I'd never resigned before. But I shouldn't get ahead of myself.

I hadn't yet applied for a passport or visa, didn't even know what was required.

I parked behind the gym and sat holding the steering wheel, thinking again about what Sandy had said. Was she right, would I ruin things for Georgia? Should I stay away because my pathetic life might be contagious? Tears clogged my throat. I opened my phone and typed a message: *Hey G, are you sure I can come to London? I don't wanna be a pain in the arse. Honestly, you can tell me.* It was after midnight in London, but that didn't mean much because Georgia worked shifts. I didn't wait for a response. I left the car, jogged up the stairs to the gym and swiped my entry card.

There were dozens of members inside and I kept my head down, in no mood to talk. It was Leg Day, and I moved into a corner to warm up with squats and lunges before working through my routine, beginning with the barbells. I moved deliberately, methodically, keeping track of my breathing and watching my form in the mirrors.

I wasn't the only one monitoring my workout. Anton was watching. Again. He was sitting on a bench press, gawking at me between sets. He made me feel like I was on a stage, forced to perform in front of him, and I loathed him for it.

Anton was a relative newbie – to the gym and to weightlifting. Taller than me and skinny, he had a long road ahead to build muscle mass. I'd shown him around during his orientation and over the next few days, he'd peppered me with questions about various machines. In his second week, he'd asked me to watch him attempt an overhead press.

'Sure,' I said. Later, I regretted being so helpful.

Anton had accepted my suggestions, adjusting his stance and the position of his hands gripping the bar. 'You could practise with dumbbells first,' I suggested.

'Nah, I want to do this.' His smile was shaky and I felt sorry for him. It wasn't easy being a bodybuilding newcomer under scrutiny.

I nodded and tried to look encouraging. 'Good stuff, keep it up.'

When I turned to leave, I felt his fingertips rake my arm.

'Thanks,' he said.

The touch was unexpected, bizarre, but I was too polite to remark on it. I returned to the front desk without another word. The next day, Anton stopped by the counter and bought a container of protein powder.

'Come for dinner with me,' he said. Bam. Just like that.

'Thanks for asking . . . but I'm not supposed to date customers,' I said.

'I'll cancel my membership right now, haha!'

'Very funny.'

'I mean it.'

'Well, I'm flattered, it's nice of you, but I'm not interested.'

I'd had six months of bad dating and was on 'a cleanse', as I joked with Erika. But even if I was dating, no part of me was attracted to Anton. In fact, he was kind of repellent.

He'd drummed the container lid. 'All right, but I'm not gonna give up, I'll ask again.'

Over the weeks, I came to dread seeing him. If our workouts happened to coincide, he'd try to soak up eye contact with me, even from the other side of the gym. Whenever he attempted conversation, I gave clipped responses. I was forced to speak one afternoon, however, because I caught him pointing his phone at me.

I stormed over. 'Dude, are you taking pictures of me?'

'No.' Although he denied it, he flushed red. People around us paused to stare.

'Delete them now,' I said.

'I didn't do anything . . . I swear.'

'Delete them, and don't ever do it again.'

Today, I kept my earbuds in and my gaze averted. More members had arrived by the time I finished my routine, the constant clink of weights a familiar backdrop, and Anton was lost in the crowd. I hung my towel around my neck and checked my notifications.

Georgia had replied: *OFC you can come! I miss ya, it'll be so good to see you. Is Mum getting in your ear? Ignore her and get planning!!*

I hugged the phone, almost sobbed in relief. Everything was all right.

'Someone looks happy.'

I startled. Anton was standing behind me.

'Yeah.' I took a step back. 'I just got some good news.'

'That's great.' He was freshly shaved, not a hair on his chin, skin slick and shining. 'You're so cute when you smile.'

I picked up my water bottle. 'I've gotta go—'

'Do you wanna grab a coffee? We could go to that new warehouse place down the street.'

I looked at him, grappling with what to say. It was important to be candid, but I didn't want to be cruel. 'Anton. We already talked about this – you have to stop asking me out.'

He smirked, shrugged. 'Come on, one little coffee.'

'I'm not interested, just leave me alone.'

'Aw, Mac, don't be so uptight.'

I felt my blood pressure rise. 'I'm not uptight, I don't want to go out with you. End of story.'

I spun and walked to the bathrooms, not glancing back but certain that he was watching. I locked myself in a stall and showered, seething under the spray. *Uptight?* In one second, Anton had gone from asking me out to insulting me. Why was it so difficult to understand that I wasn't attracted to him? He might think it was charming to be persistent, but the more he cajoled, the uglier he became.

I tried to push him from my mind as I washed and rinsed my hair. It was tempting to remain turning under the nozzle, but this bathroom wasn't my own. My shift began soon and there was a growing hum of voices as people queued for the cubicles. I wrapped myself in a towel and exited, pulled on my staff uniform and stood by the mirrors for my skincare routine. After work, I decided, I'd hop online and see what was required for a passport and visa application. Fuck Anton, fuck everyone, I was going to London. The more I thought about it, the better the idea was.

As for where I was sleeping tonight? It was time to start messaging friends.

5

BREX

I was sore from sleeping on Flynn's bedroom floor for four nights in a row, but anything was better than being in my own room, wondering if Shithead would try to sneak in.

I rolled over. Flynn was above me on his mattress, sheets bunched around his calves, facing the wall. It sucked I couldn't watch his sleeping face. His wide back was curved under his T-shirt. He was too shy to sleep bare chested when I was around.

He'd strung an old UFC quilt cover across his window, dulling the sunlight and bathing the room red. I checked my phone. Nearly 7 am. His oldies were in the kitchen, speaking loudly so they could be heard over the radio.

Flynn coughed and rolled over. 'Hey.'

'Hey.' I rubbed the crust from my eyes and sat up. 'Wanna ditch today?'

'Nah, we got the science test.'

'That's why I wanna ditch, dummy.'

'What's the point? We'd only have to take it again. I wanna get it over and done with.'

'Pfft.' I flopped back onto the pillow.

Flynn put two big feet on the ground. 'I'm gonna take a shower.'

Soon after, he snuck me a bowl of Nutri-Grain, the milk sloshing from side to side. I'd nearly finished eating when his mother walked in. She was wearing her supermarket uniform and she scowled when she spotted me.

'You're still here?' she said.

I shrugged, a milk droplet sticking to my bottom lip.

'She has nowhere else to stay,' Flynn said.

'That's not true, she's got her own home to go to.'

'But—'

'But nothing. We can't keep feeding her.'

They were talking like I was a stray dog that had wandered in.

She pointed at me. 'No more, Brex. You can visit, but you're not sleeping over again, got it? We're not made of money.'

'Mum,' Flynn said.

'No. Get to school.'

Outside his house, we paused by the letterbox. There were no clouds, no birds flying in the heat, but flies buzzed our faces.

'Sorry about that,' Flynn said.

'It's not your fault.'

'Let's go, we're gonna be late.'

'I'm not going today, I mean it.'

'Well, what are ya gonna do?'

'I'll go to The Cave. Come with me, we can swim.'

He looked away. 'Nah, I'll sit the test. I think I can do okay.'

'Screw you.' I spun on my toes and walked in the opposite direction. He didn't chase after me. After I'd turned the corner, I texted him: *sorry*

nw, he wrote, adding a smiley face. *Where ru going to stay tonight?*

dunno

I couldn't stay at Cindi's. Her parents banned me ages ago.

the cave, I guess. I'll camp out

Twenty minutes later, I reached my street. Shithead's scratched and dented car was in our driveway. Why did he have to come back to Adelaide? We never had money, hardly any food, now he was scabbing off Mum again, and I wouldn't get any sleep as long as he was around.

I let myself in. My brothers were in their undies, watching TV. 'Get ready for school!' I barked. They ignored me.

The kitchen stank of fried eggs. Mum was sitting at the table in her Nirvana T-shirt, Shithead opposite her, both of them smoking.

'Here she is!' Shithead grinned. One of his knees was bouncing so fast, it was like he was typing with it.

I went to the sink and poured a glass of water.

'Hey, I'm talking to you,' he said.

I looked at Mum. 'I thought you were working today.' Her friend Adele ran a housecleaning company and gave Mum shifts every week.

She flicked ash onto a breakfast plate. 'Where have you been?'

'I told you. Cindi's.' I didn't want Shithead to start talking about 'lover boy' again. I finished the water and went to edge past, but he put a leg out to stop me.

'Ah, let her go,' Mum said. 'She's in another one of her moods.'

Shithead took his time moving out of the way.

6

MAC
NOVEMBER–DECEMBER

I applied for a passport and working visa and spent the following weeks impatiently couch surfing with friends. Vikki, Devin, Renata, they all welcomed me warmly, and everyone was supportive and excited about my London plans. Erika seemed startled when I shared the news, but she quickly recovered. 'You're going to love it over there, it'll be really good for you,' she said.

Still, life with friends became awkward. Our relationships took on a new tinge because I was relying on them to house me. Maybe I imagined it, but after I'd stayed anywhere more than a few nights, tension crackled. None of us were able to completely relax and be ourselves because there were constant negotiations to be had: who was using the bathroom; who was prepping dinner; who was doing the washing up. Often, I slept in the lounge, presenting a literal obstacle for people to sneak around. Despite my friends' insistence that I could stay as long as I needed, I was an interloper, a charity case, surviving on the fringes of their success as fully functioning adults.

Once, I overheard Renata and Vikki talking.

'Who's got Mac tonight?'

'Make sure she gets a healthy dinner and a bedtime story.'

They were joking, I knew, but it wasn't funny.

I strived to stay out of everyone's way and avoid being a nuisance. Sometimes I'd go to the cinema alone or linger in a café, reading, so friends could have the evening to themselves.

After weeks of shifting about, Erika insisted I stay with her.

'But your parents' house is already so crowded,' I said.

'Don't be silly, there's plenty of room,' she said. 'And Mum adores you.'

Her family home was in a far leafier suburb than the one I'd grown up in. They had a ranch-style house spanning a wide block, and on weekends her mother pruned flowers while her father criss-crossed the yard with an ear-splitting leaf blower.

Erika squeezed a blow-up mattress on the floor beside her bed and kept me awake, talking into the night. 'I am so jealous that you're going to London. Maybe I should come with you.'

'Aah . . .' I didn't know how to respond. My working holiday was mine to treasure, and I didn't want the burden of a companion.

'Relax, I'm messing with you!' She laughed. 'Maybe I'll visit one day, but not right now. I've got other things on my mind . . . Theo, for example.'

I'd heard a lot about the DJ she was smitten with. 'Just ask him out already,' I said.

'I'm working my way up to it.'

I appreciated Erika's hospitality, but her house was overrun and privacy was impossible. The kitchen was always occupied, and I couldn't use a bathroom without someone knocking on the door. Her brothers stalked the place wearing headphones, eyes glued to their screens and never watching where they were going. Erika's mother had a special sympathetic face she reserved for me, like I was terminally ill. I often hid out in Erika's room, reading my Kindle. It wasn't so different from a jail cell, apart from the incense and the jumble of crystals on her windowsill. Hours crawled by. I relentlessly refreshed my emails, waiting for word of my travel documents. How long would it take? One month, two? Living in limbo was driving me batty.

I needed a break. 'I'm going to stay at a hotel,' I told Erika.

'*What? Why?* Did one of the boys hit on you? I'll kill 'em—'

'No, nothing happened, I just need time alone so I can decompress.'

'Wow. I feel so . . . rejected.'

'Don't.' I gave her a quick hug. 'You've been amazing, thanks so much. I'm the introverted weirdo, you should know that by now.'

Erika's brother Josh had appeared in the hallway as I was lugging my bags. 'You leaving? At last.'

'Josh!' Erika screeched.

'What? I'm not being rude. It's crowded here, everyone knows that.'

I was too stunned to say a word. My face burned.

Erika followed me across the lawn. 'Forget about Josh, he's a dick. He didn't mean it.'

I couldn't look her in the eye. 'It's fine, I'm all right.'

I booked into a suburban motel on a main road, the cheapest I could find, one that I'd passed many times before, wondering who the heck would stay there. The ceilings were low and the yellow carpark lines had faded in the sun. My room reeked of lavender spray, the shower cubicle glass was cracked and a framed photo of a kookaburra was nailed to the wall as if guests would try to steal it. Despite its low rates, I couldn't afford to stay for long. To qualify for a UK visa, I had to have at least $3000 in my bank account and I was scraping awfully close.

Although we'd stopped looking for rental accommodation, we still had active applications and no response so far. That's when I realised something. If I wasn't going to the UK, I could be classified as homeless.

I sat at the motel room's slim desk and searched 'homeless services' online. My pulse quickened just typing the words, like I was confessing to something. Could I actually be eligible for emergency accommodation? On a government website, I worked through an online checklist:

Have you been evicted? *Tick.*

Are you temporarily sleeping at a friend or family members' place? *Tick.*

More questions, more ticks.

I qualified.

It was official, I was homeless. I stared at the kookaburra, stunned.

The next step wasn't as straightforward. Nothing seemed to fit. I read about 'safe spaces' and 'boarding house support'. Saw photos of women with young children; old men with white beards. There was a number to call, but I couldn't bring myself to speak to a stranger. How could I articulate my situation? Besides, there were hundreds of people more needy than me.

I was due to check out of the motel the next day. I braced myself before messaging friends and asking for a bed. Let the merry-go-round begin again.

Sorry, babe, my parents are visiting this week, Renata replied.

I just started seeing someone and I don't wanna make it awkward, haha, maybe next week? Devin wrote.

Vikki and Mason didn't respond at all.

Fuck. What was I supposed to do? Book another motel night? Schlep back to Erika's, where Josh could roll his eyes at me? I refused to return to Sandy's. She hadn't phoned or texted, not a word to check if I was okay. I wouldn't continue to parade my failings in front of her. I needed to widen my options. I opened Instagram to double-check my friends list, and found a follower request waiting for me. It was from someone called @theidealanton. I examined the profile photo.

Oh god. It was Anton from the gym. His grid was mostly mirror selfies, and he had 180 followers, while he was following more than 6000. It was an odd ratio, so I flicked through his list. He seemed to only follow women my age. Hell, no! So many red flags. I rejected the request. When was Anton going to take the hint? I didn't want anything to do with him.

Unless . . . . what if he had a spare bedroom?

I fell sideways onto the mattress. Tears of laughter were better than tears of despair.

7

ERIKA

Mac surprised me with her plan to go to London. I tried to act happy and supportive, but underneath I was disoriented, let down. What about me? We'd been flat hunting together – what was I supposed to do now? Being back at my parents' house was temporary; I'd been banking on living with Mac again, and she seemed to have forgotten that.

I missed our place. I hadn't appreciated it enough. It was no luxury pad – our furniture was old and mismatched, and the fridge gurgled so loudly it woke me sometimes – but it was in an avenue lined with jacarandas not far from the city centre, making the perfect base for our mates to meet before a night out. I missed Mac's daily presence in my life, too. We were very different people but complemented each other; at least, that was my view. She was serious and disciplined, I was the optimist that helped her lighten up. I liked to sloth around but Mac was incredibly fit, a genuine gym junkie whose calendar revolved around her specific workout days. Her arms and legs were super defined – to look at her was a lesson in anatomy – and that kind of shape took commitment. Last year she'd been brave enough to go on stage at a bodybuilding show, the only time I ever saw her in a bikini. I'd tried lifting weights once and couldn't handle the boredom, it was all *struggle, grunt, rest* in a mind-numbing routine. Give me a dancefit session any day.

We'd stay friends, regardless of the flat, but I knew we wouldn't be as close as we used to be. That was depressing. Fuck our greedy landlord, fuck her holiday rental. Thanks to her, Mac had become a nomad and I was back in my childhood bedroom. How could I invite Theo here?

I wasn't the only person at Horizon who had a massive crush on him. The difference was, I was sure Theo was interested in me, too. We always had great banter after work and last week, we'd sat at staff drinks with our arms occasionally bumping. It wasn't my imagination that he didn't pull away.

'Wearing your favourite top again?' I'd teased. It was a white T-shirt with a yellow Andy Warhol banana in the centre, and he wore it regularly.

He'd pointed at his chest. 'Are you wardrobe shaming me?'

'Not at all, I'm sure you're just environmentally conscious.'

'That's right, and I think we could all do with more potassium in our diets.'

I laughed harder than the joke warranted.

Theo was a few years older than me and already a father. I visited his Instagram profile several times a day. Unfortunately, he didn't post a lot of selfies; his feed was mostly pics of nightclub crowds dancing to his sets or abstract close-ups of random items. A few pics showed his toddler daughter and he used #myworldmylife with her photos. He never showed her entire face and I adored the way he protected her privacy. Although I'd searched his profile carefully, I hadn't found any photos of his ex. It was driving me batty, not knowing what she looked like. Some people at the club said Theo wanted to get back with her, but if that were true, he would've done it already.

Recently, he posted a question in the staff WhatsApp group asking if anyone knew of available rentals because the lease on his share house hadn't been renewed. So, we had *that* in common. The replies were sympathetic but ultimately unhelpful. One bartender summed it up: *Good luck, man, it's wild out there.*

True! I typed. *I lost my flat ages ago and I'm still looking.*

That's when an exciting idea began burbling. If I could land a lease, I'd hop onto the WhatsApp and tell Theo. We could be housemates – imagine! Of course, I'd have to pitch it carefully, I didn't want to act like I'd already chosen my wedding dress.

There was one apartment that hadn't rejected us yet. It was on the ground floor of a fairly modern block, and the carport had space to squeeze in two vehicles. Sitting in my bedroom, hopeful butterflies swirling in my stomach, I phoned the agency. I was prepared to beg if I had to.

'Redmond Real Estate,' a voice said, 'hold please.'

It was another minute before the person came back on the line.

'Hi, I'm calling regarding a rental property,' I said. 'It's in Brabham Park . . . Murphy Crescent.'

There was typing on the other end. 'That's no longer available.'

'It's still on your website.'

'We haven't had a chance to update it yet. Trust me, it's been rented out.'

'Oh. We applied for it, were we successful?'

'It says here that a lease has been signed. Did you sign something with us?'

'No, we didn't . . .' I slumped against my bedhead. 'I was really keen on that place, the kitchen was so nice. Could you explain why we didn't get it?'

'Well, we had more than fifty applications. I can't really go into specifics.'

'Did the successful person offer to pay higher rent?'

'Absolutely not, that's illegal,' the agent said.

'Of course. Still, I want you to know, I *am* capable of paying more. I'm a good tenant, a great one, you'll see the reference from my last landlord on my application.'

'You sound like a lovely person, it's nothing personal, the market is just extremely cutthroat right now.'

'Tell me about it. Is there anything new available, anything coming onto the market?'

'Have you registered on our website?'

'Yes.'

'Then you'll receive notifications as soon as more locations are listed, just like everyone else.'

'Okay . . .'

I ended the call before they could hear the tremor in my voice. Kicked at the covers, watching them fall to the floor. I was stuck, so incredibly stuck.

I texted Mac: *We didn't get that Murphy Crescent place*
Not that you care, haha
Where ru?
You're always welcome here, no matter what anyone else says x

There was no immediate response. I wondered where she was sleeping lately. She'd been doing the rounds with friends, but I wasn't sure where she'd landed. One thing was certain – she wouldn't return to Sandy's. They had an awful relationship. I couldn't imagine it; I got on so well with my mum.

Normally, Mac was quick to reply to messages. I blamed Josh, the absolute dunderhead. He had no filter, and made her feel embarrassed about staying with us. I hoped she didn't think I resented her staying, too. It was the exact opposite – I loved having her in the house. It was like the sleepovers we would've had if we'd known each other when we were younger. Since we'd been flatmates, we'd pretty much become best friends. At least, I felt that way. I wasn't sure about Mac. When she stayed with me, she'd been such a great listener, letting me gabble on and on about Theo. She helped me stay sane.

But I wouldn't have her in my life for much longer.

8

MAC
DECEMBER

When I checked out of the motel, I felt more adrift than ever. Maybe Vikki or Mason would text me later and offer a bed. I decided to reach out again in a few hours.

I was rostered on for the café morning shift and arrived twenty minutes early, feeling tense because I was going to share my travel plan with Clover, my boss. She'd lost a lot of staff in the past six months and I was unsure how she'd react to my resignation.

The café sat on a street corner, its southern wing facing a busy road, the eastern side facing a green park with a trickling creek. It was popular with young mothers with prams and huge family lunches.

Clover was in the kitchen slicing fruit. 'Hello, early bird, you're keen! You can start your shift right now, if you want.'

I leaned against the opposite counter. 'Actually, can we talk for a minute?'

'As long as I can keep chopping.'

'I'm really sorry to do this to you—'

'No.' Clover put her knife down. 'You're leaving me?'

'Yes.' My voice was a squeak.

'Why?'

'I've decided to go to London.'

'London? To visit your sister?'

'Yes, but for more than a visit. I've applied for a working visa, I'd like to stay a while.' I didn't bother giving Clover the rest of my story; she'd gone this long without hearing about my housing problem.

'Well, it's understandable, you're young and you want to see the world. Still, I have to admit I'm gutted. How much notice are you giving me?'

'That's tricky. I haven't booked a flight yet because I don't know how long it'll take for my passport and visa.'

'Can you give me at least a month?'

Technically, as a casual staff member, I didn't have to give a lot of notice but now wasn't the right moment to remind her. 'I can't make any promises. It might take a month for my paperwork, but when it arrives I want to leave as soon as I can.'

Clover massaged her forehead. There were grey curls at her hairline that I hadn't seen before. 'This has come out of the blue.'

'Sorry. Do you think the others will take on my hours?'

'Leave it with me for a bit, let me think.'

'Okay. Thank you. And again, I'm sorry, truly I am.'

I threw myself into work, serving coffee and breakfast to regular diners. Some opted to sit outdoors and bask in the warm morning. I hustled to and from their parasol-shaded tables, not minding the heat. I brought a dish of water to a Cavoodle lying patiently while its owner ate berry pancakes.

When my shift was over, I checked my phone. There were still no accommodation offers from friends. I was growing worried. Maybe I should've stayed at the motel until I'd arranged something, but I couldn't waste more money.

I drove to the gym. It was my Back and Biceps day. There was no sign of Anton while I worked out, so at least something was going right for me. As I lifted weights, I felt a familiar calm take hold. There was nothing like this, eking every effort out of myself, pushing myself further. I showered afterwards, then took my place behind the reception desk. In a quiet moment, I messaged Vikki: *Hey girl! Sorry to ask again, but did you see my message last night?*

I watched the bubbles on screen as she formed her long reply: *Sorry mate I should've responded sooner but got caught up. Things are frantic at work and tbh I'd prefer alone time at home, hope that's ok? Have you tried Erika or Renata? My sched will better next week, but anyway hopefully you'll have found somewhere more long term before that. don't hate me x*

Dang. Rejected.

nw, I wrote, *hope things calm down for you x*

My thumb floated over Erika's number. But I couldn't do it.

Then I had a brainwave. I searched caravan parks online, wondering why I hadn't done it earlier. Surely it'd be cheap, and the thought of a mini kitchen and snug bed was a wholesome solution. Perfection!

But I should've known there'd be nothing available. The same people who were competing against Erika and me for a rental had thought to hit the caravan parks long before I did. How about a tent? I scrolled through the list of caravan parks that offered camping, but the only locations that allowed tents were outside the metro area. Fuck! I wanted to throw my phone onto the floor.

Outside in the carpark, I squinted in the sun. It was the type of sizzling, breezeless day where birds languish in the treetops and not a leaf moves. Heat created a shimmering haze over the bitumen. I walked to my car, cranked the air-conditioner and drove from the gym with no particular destination in mind. Thank god for my Ford, thank god there was something reliable in my life, something I owned. It was at least one roof over my head.

As I drifted towards the traffic lights, I was hit by a fresh idea.

I could sleep in my car.

⸻

My Ford Fiesta had grey fabric seats. I tested out the sleeping options. First, the back seat, curled onto my side. There wasn't much space to stretch my legs and the bench had an unsettling backwards tilt. Next, the driver's seat. It was more visible, yet more comfortable, and if I reclined it all the way back and wedged a pillow between my head and the door, it'd be possible to nod off. Being behind the steering wheel was a bonus too, if I needed to take off suddenly.

I chose the carpark of a suburban sports club in Adelaide's west, where I was most at ease. I'd driven past the club often, it was my patch. The venue felt safe: a community facility with a thirsty cricket pitch, perimeter lighting, a toilet block I could use before I left at dawn. The neighbouring houses had neat gardens and multiple cars tucked in driveways.

Close to midnight, I parked behind the low, white-painted clubrooms. The surrounding streets were peaceful and silent. I lay a sleeping bag alongside me – using it for padding rather than warmth. I inched the windows down, otherwise it would have been unbearably hot. Got comfortable and dozed on and off, wondering what my family would say if they could see me. Georgia would call me a bloody nutcase. What she wouldn't realise was, this was a reprieve. It was for one night only, one secretive night of blissful autonomy.

I fell asleep.

And then.

BOM, BOM!

Detonations from above.

My body jerked to attention, heart racing.

BOM, BOM!

Someone was bashing the car roof.

'Hey, whatcha doing?'

Ogling eyes stared from the other side of the glass. I shrank away. It was a guy in a torn sweater and woolly beanie, younger than me. He sat astride a BMX and rested one elbow on my car door. I checked the locks were down and shifted my seat upright.

'What do you want?'

He leaned in, relaxed, as if we were meeting at a birthday party. 'Just sayin' hello. Looks comfy in there.'

A second guy on a bike appeared at my passenger side, wearing a black tracksuit. Shit, how long had they been watching me?

'Got any ciggies?' the first guy said.

'No, I don't smoke.' I reached for the ignition key.

'Wait!' He hooked his fingers through the window gap. 'What's your name? I'm Lenny.'

'I've gotta go,' I said.

'Aw, why? We're harmless, stay and talk.'

I thought I'd prepared for this moment, that I'd be able to jump into driver mode at the first sign of anyone hassling me. I was wrong. My body shook, my fingers were fat while I fumbled with the key, until at last the engine fired and the dashboard lit up.

Lenny, still clinging onto the window, angled himself so his chin jutted in. 'C'mon, sexy, switch off the car, you're gonna wake the neighbours.'

His mate dropped his bike and pushed on my bonnet, the car dipping with the pressure.

'Stop it!' I barked. 'Get out of the way!'

He didn't budge. As I checked over my shoulder and put the car into reverse, Lenny fell away from the window. I was terrified of running over one of them, yet part of me wanted to crush them, too. The tyres slid on gravel as I switched into drive and rushed for the gates.

THUMP!

They'd thrown something and it had bounced off the boot.

I navigated onto the street and pressed the accelerator. Turned corner after corner, not bothering to use indicators, until I reached a major road and its comforting, blazing street lights. Tore along for a few minutes before reducing speed, eventually veering into a giant shopping centre carpark. I stopped but kept the engine running, and covered my face and sobbed. When the adrenalin finally dissolved, I sank back. Only then did I realise I'd been driving without headlights on.

I turned the engine off. Sat watching dawn bloom behind the buildings and the staff of the nearby café arriving for the breakfast shift. Promised myself I'd never sleep in the car again.

9

BREX
FEBRUARY

There was good news, and shit news.

Mum and the boys were going to Port Augusta for a few nights. My Aunty Paula'd had her first baby and begged Mum to come help out. I talked her into leaving me behind.

'I've got school, and high school's important,' I said. As if I cared.

Mum sighed. 'All right, fine.'

I couldn't wait to have the house to myself. I planned to invite Flynn over, but then Mum wrecked everything, as usual. She said Shithead would drop by to check on me.

'I don't need him, tell him to leave me alone!' I said.

'Don't be silly. You're still a kid, you need supervision.'

'He needs supervision!'

'What do you mean by that?'

'He's a creep, I hate the way he looks at me.'

'You hate the way everyone looks at you.' Mum pulled a sports bag from her wardrobe.

'What if he tries something?' I said.

She looked at me. 'Has he ever tried anything?'

'Not *yet*.'

'He's been back for months and he hasn't put a foot wrong. Stop trying to stuff this up for me.'

'You don't care about anyone but yourself!'

I ran to my room and shoved clothes into my own bag. I couldn't stay here. I texted Flynn: *can I stay at yours tonight?*

He replied straight away: *we're having a family barbie, sorry*

I could come, haha

Mum will freak

I threw my pillow onto the floor. I hated Flynn's parents so much.

I rolled up a blanket and tried to cram it into the bag. It wouldn't fit, so I removed the clothes, except for the underwear. Waited until I heard Mum in the shower, then slung the bag on my back and snuck through the kitchen, swiping a pack of cigarettes from the table on my way out.

It was burning hot outside and I hurried to the mall, wishing I had my baseball cap for shade. I stashed my rucksack behind a skip in the laneway. Mooched into Woolies, soaking up the air conditioning. Hid by my favourite column and shoved a Red Bull and a Snickers down my pants. I nabbed a ChapStick on the way out, too. If grades were given out for shoplifting, I'd definitely get an A.

There were three other passengers on the beach bus, and I chose the back row. Stuck my earbuds in and by the time I'd finished the Snickers, we were out of the 'burbs and in the 80 kilometres per hour zone. I hit the bell for stop 96, jumped down the steps and into the blinding sun. Streams of traffic passed in both lanes, and I waited for a gap before running across and into the scrub. I cracked opened the Red Bull and nodded along to my playlist, soon reaching the dunes. Went straight to The Cave and its cool shade.

This was our spot – Flynn, Cindi and me. We'd been coming since last summer and although we sometimes found empty beer cans or fresh smoke butts, we'd never bumped into anyone else here. Our initials were painted by the entrance, mine at the very top. We'd used a spray can that Cindi found in her dad's shed. The firepit looked just as we'd left it, and I sat on my favourite flat rock, opened the new ChapStick and smeared my lips. Folded the cardboard packet as small as I could while I watched the waves. Thought about getting into the water, but I didn't want to go alone. I'd missed all the school swimming lessons and preferred it when Flynn and Cindi were treading water around me.

My phone hummed with a message from Cindi: *where ru*

I wrote: *Cave. Coming?*

Maybe

Please!! I'm bored

All right. meet u later

Then I messaged Flynn too: *forget the bbq, come to the cave. I'm here now, gonna camp out tonight*

My phone was at 15 per cent battery. I thought it was charging last night, but I mustn't have plugged it in properly.

I left my bag hidden in The Cave and moved onto the rocks, watching my feet carefully so I didn't end up on my arse. The construction site appeared. We'd never gone in, the fence was too high, and it looked empty and kinda boring. But I bet there were power outlets inside.

I followed the fence, searching for an entrance, feeling the sweat build up under my clothes. Turned a corner, the beach behind me, one tired foot in front of the other. Around another corner, I found a dirt carpark. There were gates with thick metal chains securing them together, so I walked back the way I'd come. Nearer the beach again, I leaned into the wire, feeling it flex like a trampoline. I tried to get a better look at the buildings. Now that I was closer, I was starting to like the idea of getting in and exploring. If I sent some selfies to Cindi and Flynn, they'd lose their minds.

I studied the wire, meshed together in small rectangles. When I looked up, I felt dizzy.

The fence was high, way taller than Flynn. But I was a good climber.

I kicked off my sneakers and slipped one foot through the grid. It only just fit; lucky I had narrow feet. My toes curled around the wire and I hauled myself up, testing things out. The steel was thin and uncomfortable, but my socks protected my soles a little. If I scrambled up real quick, it wouldn't hurt too much. I tossed my sneakers onto the other side. I was committed now.

Halfway up, my feet were screaming and arms burning. I moved faster. Getting over the top was the scariest part; laying my gut onto the metal and rotating around. When I lifted a leg the whole structure wobbled wildly; I was sure I'd fall and break bones, so I hugged the fence like I was in love with it. I swung one leg over, then the next, putting my socked feet into the wire again. When I was closer to the ground, I let myself drop, which was a dumb idea because I hurt my feet on the landing and fell onto my butt. I sat on the dirt rubbing my sore bits, looking to see if anyone had spotted me. Then I collected my sneakers and put them on.

I was in! I took a quick selfie and sent it to our group chat: *Look where I am!* Then I tucked the phone away because I needed to save battery. I hurried to the buildings. There were three main ones, and the shortest one in the centre was topped with several giant spikes that reached towards the sea. They didn't seem to be part of the building, but a bizarre add-on. I had no idea what that was about, but I was curious to go inside.

On the way, I found a ginormous hole in the ground. WTF? Outside the perimeter, I'd never seen it before. It was like a bomb crater, except the sides were cement instead of dirt, and it was stained with old puddles and clumps of leaves. What were they building here? Nothing made sense. Cindi thought it might be a hotel, but this was a stupid spot for one, so far away from everything.

I avoided the hole and jogged to the centre building. It had wide sliding doors, but of course they weren't working. Newspaper had been taped to the glass. I found a gap and put my nose close. Inside, it was all bare floors and fuzzy shadows. There wasn't any furniture, but a tall counter stood in the middle.

I continued around the side, finding a thin alley between buildings. There was one wooden door. I assumed it'd be locked, but I tried the handle just in case.

And it opened.

I chuckled quietly. This place was awesome, I should've climbed the fence ages ago.

I entered a short corridor with plain unpainted walls, and two open doorways at the end. I stopped to light a ciggie, then chose the left exit, which led to a stairwell. It was muggy in there. I took the stairs down and went into a corridor with a low ceiling and row of closed doors. There were exposed pipes and bright lines painted on the floor, like a sports court. I tried the first door. It was locked, the second and third, too. Interesting. There was something worth hiding down here. I made it all the way to the end without being able to open a single one, but I did find a sign on the last one: *SITE SUPERVISOR.*

Cool.

I finished my cig and crushed it under my shoe. Messaged Flynn and Cindi: *bring tools*

Flynn wrote: *??*

I wrote: *there's rooms we can break into*

He gave a thumbs up.

I returned to the stairwell and plodded up slowly to reach the first level.

Woah. There was a massive open area, the same size as heaps of classrooms strung together. Pillars, thick enough to hide behind, were holding up the roof. It smelled similar to The Cave: dust, dirt, emptiness. I turned in circles but couldn't see any power points to charge my phone. I walked to one boarded-up window, tried pulling the panel away, but it was stuck. I wandered the floor for a while, checking for anything worth nicking. Nothing. Boring.

Maybe I could get up on the roof. That'd make a better selfie!

Back in the stairwell, I climbed to the very top. There was a sign on a closed door:

Roof Access

Authorised Personnel Only.

I pushed the metal bar and exited.

Woah again.

I was out in the open, high above everything. Wind blew my fringe into my face and sunlight pinged off large aluminium cubes with thick vents. Air conditioning, maybe. There was a low wall all around, and I shuffled carefully to the beach side, where the steel spikes jutted out. Peering past them was like being behind giant prison bars. Further on, I saw the familiar lumps of seaweed, the rocks, the dunes where The Cave was hidden. Closer up, the crappy garden was full of sad-looking trees and tons of weeds. I swept my phone around, recording a video: 'What's up? Check me out!'

Cindi and Flynn would be impressed. Again, I wished they were here, especially Flynn. He'd like this view. I couldn't wait to show them later.

The wind tugged harder, and I started walking in a half-crouch, scared I'd be swept away. I aimed for a little brick hut. Wondered what was inside; maybe I'd finally find a power socket. I could sit while my phone was plugged in, sheltered from the weather.

The hut had a door covered with safety messages. It was padlocked. Bugger.

My phone vibrated with a message from Cindi and I opened it as I walked.

I turned a corner and found a dirty white shoe.

The shoe moved.

10

MAC

It was a Sunday, a day off, and I was battling the sharp loneliness of my situation. I'd spent the night at Renata's after begging for her sofa once more, leaving a thank you note on the kitchen table and departing before she even emerged from her bedroom.

I decided to get out of the city. The sun was a bright ball and I took the coastal route south, listening to the radio. The music was interrupted by a news broadcast. Oodnadatta, near the centre of South Australia, was experiencing torturous heat yet again. Forty-five degrees; ouch. The next story was about an escaped prisoner called Curtis Timothy Burbank.

'Burbank was serving an eighteen-year sentence for the brutal 2005 kidnapping and killing of Adelaide man Damien Warlock,' the newscaster said.

I'd never heard of either of them, but then I would've been too young to take any notice.

'Burbank escaped yesterday during a pre-release work program,' the bulletin continued, 'and was last seen wearing correctional services green track pants and T-shirt, with white shoes. He is forty-two years of age, 172 centimetres tall, of average build, with greying brown hair. Police have cautioned members of the public not to approach Burbank, who is considered highly dangerous. If anyone sights this individual, they are urged to get in touch with police via Crime Stoppers.'

If you asked me, a fugitive wouldn't be hanging around. He'd probably fled interstate already.

I drove for another thirty minutes, parking at a beach I hadn't visited in years. Changed into bathers in the public toilet, pulled on a hat and claimed a spot on the sand in the shade of a retaining wall. After a swim, I lay down, mulling over the constant question: where was I sleeping that night? Which of my friends would I hassle? I'd spent months relying on their kindness and patience, and had no doubt they all now dreaded seeing my name pop up on their phones. Except for Erika. I supposed I'd have to live on her bedroom floor again.

Groups of people gradually took over the beach, setting up tents and cabanas, laying out blankets, sharing food. Toddlers were chaperoned into the shallows. One family began playing cricket, the fielders encroaching closer and closer. The ball thudded near my feet and everyone watched as I threw it back. I packed my things. Was there no peace for me? I had no home base, didn't belong anywhere. I dashed across the scorching sand towards the carpark, angry with myself for the tears pooling behind my sunglasses.

Getting into the Fiesta was like entering an oven, the steering wheel too hot to touch. I sat with windows down and air conditioner rushing until the temperature became tolerable. Then I set off for further along the coast, no specific escape in mind. The suburbs thinned until they were replaced by tawny scrub. To my left, advertising hoarding for new housing developments, winery signs and a quarry. To my right, a series of hills with occasional glimpses of glittering sea.

Then, a small, faded sign: *Barren Cape Resort.*

And another: *Barren Cape Resort entry 500m.*

Acting on impulse, my hands turned the wheel, giving me an immediate thrill. There was nothing illegal about taking this route, yet it seemed subversive. Warped trees and bushes crowded in and I reduced speed. After a minute, I neared a sign decorated in dried mud: *Barren Cape Resort. Visitors must report to Supervisor's Office.*

I saw a series of signs with the names of building companies. The vegetation fell away and space opened up; an unsealed carpark. A fence stretched in both directions and two huge, multi-storey buildings brooded behind the wire, their grey backs to me.

I parked, buzzed my window down and listened. Was it surf I could hear, or was I imagining that? Searing air flooded the car, followed by a buzzing fly, but there were no voices, no motors. The coast was on the further side of the complex; mine was the only vehicle. I slathered on more sunscreen, jammed on my hat, and exited. Couldn't see any signs of life, nor any security cameras. Collected my towel and bottle of water, went to the gates and noted the huge padlock. There was a vast gravel space on the other side, shrivelled weeds poking through. Perhaps a carpark for construction workers. Tin signs were cable tied to the fence: notices about private property, hazardous materials, instructions for wearing safety gear.

I meandered along the eastern perimeter and at the corner of the fence, I continued towards the bay. The path's colour morphed from bronze to vanilla. To my left, silvery saltbush vied with golden grass. I could smell the sea. I lifted my feet, taking care over rocks and the occasional furrowed ground. The resort took shape on my right. There was a smaller building tucked between the two multi-storey edifices, all with boarded-up windows. A flat, cleared area, perhaps intended for lawns, bars, a restaurant or two. Listless palm trees watched over everything. You can't have a resort without palms, right?

When the fence ended, I threaded my way through spiky grasses and crested a rise. Laid out in front of me was a cove as empty as the resort itself, about 300 metres wide, with rocky outcrops at either end. The sand was strewn with mounds of seaweed that looked like dormant, hairy beasts. No room for beach cricket here.

What apparently qualified this spot as a 'cape' was the southern perimeter, where a high cliff jutted like a wall into the sea. From where I stood, the cliff appeared unsuitable for walkers. You'd have to clamber over sharp ridges and chasms to reach the lookout point.

I scoped the bay from one end to the other. Thought I heard a car engine, froze. The sun beat down on my head I could feel my bare shoulders smarting. If there had been a car, it'd driven past now. I was alone.

Dropping my things, I stripped to my bathers and waded into the foam. It was biting cold and seaweed swirled around my ankles as I tackled the slick stones. Aha. This would be why Barren Cape wasn't super popular. There were lots of beaches along this stretch of South Australia, most with gentle shores and clear blue water. Not to mention closer to the CBD. Barren Cape was an underwhelming spot in comparison. Maybe the resort developers weren't fully aware, maybe they didn't care. Any guests might have spent more time by the pool or in the cocktail bar than on the shore, and of course they would've had the immense sea views from their windows.

Once I was waist deep, I began to swim. It was glorious to have the sweat washed away. I floated, bobbing with the sea, hair fanning in the water. Couldn't help grinning. A beach all to myself.

I lifted my head and studied the resort. No sign of movement. The buildings looked back at me. Still, hollow, yet not foreboding or unsettling. In fact, I felt sorry for the place. It was neglected, unloved.

It was calling out to me.

11

BREX

I yelped and backed away from the shoe. It was connected to a leg, connected to a man in ugly track pants and T-shirt. I reversed, fast, but he lunged and grabbed the back of my neck.

'Shut up,' he hissed.

'Let go!'

He slammed me against the wall of the hut and pressed a forearm across my chest. He was old, about Mum's age, with greasy hair, and he needed a shave. 'I said shut up! Cool it, I'm not gonna hurt ya.'

He was already hurting me, the dickhead. I tried to push him away but he pressed harder, threatening my breathing. I screwed my eyes shut, not wanting to see him, not wanting to smell his rank breath.

'Stop fuckin' strugglin', stop bein' stupid!' His voice was low, rough as a smoker's. 'I'll let ya up, just be quiet.'

I forced myself to be still. It wasn't easy; I wanted to claw his face, and the pressure of his body against mine was revolting.

After a minute he relaxed his hold, shifting off, but still pinning me. 'Good, easy does it.'

I curved away from him, bracing for a slap. 'What do you want?'

He nudged my foot. 'Give us ya phone.'

'No.'

He kicked my shin.

'Ow!' I removed the phone from my pocket and held it up, hating him.

He snatched it from my hand. 'Battery's nearly dead.'

'I know.'

'Look up.' He shoved the screen in my face and my phone unlocked. 'Don't move.'

I watched as he typed, reciting numbers under his breath. His fingers were decorated in tiny, faded tattoos.

We could both hear the response: '*The number you have dialled is not in use.*'

'Fuck.' He dialled again, more slowly. He was barely taking notice of me, and I looked across the rooftop, thinking about the distance to the stairwell door. It would've been a good time to run, but my legs wouldn't move. I thought about screaming, but we were far away from anyone. Who was he? He looked homeless – and smelled homeless, too.

'*The number you have dialled is not in use.*'

'FUCK!' He glared like it was my fault. 'How do I look up a phone number?'

'I dunno,' I mumbled.

The dude rapped me on the scalp. It wasn't a full punch, but it lingered. My blood boiled; I hated being hit on the head.

'Whaddya mean ya don't know?' he said. 'You can use the internet, can't ya?'

'I've never searched a phone number before.'

'Fuck's sake.'

'Why don't you message them?'

'I don't have *their number*,' he chanted, like I was dumb.

'I mean on WhatsApp or Messenger . . .'

'Do I look like I'm on fuckin' WhatsApp?' He stomped in circles, scratching at his bottom lip, then slipped my phone into his pocket.

'Hey, give it back!'

He stepped close again. 'Who are ya here with?'

'Nobody.'

'Seen anyone else?'

'Nah.'

'Got anythin' to eat?'

I knew it. Homeless. 'Does it look like I'm carrying food?'

Wallop! He punched me in the shoulder. I cried out, grasping the aching skin.

When I looked up, the dude was walking towards the edge of the roof, looking around like he was searching for something.

It was my chance. I jumped to my feet and ran.

12

MAC

After that first lone swim at Barren Cape, I sat on the sloping sand, my towel protecting my shoulders from the sun. I waited for other beachgoers to arrive, but the cove remained deserted. Two jet skis buzzed past in the distance, neither slowing down nor showing any sign of interest. Like the tall, echoey buildings behind me, the beach was effectively abandoned.

I shaded my phone and did an internet search: *Barren Cape resort.*

A flood of news articles appeared. A few years ago, a consortium of Australian and international developers decided it was an excellent idea to build a luxury resort at Barren Cape, 40 kilometres south of Adelaide. They were wrong. A global pandemic arrived, travelling was restricted, then trade was interrupted and the cost of building projects soared. When the developers tried to sell, nobody wanted to buy. The cost of tearing down and removing the half-finished resort was almost as exorbitant as the build.

The most recent news articles were months old, announcing a court case between the developers, local council and state government. There was a story about an action group that was calling for the place to be torn down. A community spokesperson was quoted: 'We were promised a jewel on our coastline but instead we're left with Soviet-era concrete blocks spooking everyone.'

I found the official website for the resort and read marketing spiels spruiking unrivalled luxury and attention to detail. The resort would boast a connected string of swimming pools; a day spa with professional beauty staff; a vegan and gluten-free café and five-star restaurant; one garden bar and one rooftop bar. A sunken lounge in the lobby, plus an amazing hanging fireplace. There were mock-ups of the guest rooms. One block, called Callista, would be dedicated to opulent two-storey suites with enormous floorspace and a spa bath on each balcony. The other, to be called Semira, contained more standard hotel rooms and was four storeys, more of an apartment block versus Callista's more spacious penthouses. I wasn't sure of the significance of the names; perhaps the quirky marketing was part of its demise. There were artist's impressions of the interior décor: a lot of gold and mild green hues – glitz meets aloe vera.

I left the website and found a map of the area, zooming in and out and reminding myself of the nearby towns and holiday sites. Barren Cape was set between two hotspots: Carnaby and Mistle Beach. As I expected, it was the duller, overlooked cousin. For one thing, it was by far the shortest stretch of sand and a catchpoint for seaweed. And it was hemmed in by steep hills and thick deposits of limestone, which explained the lack of suburban sprawl.

I pulled my T-shirt and shorts on and returned to the fence. The temporary panels – if they could be called temporary after being in place for so long – were two metres high, each supported by yellow concrete footings. I moved in the opposite direction from where I'd arrived, onto a concrete path running parallel to the beach. It'd be too kind to call it an esplanade, but it was wide enough for pedestrians and cyclists to share. It ran past a public toilet and I checked inside: three cubicles, three sinks and two showers. Cold water only. The stainless steel was bright, barely used. I kept walking.

The sea-facing side of the fence ended at bush-covered hills that rose as a natural barricade. Lower down, nearer the sand, the cove was covered in rocks. Hot, I had another swim, floating and thinking.

I returned to my towel and phone. Almost shrieked when I saw a person walking towards me.

They approached from the south, walking just out of reach of the incoming tide. Short in stature, wearing a baggy blue top and shorts. Cropped hair – apart from a long fringe that whipped in the breeze, which they regularly pushed out of their eyes. As they neared, lining up with me, I could see it was a teenager. How did she get here? We were a long way from the suburbs, although there was a bus route nearby. I had a twinge of sadness. Why was this kid walking this remote bay alone?

That's what made me lift a hand in greeting.

She waved back.

I imagined she'd continue walking and was surprised when she approached.

When she was within speaking distance, she said: 'Hi.' She looked to be fourteen or fifteen and was tearing a strand of seaweed apart with black-painted fingernails.

'Hello,' I said.

'Haven't seen you before,' she said.

I smiled. 'I haven't seen you, either.'

She didn't smile back, her gaze avoiding mine. 'You going for a swim? I can mind your stuff.'

'Nah, that's all right,' I said, 'I've already been in.'

'You can trust me.'

The cheek of the kid, I'd only just met her! 'What about you – have you been swimming?'

'Not with old perverts like you around.'

We chuckled. She had tiny teeth and her loose Quiksilver T-shirt hung over her shorts.

'You here alone? Where are your friends?' I asked.

'Where are yours?'

'Ha, fair enough.'

'I like being here alone.' She let the seaweed drift to the sand. 'Got anything to drink?'

I opened my pack and offered my water bottle. She guzzled half of it, then jabbed a thumb at the buildings beside us. 'Do you go in there?'

'Of course not. You?'

'No. That would be illegal.' She shifted closer and I caught the scent of cigarettes. 'Do you have any money I can borrow? My metro card's run out.'

I looked at her. 'Are you for real?'

'Hundred per cent. I can't get home.'

'I don't even know you.'

'My name's Brex, short for Brexleigh. *Do not* ask me about the world's worst bogan name.'

'You want bogan names, you should hear my middle name.' This wasn't something I shared often, yet it felt right in the moment.

'Go on then,' Brex said.

'Promise not to give me shit.'

'Spill!'

'Starlette.'

'What now? Scarlet?'

'No. *Starlette*. S-t-a-r.'

Brex cackled, tilting her head back. 'No way!'

'It's true,' I said. 'My parents must've thought . . . oh, god knows what they were thinking.'

'I'll call ya Star for short.'

'Well, it's marginally better.'

She angled her head like an appealing puppy. 'So how about it, Star? Got any spare change . . .'

'It feels like I'm being scammed,' I said. 'I met you sixty seconds ago and you've got your hand out.'

'It's only four bucks, it wouldn't make any difference to you.'

'I'm not a Boomer, I don't carry cash with me.'

She dropped her smile and stared intently, eyeliner too thick on her lower lids. 'Looks like I'm hitchhiking then. I wonder who'll pick me up. I hope it's someone nice and not someone *murdery*.'

'What would you have done if you hadn't met me on the beach? How were you planning to get home?'

'I thought I had more credit on my metro card, honest. Mum was gonna top it up for me – she's always forgetting. She says I use it too much, that I should get a job.'

I nodded. 'My mother made me get a job when I was in high school. It was a good thing, having my own money, but at the time I hated it.'

'Mums suck.'

It was my instinct to correct her, but I checked myself. 'Yeah. They do.'

I sighed, dug into my wallet and touched my emergency fifty dollar note, folded into quarters. It was a lot of money, but the only cash I had. Did I really want to hand it over to a stranger? When I glanced at Brex, all the sass had disappeared. She looked worried and defeated, and was far too young to look like that.

Slowly, I withdrew the note. She lit up.

'This is all I have apart from my credit card,' I said.

'I accept card,' she joked.

'You better use this for transport and not smokes.'

'I will, I promise, you're the best, a lifesaver!' She snatched the fifty and tucked it into a bra strap. 'Thanks, girlfriend.'

My fingertips tingled after her swift move. It was like I'd just been robbed. 'Put *all of it* on your metro card, okay?'

'Aw, and I was gonna buy crack.'

'I'm serious.'

Brex began walking. 'I gotta dip. See ya, *Starlette*.'

'See ya, *Brexleigh*.'

She headed for the rocky end of the beach. It was the opposite direction to the road and bus stop.

'Where ya going?' I called out.

'I like going this way.'

'Okay . . .' The kid knew the region better than I did.

Of course, there was a good chance she'd spend my fifty on something else. I chuckled, thinking about her audacity. At her age, I never would've wheedled money from a stranger. I wouldn't be out here by myself, either. She'd said she enjoyed being alone at Barren Cape. What was she hiding from? I would've liked to tell her that school doesn't dictate what happens in your life, you'll soon forget the bitches and the bullies. But that was making assumptions, and I reckoned she would've teased me if I tried to dispense wisdom. Anyway, what did I know? I was a homeless university dropout.

I wondered if Brex had ever attempted to break into the resort. She struck me as the type of person who would try.

I sat and checked my phone. There was a text waiting from Erika: *Where ru staying tonight?*

I ignored it, instead searching online for the nearest hardware store. There was a regional outlet a quarter of an hour away. My skin tingled. Was I really doing this? Was I really going to break in?

13

BREX

By the time Flynn and Cindi got to The Cave it was way past dinner. I'd finished crying about the old man stealing my phone, but I was still fuming. I thought about all the names I'd call him if I ever saw him again. How dare he touch me, how dare he keep my fucking phone! Mum gave it to me when she was finished with it and there was zero chance of her replacing it. The fifty dollar note that I'd scammed off the chick on the beach made me feel better. So slick and pretty. I studied the portraits on both sides, the transparent strip with a swan etching. Still, it wouldn't get a replacement phone.

Cindi scowled when she saw me. 'What's up with you? Why haven't you been answering our messages?'

I hung my head and tried to hide my bloated face. 'A man nicked my phone.'

'What man?' Flynn said.

I shrugged. 'I dunno, a homeless dude. I climbed the fence

and went inside one of the buildings. I was up on the roof and he surprised me, grabbed me.'

Cindi gasped. 'Did he hurt you?'

'Yeah! He punched me, kicked me.' I showed the horrible bruise on my shin.

She lowered her voice. 'Anything else?'

'Nah. I ran away.'

Flynn put his backpack on the ground and I heard the clink of metal. He'd remembered the tools. He stepped close and hugged me. He was wearing his usual long T-shirt and Adidas shorts, and I could feel dampness on his back. I wanted to stay cocooned, but he stepped away.

'Is he still in there?'

'I dunno, maybe.' I opened the pack of smokes and handed them around.

'What does he look like?' Flynn said. 'Was he alone?'

'Yeah, he was alone, but he used my phone to try to call someone. It didn't work.'

Cindi sucked on her ciggie, then coughed. 'What are we gonna do?' She was looking at Flynn.

'We're gonna go in there and get her phone back,' he said.

'What if he's not by himself anymore?'

Flynn hitched one shoulder. 'Dunno. Let's just see what we see.'

I dabbed my nose on the collar of my T-shirt. 'Okay, this way.'

We walked over the rocks. The tide was low and the crossing was easy: there were no pools to avoid. Though it was later in the day, it hadn't gotten any cooler. The sun would be up for another few hours; my mouth was dry and skin sticky.

I led them past the toilet block to the fence.

'How did you get over?' Cindi asked.

'Took my sneakers off and got a grip with my toes.'

'Ha ha, ya bloody koala.'

We all ditched our cigarette butts. Cindi got her phone out to film me. I threw my shoes over then clambered up, faster this time, because I'd practised. Cindi went next, going up fast because she's what Mum calls 'skinny as a rake'. She was wearing a red lacy singlet that she'd been eyeing off in Valley Girl last week, plus belted shorts, and when she landed on the dirt she spent time dusting off the outfit and fixing her straps. Cindi's parents gave her money for clothes. I hated her for it, even if she was one of my besties.

'I dunno if I can do it,' Flynn said.

'Sure ya can,' I said. 'Use ya muscles.'

'Don't film me.'

Cindi put her phone away.

I checked over my shoulder, up at the roof, but couldn't spot the old dude.

'I'll chuck my bag first,' Flynn said. 'Watch out.'

He gripped the top handle and spun like an Olympic hammer thrower. When he let go, it collided with the fence, still on his side. Cindi and I couldn't help ourselves, we fell about laughing. She did her usual snorting.

'I'm sorry.' She crossed her legs. 'But that was too funny.'

Flynn told us to fuck off. On his second try, the bag cleared the fence and raised dust on its landing.

'Yay!' Cindi said.

Flynn's foot wouldn't fit in the wire grid. 'See?'

'Take your shoes off.'

'That won't help.'

I looked around. There was nothing to stand on, nothing to boost him over.

'Give it a go,' Cindi said.

Flynn cricked his neck, tilting his head one way, then the other. He walked towards the beach and swung his arms in a warm-up. Then he ran, throwing himself at the fence so hard it sent jangling shockwaves along the wire. He got a metre high before his feet lost traction under him and he slid off.

'You can do it,' I said.

He went through the same prep routine, glaring at the wire like he hated it.

BAM! He jumped on again, the toes of his sneakers propping on the horizontal struts. Scramble, scramble, hands clawing. He dragged himself onto the fence top, and Cindi and I urged him on.

'You got this!'

'Almost there.'

Flynn dangled his legs over, lowered himself closer to earth, then dropped. He staggered for a sec, but we were running and ready to grab him.

'Yes! Told ya!' Cindi said.

Flynn straightened his clothes. 'There's no way I can climb back out. We live here now.'

We all giggled. Hours ago, the world sucked and I hated everything, but now something bubbled in my chest. I couldn't stop smiling and I wouldn't want to be anywhere else.

'Come on, this way,' I said. 'Keep a lookout.'

Cindi pointed at the tallest building. 'Are we going in there?'

'Nah, the middle one.'

We entered the thin laneway I'd found before. I pushed the door open and we snuck in.

'I thought you said we needed tools,' Flynn said.

'There's locked doors in the basement,' I explained. 'We'll look later. Let's get my phone first.'

As we climbed the stairs, I heard the tapping of their sneakers behind me. I paused at the roof door. 'You ready?'

'Yeah,' Cindi said.

'Be careful,' Flynn said.

The wind blew hard when we exited. With so much bright sky – plus the sea ahead of us – it was like being trapped inside a blue dome.

'Wow, sick.' Cindi slipped a tie from her wrist and pulled her hair back.

Flynn and I scanned the rooftop. 'Can ya see him?' he asked.

'Nah,' I said.

Cindi went to towards the steel spikes and gazed through. 'What is this? It's epic.'

Flynn went to join her.

'Watch where you're stepping,' I said.

There was scuffling behind me.

Before I could turn, a thick arm roped my neck and yanked me backwards. It felt like I was falling through space with no control. I could hardly breathe.

The old dude hissed in my ear: 'You dumb bitch.'

14

MAC

The tools were cheaper than I'd expected. I paid at the hardware store self-checkout, juggling everything in two arms as I left. At a nearby supermarket, I bought more bottled water and snacks. Put them in the car, then ducked back to the store and grabbed a two-pack of toilet paper.

I stopped for a burger and sat at a high bench with a view of a carpark. The sun winked between Norfolk pines, turning them into picturesque silhouettes. People rushed past, ferrying bags of food; people with someplace to be. People with homes.

At seven o'clock, I began to drive. I didn't want to park my car right outside the resort gates because that would create suspicion. Eventually I found a suitable location – a layby marked by a blue tourist sign. It was nothing more than a semicircle loop away from the road. There were no facilities besides two picnic benches, and no other cars. I parked near the exit. It'd still be light for a while, so I remained behind the steering wheel, sitting tensely and trying to read an ebook.

It was twilight when I assembled my new supplies and strung bags over my shoulders. I set out, trudging on the gravelly verge, wincing at the traffic speeding past and hoping I didn't attract curious glances. It took fifteen minutes to reach the resort sign. I waited for the road to quieten before I took the resort road. It became darker, crickets sang, the drone of vehicles fell away.

I arrived at the fence and scanned one last time for cameras or security alarms, thinking I might see red lights blinking. Maybe I was hoping for something to talk me out of this craziness. But it was all clear. Drained of sunshine, the site didn't look so harmless anymore. There were too many concealing shadows and the wind had picked up, wailing like a warning between the buildings. I took a deep breath and continued towards the sea, stopping midway, my heart pumping like I'd just stepped off the treadmill.

Shit, shit, shit.

I removed a spade from my bag, still bearing its store stickers. The fence grid was too compact to slip a shoe into; impossible for me to climb. So I was going under.

I cringed at the sharp ringing of pebbles as I dug. The ground was too hard and dry to penetrate, so I relocated ten metres further on. The soil was more cooperative there, although it still took a massive effort. My palms hurt, pummelled by the effort. I didn't intend to dig far, only enough to squeeze through. When it was time to test the gap I'd made, I put the shovel to one side and checked my surroundings again. Then I lay facing the early stars. Wriggled backwards head first, scrunching my face and holding my breath, waiting to be showered with dirt. I got as far as my boobs; they wouldn't fit. I withdrew and dug deeper and, on the second try, I made it through. I experienced such a rush that I fist-pumped the air – not something I'd normally do.

I swore. I'd left my gear on the other side of the fence. Real clever. I knelt, scrabbled for the shovel and pulled it towards me. I couldn't reach anything else and had to slither under to retrieve it all.

When I was done, I dusted myself off and stared at the massive buildings. In the fading light, they didn't look as benign as they had that afternoon. I pulled on my backpack of tools, crouched like a commando and raced towards the nearest structure, a small shed. What was it used for – temporary storage, utilities? I sheltered against it for a moment, acknowledging the terror in my stomach, the craziness of the situation. But I'd come this far, I had to keep going. I sprinted to the first of the two enormous buildings, Callista, earmarked for the luxury suites, all blank walls and balconies towering above me. Grey, brooding, more of a dystopian prison than a pamper palace. To my left was a sinuous canyon, which I assumed was the swimming pool I'd seen in the online marketing material. There was a wide lagoon shape at its centre, then lanes peeled off into teardrops at either end. I supposed there'd be a variety of depths, though nothing seemed an obvious children's pool. Perhaps this was intended to be an adults-only resort.

I dashed over open ground until I reached the narrow central building – the lobby and administration area, according to the website. Angular metal poles decorated the roof in a specially commissioned industrial artwork, but the V-shape made me think of robotic wings that were set to lift the lobby away.

It was a good distance until I reached the northern block, Semira, where low concrete walls jutted at regular intervals. The plan had been for the ground floor rooms to have private courtyards; the artist's impression showed gleaming decking, hammocks, outdoor showers and gardens of healthy succulents. I hid in the final, dusky courtyard and settled my breathing. Both the doorway and window were boarded up and there was a slight ceiling overhang. In the dying light, I read an orange and black sticker: SECURITY. *This area is under 24-hour surveillance.* Pipes protruded from bricks.

My ponytail had become loose and hair strands tickled my neck, annoying and unnerving. I retied it as I sheltered against the building, still warm from the day's heat, thinking about abandoning my scheme. At this point, I'd only dug a ditch. If I was caught, that wouldn't be so terrible, but if I broke into a building that was a whole different ball game. I could face criminal charges.

Curiosity and determination spurred me on, however. This wasn't the crime of the century; if a guard spotted me there was a good chance they'd simply march me off, not bother to even write a report.

Of course, there could be other people here besides guards, but they'd be equally worried about me. Right?

I approached the nearest window and squinted at the plywood. It'd been tacked to the frame and didn't look completely impenetrable. My new pair of pliers came in handy; I used them to wrest the nails away. Once the board was removed, my courage wavered. Palm fronds scraped eerily nearby, and the yawning space in front of me was suddenly untrustworthy. Was I sure this was something I wanted to do?

I thought about all the sofas I'd slept on. My awful night in the car.

Not giving myself a chance to second-guess, I climbed over the ledge.

I was in.

The chamber was square, generous in size, aided by the extraordinarily high ceiling. It was also tepid and stuffy. I stood while my senses adjusted. It didn't smell unclean – rather, there was an absence of scent. Maybe a smatter of dust, far-off salty sea. Grit raked my sneakers. The walls and floor were unfinished concrete. I edged through a gaping doorway into an even darker space and the beach became hushed. A corridor stretched away to my right, more of an underground tunnel. I flashed my phone light into the murkiness and spied open doorways. Doors hadn't been installed here. Each room was designed to face the sea. There was no rubbish, no graffiti on the walls, no mattresses or any signs of squatters that I could imagine. As I'd thought, this was too far from the city. Forgotten.

Available.

To my left, a couple of metres away, a printed map and safety posters were stuck to a wall. One of the posters displayed the staircase symbol. I entered. It didn't smell of urine like carpark stairwells often did. It was airless and close, yet clean. Another good omen. I climbed with one hand on the metal rail, trying to ignore the frightened quivering in my quads. I reached the first level and discovered another dim corridor of open doorways. The second level was the same. At each ascent, the atmosphere became warmer and my skin clammier.

The top level was different from the rest.

My phone light revealed a long series of closed doors. Actual doors. I stopped in surprise. This level was nearer to completion than the others.

I grasped the first handle, held my breath as it turned.

The room was a duplicate of the one on the ground floor, with wood panelling covering the tall window. I retreated, moving on until I reached what I estimated was the centre of the building. Stepped into the room and shut the door behind me.

I felt a mixture of delight, pride, relief. The security fence, the warning signs, shuttered windows – they hadn't kept me out. There was still an underlying dread, but I ignored it. I walked cautiously in the gloom towards the far wall. Selected my pliers again, and used them to ease one panel away.

It revealed the balcony.

'Wow.' The sky was huge and glittering, reserved only for adventurers, only for people willing to risk it. Like me.

I pressed a shoe to the deck, testing its stability. It was solid, so I ventured out, holding the balustrade tightly. I had a feeling of being on a precipice where no one had stood before. The balcony was about four metres long and only a metre-and-a-half wide. I tuned into the *whish, whoosh* of the waves, rhythmic and hypnotic. Directly below, the resort garden was an overgrown meld of indecipherable shadow.

Far away, Adelaide glowed, home to more than a million people. Except me.

15

BREX

My fingers clung to the arm choking me, trying to tear it off. It was impossible to speak. I saw a flash of green, smelled the recent familiar stink. It was the old man who stole my phone.

Flynn spun around. 'Fuck.'

Cindi shrieked. 'Let her go!'

'Stay back.' The man clinched me harder. 'Did ya call the cops?'

'Cops? No, but we will.'

My heels slid beneath me as I fought to get loose. His fingers threaded through my hair, yanking so hard that I yowled.

'Stop, you're hurting her!'

'Shut ya trap.'

Flynn inched forwards, Cindi too.

'Stop fuckin' movin',' the dude snarled.

'What do you want?' Flynn said.

The arm tightened again. 'Take me to ya car.'

'We're kids, we don't have a car.'

'Bullshit.'

'It's true!'

'Phones. I wanna see 'em, chuck 'em on the ground.'

'You're not having our phones too,' Cindi argued.

'And the money. Give us ya wallets.'

Slowly, Flynn lowered his backpack.

'Don't give him a single thing!' Cindi said.

I felt the rise and fall of the bloke's chest as I struggled with my own breathing. My eyes were bulging. I tried to communicate with the others but couldn't form any words.

Flynn had unzipped his bag, but he didn't remove his phone or wallet. Instead, he pulled out a pair of bolt cutters, long and hefty.

'Don't ya fuckin' try me, I'll rip her head off.' The man tugged me backwards.

The pain was excruciating; his warning felt too real.

'I've killed before. You're just a bunch of stupid kids.'

I didn't think it possible, but the chokehold tightened even further. My vision went blurry.

Cindi was hopping from foot to foot behind Flynn, almost dancing. I'd seen it before. She was riled up, about to freak out, nails digging into her palm. 'Let's get him,' she muttered.

I stopped struggling and raised my feet, no longer supporting my own weight. Pain shredded my neck; my scalp scorched where his fingers still caught my hair. The dude sagged and swore, tried to hoist me. We lurched and he fumbled his grip.

Oof!

Flynn bowled into us and we all fell. My left side slammed onto concrete and I cried out. The dude released his hold and

I jabbed an elbow into him before rolling away. Cindi flew past me and kicked him. Flynn climbed onto his chest and raised the bolt cutters skyward. I turned away, curving myself like a snail.

One, two, three, four . . . Sickening squelches.

'Get him!' Cindi yelled.

. . . five, six.

CLANG. The bolt cutters fell to the ground.

When I looked, Flynn was still sitting on the dude, who was flat on his back and unmoving. Cindi toed his legs. There was no response.

Flynn climbed off, backpedalling on his arse and kicking out as if spiders were crawling after him.

I rushed to his side. 'Are you okay?'

His mouth hung open but no words came out. His eyes were round as Poké Balls and there were flecks of blood on his cheek.

'Here.' I used a sleeve to clean it off.

Cindi looked down at the guy. 'Oh, fuck.'

'Is he okay?' I said.

'Dunno, I'm not touching him.'

She joined us and we sat in a huddle, listening to our frantic breathing.

'So, that was him,' Cindi said.

'Yeah.'

Flynn sniffed and wiped his eyes. 'He's wearing a Corrections uniform.'

I glanced at the green outfit, the cheap slip-on shoes. 'You mean, like, jail?'

'Yeah. My uncle wore the same thing when he was on remand.'

'Do you think he, like, escaped, or did he just get let out?'

'Doesn't matter. Now I'm the one going to jail,' Flynn said.

'No way, not gonna happen.' I squeezed his hand. It was hot and damp. I stared at the distant ocean and tried to think of all the ways we could get rid of a body.

16

MAC

On my first night, I found it difficult to sleep. Not surprising, really.

The inflatable mattress was double-bed size but I hadn't inflated it enough, especially for my weight. It sank a little, becoming an overly warm cocoon. And of course, I was anxious. Despite the wedge beneath the door, I lay awake, worrying about someone stumbling across my hideout and asking what the hell I was doing; a security guard throwing me out, maybe reporting me to the police. Even worse, being threatened, robbed or assaulted. I reassured myself that the resort was empty and of no interest to anyone. Tried to think cosy thoughts, like how I'd make the cube more habitable. I didn't need much, the situation was temporary – my passport and visa would come through soon. Still, I could improve things with a few kitchen items.

Everything calmed. I felt myself drifting into sleep.

I woke to laughter floating into the room. I sat up and scanned my moonlit surroundings, wondering if I'd been dreaming. I'd left the balcony uncovered so the sea breeze could erase the day's heat. Seconds later, it was unmistakable. People hooting.

Terror shot through my veins.

I scrambled across the room and crouched on the balcony, my eyes sweeping the grounds. Who was it? Where were they? There were no shapes moving below. The cackling sounded again, followed by a squeal. Not coming from this building, but further away, on the beach. I eased up to get a better view and spotted a weak flash of light. Maybe a phone, maybe a cigarette lighter, it was there and gone, just enough to judge it wasn't inside the development. There was upbeat conversation. Another light flickered, wavered, then grew. A fire. Shapes took form – about a dozen people standing and watching the writhing flames. I saw drink cans being passed around.

A late-night beach gathering. Great.

I couldn't tell if they were young or old, fishermen or youths, they were too far away to get a good look. I sat on the cold floor, monitoring them, ignoring the goosebumps on my arms and legs. Heard snatches of sentences, nothing that made sense. How long were they going to stay? I was used to broken sleep these days, waking in all sorts of unfamiliar spots, but this was unsettling. Potentially dangerous. Would they enter the resort? For all I knew, they were squatters and had set up in Callista or the lobby. I cursed, annoyed that I hadn't investigated every space before moving in.

Keeping low, I retreated to my room. I could sneak outside, stick to the shadows and leave the resort without being noticed.

The party people were probably focused on their fire. But what if they spotted me? They outnumbered me, they were drinking; I had no idea what kind of people they were. No, it was safer to stay here and hide.

I lay on the sleeping bag, ears attuned to any changes. I hoped parties weren't a regular thing here. My thoughts drifted to the flat I'd shared with Erika. We'd had parties. Nothing massive, just a few close friends squeezing into the tiny lounge, everyone bringing their own booze. Erika always wanted to kick on, she'd wail dramatically whenever I began to wrap things up. Sometimes, she moved the party onto a club. 'Come on,' she'd say, 'let's leave Mac to get her *beauty sleep*.' While she might've thought she was having a cheeky dig, I actually appreciated it. I wasn't keen on the 'introvert' label, but there was definitely a limit to how long I could hang out with people. My favourite moments living with Erika were the nights she was rostered on to work at Horizon and I had the flat to myself. I streamed the shows I wanted to watch, pausing or rewinding as I liked, not having to answer any of Erika's questions or discuss plot points. I pushed the coffee table out of the way and did yoga on the rug. Perfection. I'd love to live by myself, if only I could afford it. From what I now knew of the rental market, finding any flat – let alone a solo one – was impossible.

A loud clinking startled me.

Sliding from the bed, I returned to the balcony and peered out.

A person was clinging to the fence on the beach side of the resort, their arms spread like a sugar glider. It seemed like a man, tallish, around my height. The wire shuddered and the others stood laughing on the footpath. The climber thrust his shoes against the wire and tried to heft himself higher, while I watched anxiously. If I couldn't scale the fence, surely he couldn't either. I considered the door behind me, wedged closed but not lockable. The ground-floor window with the board I'd removed. It was a resort, with multiple levels and hundreds of rooms. What were the chances of them finding me?

Far better if they breached the fence.

A second later the climber lost his grip, sliding to the ground. His friends laughed and two bent over to help, still cackling.

'Please go away,' I muttered.

Another party person broke away from the others. The esplanade light shone on his bald head. He stopped inches from the fence and kicked it, making it sing, then froze, staring in my direction. He was too far for me to make out his features and I was invisible in the darkness, but I could've sworn he was looking straight at me.

It was curious how a simple unflinching gaze could be so spine-tingling.

'Hey!'

A man in boots and hi-vis vest appeared. A security guard. Shit, where did he come from and at this time of night? I put my back to the wall, wishing I'd stayed in my room rather than exposing myself on the balcony. His torchlight swept over the crowd. All adults, from what I could see.

'Get away from the fence!' he commanded.

I waited for them to obey but instead the group faced him. He stopped in his tracks. Words were exchanged, torn away by the wind before I could hear them. The bald man stepped forward and shoved the guard in the chest. His torch fell to the ground and they grappled.

I gasped and shrank back. Should I call the cops?

Before I could make a decision, others broke up the fight. The bald man was coaxed away and the group retreated along the esplanade. Casual, unworried, chuckling, but at least the mob hadn't beaten the poor guy to a pulp.

The guard collected his torch and waited until they'd vanished. I didn't dare move in case he spotted me. He stood glaring after the gang, before stomping to their abandoned firepit. He kicked sand over the flames until they were smothered. I tracked him as he walked in the direction he'd come from, torch beam bouncing, rounding the corner and continuing towards the carpark. Only when his light had vanished did I dart back inside.

17

BREX

The sun was going down, and we still weren't sure what to do with the body. Our first idea was to bury it, but we didn't have a shovel.

'Chuck him in the ocean,' Cindi suggested.

'We'd never get him over the fence,' I said. 'Anyway, he'd come floating back.'

'What, then?'

'We could burn this building down.'

'It'd attract all the firies, as well as the cops,' Flynn said.

'Well, you come up with a great idea, then! I'm hot, I'm hungry, I'm fucking over this.' I walked to an air duct and sat down.

'Chill,' Cindi said.

'You chill!'

'Stop fighting,' Flynn groaned.

We stayed silent for a while. My hair flew about in the wind, making me even angrier.

'Let's leave him up here,' I said eventually. 'Nobody comes here, let alone onto the roof. We can roll him out of sight.'

'Ugh. I can't even look at him.' Cindi made puking noises.

I gawped at her. 'You beat him up, but you can't stand the sight of blood?'

Flynn stood. He looked ill. This was my fault, none of it would've happened if I hadn't climbed the fence. 'All right, let's put him under one of the vents,' he said.

Still, nobody moved. I didn't want to admit Cindi was right, but none of us wanted to touch the guy.

'I'll cover him a bit first,' I said. 'Anyone got a plastic bag?'

Cindi dug through her backpack and passed me one. It was semi-transparent, but would do the job. She hurried away as I knelt by the body, my eyes trying to avoid his pulpy face, his slick hair, the weight of his bowling ball head . . . It made my skin crawl. 'Oh god.' I almost dropped it and ran. But I had a job to do – for all of us. I tied the handles beneath his chin. Then I patted his pockets and found my phone. There was a new crack in one corner of the screen, but it lit up okay, showing the list of missed messages from Cindi and Flynn. There was no wallet or anything else.

'Look.' I pointed at the shoes. *DCS* was stamped across the soles in big letters.

'Department of Correctional Services,' Flynn said. 'Told ya.'

'What was he even doing here?' Cindi scowled.

'Nothing, anymore.'

'Right, let's get this over with.' Flynn crouched and grabbed the bloke under the arms. The head lolled to one side.

'Need a hand?' I said.

'Nah, I got this.'

He dragged the body across the roof and dropped it alongside one of the air ducts. I followed. 'Shit. The gap's too small,' he said.

'What are we gonna do?'

'Leave him for now, we'll come up with a proper plan later.'

'Hey, Cindi – give us your water.'

She passed her bottle and I washed blood off my fingers. The bolt cutters were lying nearby and I doused them too. I went to tuck them under one arm, but Flynn held his hand out.

'Give 'em here. I'm okay.'

'Sure?'

'Yeah.'

Cindi put her backpack over her shoulder. 'All right, can we *please* go?'

'Hell, yes!'

We hurried inside. I turned to check the door. 'Is there any way we can lock this?'

Flynn fiddled with the handle. 'Nup, doesn't look like it.'

'Come on, already!' Cindi said.

We continued downstairs, leaving the wind and harsh daylight behind. My hand stroked the phone in my pocket. I'd taken back what was mine and the old guy was dead. Bet he didn't see that coming. Did that make me gangsta? If so, why did his skull still tingle on my fingers? Why were my legs weak? I hoped the others wouldn't notice.

'Come on, I'll show you the basement and the locked offices,' I said.

'Aren't we going home?' Cindi said.

'You can, if you want. I've got nowhere else to go.' I flung a look at Flynn.

'I'll stay with Brex,' he said.

Cindi thought for a moment. 'Fine. I'll hang out a bit longer.'

When we reached the bottom level, Flynn took a torch out of his bag and shone it forward.

'Here.' I tapped the *SITE SUPERVISOR* sign on the door.

'Out the way.' Flynn dug through his tools, trying a skinny screwdriver first, jamming it into the lock. It slid off and did nothing. Then he got out the bolt cutters.

'What are you doing?'

'Stand back.'

He lifted the cutters over his head and brought them down hard, like a long hammer. Nothing happened at first, but after a few more blows, the doorhandle was scratched and lopsided. Still, it held.

'I've got another idea.' He positioned the bolt cutters behind the handle and pulled back, using them as a lever. Cindi and I stepped away and it was lucky we did, because the door splintered and screws went flying.

'Yes!' I said.

The handle hung loose. Flynn barged his shoulder into the wood and it gave way. He stumbled in and we followed, finding a windowless room barely bigger than my own bedroom.

'You did it!' Cindi said.

Flynn was rubbing his shoulder.

'Okay?' I asked.

'Yeah, I'm fine,' he said.

'Check it out,' Cindi said.

There was a desk with a kettle and mugs. A spinning office chair, a two-seater sofa, a filing cabinet with deep drawers. I pulled drawers open, finding folders of safety information. In another, there was a builder's hardhat and two hi-vis vests. In the last drawer I found a large can. I lifted it out carefully, like a homemade bomb. It was covered in Christmas wrapping, not heavy, and the lid was sealed.

'Popcorn,' I announced. 'Who gives popcorn for Christmas?' There was an unopened tin of shortbread, too.

Cindi was the winner, though. 'Look what I *foooound*!' she sang. It was a set of keys from the desk.

'Give 'em here,' I said. She tossed them to me and we returned to the corridor. One by one, we opened every door. It was fun not knowing what might be behind each one. And a good distraction from what had happened on the roof.

We found a room of machinery and electrics, everything switched off and silent. 'The plant room,' Flynn said. Another room obviously belonged to the cleaners, with shelves, mop, broom, a bucket and bottles of detergents. There was one long room with bricked cubicles and drains in the floor, we thought maybe a staff bathroom, but the toilets and showers hadn't been installed. We didn't find a safe or cash box anywhere. That was a big, fat disappointment. There wasn't even a vending machine or drinks fridge. The best thing we found was a CB radio, but there was only one, so it was useless.

'Let's go have a ciggie and eat the popcorn,' I said.

Cindi smiled. 'Yeah, let's hang out in our crib.'

Flynn set the torch on the desk so it acted as a lantern, then we pushed the sofa in front of the door. I squished between the two others and offered Mum's cigarette packet. My hands shook when I lit my own.

Flynn was studying his phone. 'I found the guy.'

We looked at his screen.

'Gawd, it's him,' Cindi said.

'Curtis Timothy Burbank,' Flynn read from the news article. 'What a wanker.'

'He escaped from jail – well, he was outside jail at the time, gardening.'

'What did he do?'

Flynn scrolled. 'He was in for murder.'

We all stared at each other.

'This beach was perfect for him to hide from the cops. Brex, did you say he tried to call a mate?'

'Hang on . . .' I checked my call log. The old dude had tried the same number again and again. What an idiot. 'It didn't go through.'

'Did he use anything else?' Cindi said.

I checked a few apps. 'Doesn't look like it.'

'What if the cops track him here?'

Flynn stamped out his ciggie, even though he hadn't finished it. 'They would've been here ages ago.'

'We did the world a favour,' Cindi said. She opened the popcorn, her fingers dived in, then she passed it to me. It was soft but salty. Good.

I pulled my legs up and leaned against Flynn. 'I like it here. I think I might move in.'

'Yeah, it's better than your house,' he said.

'A room with a window would be better,' Cindi said.

'This is safer,' I said. 'It's a . . . whatchacallit.'

'A bunker, a vault,' Flynn said.

'Yes! Like Fallout. I'm ready for combat.'

18

MAC

I checked the morning view from the balcony – there was no one in sight. After two nights at the resort, I was happier than I had been in weeks. Triumphant. I was doing it, I'd broken all the rules and carved out my own space. I'd even returned to the same hardware store and bought a one-element camp stove and a coffee pot. It was all very civilised.

I pulled on bathers and walked to the sand, weaving my way between the humped seaweed creatures to swim at my private beach. The day was already warm and the waves barely moved, lethargic in the summer air. I wondered if I'd see Brex again, until I realised she'd probably be at school. After swimming, I washed the salt and sand off my body in the public shower. The taps shone, the polished cement gleamed beneath my feet. This was far superior to the crummy motel I'd stayed in.

I worked a morning shift at the gym and then did a workout, all the while thinking about the resort, with a silly mysterious smile on my face. I was getting into my car afterwards when my phone hummed with a call. Although it was an unknown number, I was used to answering them while Erika and I were flat hunting. 'Hello?'

'Hello, Mac?'

I didn't recognise the male voice. 'Who's this?'

'Anton. From the gym.'

I glanced around, as if he'd be nearby. 'What are you doing calling me? How did you get this number?'

'Please don't be mad, I just want to talk.'

'Talk about what?'

'Can I see you? Let's meet—'

I didn't get to hear what Anton was proposing, because I hung up. Then I blocked his number. The nerve of him! When was he going to stop? Clearly, I hadn't been firm enough, but I couldn't think of what more to say. Wasn't a constant string of *No* enough for him? I didn't want to have to report him to my gym boss, Sabina, but I would if the harassment continued.

That night, I told Erika about Anton.

We met at our favourite taco place, mini red lanterns on every table, plates of piled food in front of us.

'A guy at the gym has been asking me out, he won't leave me alone,' I said. 'He somehow found my phone number and called me. He sent me an Insta request too. I'm blocking him left, right and centre.'

Erika wrinkled her nose. 'What a creep. Have you reported him?'

'To who, the police? He's not a criminal, it's just annoying.'

'What about the gym management?'

I shrugged. 'Feels a bit drastic at this point.'

'Well, let me know if you need backup.'

'Thank you, I will.'

We talked about the misery of our failed flat hunting, my plans for London and then Erika's favourite topic – Theo.

'So, you still haven't asked him out?' I said.

'Gimme time.'

'He'll say yes, you know. Of course he will – you're gorgeous.'

'Aw, thanks, babe. How about you? You haven't hooked up with anyone for a while, unless you're keeping something from me . . .'

'I'm not exactly in the state of mind to see anyone.'

Erika balled up her napkin and dropped it onto her plate. 'So, are you gonna tell me where you've been staying?'

'Ha, you don't give up, do you?'

'Of course not. You won't share, now I'm worried and, frankly, a little bit hurt. What's with all the mystery?'

'There's nothing to worry about, E, I'm completely fine.' I pulled my drink close and sucked from the straw.

'Please, just tell me.'

My irritation flared. Why couldn't she stop the interrogation? I didn't want anyone to know about the resort. 'I'm staying with a mate.'

'Who?'

'You don't know them.'

'Babe, you're such a bad liar. I know all your friends. Have you actually met someone, is that it?'

I snorted, shook my head. 'Please, drop it.'

When the meal was over, we walked outside. Insects buzzed the street lights, laughter floated out of the neighbouring restaurants.

Erika sidled up to me. 'This is your last chance to confess. Where are you staying?'

I pretended to laugh and moved towards my car. 'Have a good night.'

'I'm going to discover your secret!' she called after me.

19

ERIKA

Mac's car left the kerb and I kept my eyes on her tail-lights as I got behind my own wheel. I pulled out sharply after her, all my senses alive, turning right at the first street, just as she'd done. We arrived at South Road. Mac turned left and I kept following.

I *had* to know what she was hiding. Maybe she had a new guy and wanted to keep it low key. Maybe she'd found accommodation in a halfway house and worried about what people would think of her. Which was ridiculous – I'd always support Mac, no matter what.

Although it was night, I couldn't assume she wouldn't spot me, so I drove with calculation, letting other cars get between us. We reached the Cross Road intersection, and if Mac was going to Sandy's or Renata's, she would turn right. She didn't, though, and we continued on . . . until I was caught by a red light. I cursed as Mac cruised into the distance. We were separated, game over. There were countless suburbs she could disappear into.

Still, when the lights turned green I surged forward. I decided to stay on South Road until the Tonsley intersection and if I didn't catch up to Mac by then, I'd go home.

Seconds later, I spotted her red roof and the familiar S998 of her numberplate. She'd been held up at the next set of lights. Yes! I stayed tucked behind a white van, all the way past Tonsley and onto the Southern Expressway where the speed limit hit 100 kilometres per hour. I was confident Mac wouldn't glance back and see me, more intent on driving safely. Even if she did, she would hardly pull over in the fast, multi-lane traffic.

I glanced at my fuel gauge. Three-quarters of a tank, no sweat. If we remained on this route, we'd be in the beachside suburbs soon. I watched as Mac ignored the exits for Christie Downs and Noarlunga. Soon, we were nearing Aldinga, no houses on the roadside, just scrub. The ocean was hidden beyond the hills; this was summer holiday territory. Intriguing. Surely she wasn't renting a beach house. That'd be incredibly expensive.

Then Mac disappeared. *Poof!* Her car was gone.

I leaned over the steering wheel. There was a silver sedan ahead, a four-wheel drive further on, but no sign of Mac's Fiesta. I couldn't see any obvious turn-offs, either. *Shit.* I'd failed, I'd lost her, and I was more worried than ever. It should be easy for Mac to tell me where she was living, so her refusal meant there had to be a problem. What was she hiding? Why couldn't she talk to me?

I waited for a safe spot for a U-turn. Turned in a tight arc and paused on the roadside to wait for the lane to clear before joining it. I raised the volume of the stereo, resigned to a boring drive home, and spotted a figure walking my way. Odd. Who'd be a pedestrian out here, especially after sundown?

As I flashed past, I recognised Mac's sculpted form.

Without really thinking, I blasted the horn. In the rear-view mirror, I saw her whirl around.

'Where the heck are you going?' I muttered, as if she were in the car with me.

I saw a *'Take a Rest and Refresh'* tourist sign, turned and pulled into a wide layby. There were a couple of wooden picnic benches. Further up, Mac's car was nestled alongside a row of trees.

It made no sense.

I parked, jumped out and ran to the road. Mac was marching towards me, muscled arms swinging, looking ready to rumble. When we were within a few metres, we began flinging questions, our words tumbling over each other.

'What are you doing all the way out here?'

'You *followed* me?!'

We paused, panting and staring.

'Please tell me what's happening,' I said. 'I care about you, babe. Why are you leaving your car here, where the hell are you going?'

'It's none of your business. This is my life, it's nothing to do with you.'

This was more serious than I'd thought. 'Please, Mac, help me understand. What's the deal?'

'Go home.' She jabbed a finger.

'No. I'm sticking with you until I find out what's going on.'

We suffered in our standoff for a minute.

'Argh!' Mac stomped a foot. 'Okay, you've got to promise not to tell anyone.'

'Promise.'

'And don't criticise me, don't ask questions, don't dare laugh, I mean it.'

'Why would I laugh?'

'Erika.'

'Okay, I promise – no telling, no laughing.'

We returned to the rest stop and sat on the picnic table under the glow of a park light. Mac nestled her backpack between her feet. She gazed into the distance, refusing eye contact. 'I found a place to stay.'

'Without me?' It hurt.

'Give me a chance to explain, please. It's not . . . straight-forward. I've kept it quiet because it's . . . not a typical home.'

'How'd you mean? It's not a *commune* is it? Or a sugar daddy situation?'

'This isn't funny, it's no joke.'

'I know, I'm sorry.'

'Do you swear you won't tell anyone?'

'I swear.'

Mac opened her phone. 'It's easier if I show you.'

I leaned in and saw a news headline: *Resort Deal Collapses.* Mac scrolled through a slideshow of dreary buildings, ending with an image of a sandy shore and wire fence in the background.

'You remember they were building a resort at Barren Cape?' she said.

'Nuh.'

'Well, they were, until the development failed and now it's basically mothballed. There's all these empty buildings right by the water, not far from here.'

'And?'

'I've set up camp in one of the rooms.'

'Um . . . somebody's renting out rooms even though it isn't finished?'

'No. I snuck in.' Mac fiddled with her phone, avoiding my stare.

'You *what*? You broke in?'

'Well, I didn't actually break anything, I moved some obstructions—'

'And you're sleeping there? How? On what?'

'A blow-up mattress. I'm all organised, it's quite comfy actually—'

I grabbed Mac's wrist. 'Are you insane?'

She twisted out of my grip. 'See, this is why I didn't tell you.'

'You'll get caught, babe, you'll be in deep shit. Isn't that trespassing or something?'

'There's no cameras. I've seen a security guard but only cruising by on the beach. I don't think he expects anyone to be inside – either that, or he's lazy. Maybe he's too busy, he could have heaps of sites to visit. Plus, I leave my car here in the layby, I don't park it outside the gates. It's not far to walk.'

'Basically, you're squatting.'

'I s'pose so, if you wanna use that term.'

'You're, like, a homeless person.'

Mac snorted. 'In case you haven't noticed, Erika, that's exactly what I am, a *homeless person*.'

'You have choices, though! Come back to my place.'

'Thanks, I appreciate it, but I'm not doing that again. I'm not relying on mates, I'm not going to be a burden. Besides, you know your parents' house is chockers.'

'It might be crowded but at least it's legal!'

Mac picked up her bag. 'Thanks for everything, but this is exactly why I didn't tell you. You don't get it. I've had enough of staying in other people's houses, I *can't do it anymore*. The resort is my own private space, as bizarre as it might seem. And it's only until my travel papers come through.' She headed for the road.

'Mac! Wait!' I trotted beside her. This was my fault, I'd let her down, I should've kept closer tabs on her. Mac was just so tough, so independent, nothing fazed her. Now it was clear she was going loopy – living at an empty building site.

She kept marching and I moved double-time to keep up with her. We reached the road, car lights whizzing by in both directions.

'What about a shelter?' I said. 'Emergency accommodation, whatever they call it. I know it seems drastic, but—'

'I looked into it, and I'm not doing it.'

'Camping?'

'There's nowhere to camp in Adelaide.'

I sprinted ahead of Mac, forcing her to stop. 'You shouldn't be squatting, surely we know someone with a spare room—'

'No, Erika! I told you, I'm not begging for favours anymore.'

'I'm talking about friends who love you and support you.'

'You have no concept of what I'm going through. It's demeaning, I'm such a loser. I know everyone jokes about me behind my back.'

'We don't!'

Her hands were bunched into fists. 'I refuse to parade my failure in front of people any longer.'

'Okay, I'll stop badgering,' I said, my voice gentler. 'I don't mean to hack on you, I'm just concerned.'

'It's under control.'

'Fine. But if you insist on returning to that place, please do something for me.'

'What?'

'Take me there. I want to see it. I want to make sure it's safe.'

20

MAC

'It's way darker than I thought it'd be,' Erika whispered.

'There's no house lights or street lights, that makes a huge difference,' I said.

'Oh. Of course.'

My anger simmered. Erika had tailed me all the way to Barren Cape; did she have any idea how messed up that was? Since the party people episode, I'd enjoyed two peaceful nights at the resort, arriving after sundown, rising early for a dawn swim. My rudimentary home provided everything I needed for the few hours I was there each day. I'd grown accustomed to its noises, and the isolation was meditative. It was more like paradise than *squatting*, as she'd so offensively described it. Why should this place go to waste?

Yet while I resented what Erika had done, a tiny part of me was grateful too. At least somebody cared. No other friends had checked in on me, petrified that I'd ask for accommodation. Sandy had messaged, asking about my London plans, but she hadn't asked where I was sleeping.

'Look, I'm not *forcing* you to do this, you followed me here, you can change your mind.'

'I'll be fine,' Erika said. 'If you've been going inside, I can do it too.'

'Just remember, don't breathe a word to anyone.'

We crouched by the fence and I dragged the camo branch away and gestured at the ditch. 'Here.'

'*Under there!* Will we fit?'

'I've been under heaps of times. Watch me.' I removed a light jacket from my bag and pulled it on. Then I leaned like a shotput thrower and sent the bag high over the fence. I lay and slithered beneath the wire, earth raking at my clothes.

'Easy as,' I said, getting to my feet.

'All right, here goes . . .' Erika took a breath as if preparing for an underwater dive. She copied my method, lying and facing the stars. 'Shit . . . *ouch*.' Her hair and clothes collected soil but she pushed through. I helped her to her feet and she dusted her shorts before grabbing my wrists and shaking me gleefully. 'We did it, babe!'

I laughed softly. 'I know. Let's keep moving.'

The gust lifted hair into my face; I tucked strands into my collar as I led the way. I stared hard, trying to decipher shapes, the breeze drying my eyes as we inched forwards, one hand out in front as we crossed empty ground.

'Can we use our phone lights?' Erika said.

'No, we could be spotted. I saw a security patrol on my first night.'

We neared the first wall. Erika looked up. 'Is your room in there?"

'Nah, not that one,' I said. 'That's the Callista building, it was going to be luxury suites – double-storey rooms, with their own fireplace, separate lounge, bathtub on the balcony, the lot.'

'Nice! Why didn't you choose that?'

'I wanted to be tucked further away from the carpark. Mine is the next one along, it's called Semira.'

'Are they named after famous women? I don't recognise those names.'

'Apparently they're planets. Or stars, I can't remember . . .'

'Seems as huge as a planet right now.'

Erika was right, Callista loomed over us.

'The swimming pools are up ahead,' I said. 'Be careful, you could fall in and break something.'

'Pools?'

'Well, *pits* for the pools.'

'Hold my hand?'

'Argh, okay.' I did as she asked. Her hand was damp but I didn't drop it.

We skirted the void cautiously. 'So much for safety regulations,' she said. 'Shouldn't it be fenced off?'

'The whole joint is fenced off,' I reminded her. We dropped hands, continued creeping and reached the shorter central building with steel artwork on top. 'That's the lobby and reception area.'

'What's in there?'

'Dunno, it's all closed up, I haven't gone in.'

'Aren't you curious?'

'I stick to my space, I'm not here to go exploring. The smaller my footprint, the less chance of getting caught.'

'Let's hope that never happens.'

We reached Semira with its low courtyard walls. 'This reminds me of our family holiday in Fiji,' Erika said. 'We had our own private patio.'

In the final courtyard, I fished around in my bag and pulled on my headlamp.

'Woah, you really are prepared,' she said.

I donned my gloves and she watched as I wrangled the window board and guided it to the ground. 'This is how we get in,' I said.

She tittered. 'I'm shitting myself. This is the beginning of a true crime podcast.'

'Get a grip.'

I climbed into the darkness and she climbed after me. When I replaced the board we were immediately shielded from the wind and waves, like shutting ourselves in a box.

'Fuck.' Erika shivered.

'You can use your phone light now.'

She directed it at our feet. 'Any rats? Snakes?'

'Nah, there's nothing here for them to eat.'

'Do you know or are you guessing?'

I ignored her, because I was totally guessing. We headed further in and Erika gasped at the length of the corridor. 'Far out, it really is a hotel. There's no doors, though.'

'There are, where we're headed,' I said.

She baulked at the entry to the murky stairwell. 'I'm not going in there.'

She was trying my patience. 'How are you getting to the top floor, then? Climbing a drainpipe?'

'Can't we stay down here?'

'I'm set up on the top floor. And like I said – it has a door.'

'*Okaaay*. I guess I can take the stairs of doom . . .'

21

ERIKA

We climbed the steps, our phone lights occasionally crisscrossing. Never in a million years did I expect to be exploring a derelict building site after sundown. Mac was the only person I'd willingly follow here. If she said this was okay, I trusted her.

The temperature rose the higher we climbed and I began sweating. 'How far?'

'Nearly there.'

On the uppermost level, she counted aloud as we walked the corridor. '. . . seven, eight, nine, ten.' She opened a door.

'It's not locked?' I said.

'No, they didn't install locks, I guess they didn't get that far. And they'd be expensive, they'd probably get stolen.'

Inside the room, she switched on a lantern. 'Home sweet home.'

'Woah.' My eyes widened, taking everything in.

'Well. What do you think?'

'It's . . . nice.'

Mac laughed. 'Oh my god, you're so spun out right now.'

She wasn't wrong. I don't know what I expected, but seeing the temporary shelter within these four walls had me stunned. The neatly made inflatable bed, a teeny stove, a cardboard box of food. There was even a battery-powered phone charger. But no matter how Mac dressed it up, this was a bare room in a construction site. The floors and walls weren't even finished. There was no electricity, no running water. No security. And she'd spent days here already, all alone, without telling anybody.

I dabbed my eyes.

'Are you *crying*?' Mac said.

I couldn't stop, the tears flowed. 'You shouldn't have to live like this.'

She gently elbowed me. 'Hey, I'm all right, it's not that bad.'

'We've let you down, all of us. What's wrong with us?'

'Don't feel sorry for me. This was my choice, I want to be here. It feels like it's mine.'

'Only, it's *not*.'

Mac scowled and stepped away. 'This was a mistake, I shouldn't have brought you here, you're making this all out to be far bleaker than it is.'

I dried my face on one sleeve. 'I'm just a bit sad, you know.'

'Sad?'

'How can you sleep here? Aren't you scared?'

'I was creeped out at first, now I actually feel safer here than a lot of other spots where I've slept, including my car.'

'You slept in your car? Mac!'

'It was an experiment, a last-minute thing . . . I don't wanna talk about it.'

I waved my hands at the room. 'How can *this* feel safe?'

'It's great, there's nobody around to bother me.'

'Nobody around to hear you scream . . .'

She shook her head. 'I knew you wouldn't get it. You should go.'

'I'm sorry, don't be mad, I'm just wrapping my brain around this.' I cruised in slow circles, looking at everything twice. There was a door in the far corner. When I looked in, I saw the shell of an en suite. This was some Third World setup I was looking at. I knew people were living in vans, living in tents; I never imagined my bestie would become this desperate. 'Does your mum know you're here?'

Mac scoffed. 'Are you kidding? I wouldn't tell her.'

'She'd help you if she knew.'

'I wouldn't be so sure. Anyway, I don't want her help – and you better not say a word. Swear to me.'

'Okay, okay, I promise not to tell her.'

She turned the lantern low. 'There's something that'll cheer you up. You haven't seen the best part yet.'

'Oh, yeah?'

She removed a large rectangle from the wall, leaving it propped on the floor. I hadn't realised that double doors were hidden there. 'Come on,' she said, beckoning me to a skinny balcony.

'Is it safe?' I said.

'Of course. It's stable as.'

I joined her, moving my feet tentatively. When my eyes clapped on the view, I forgot my fear. We were standing under a wide, starry sky. City lights shone to our right, bushes and grass swayed serenely below us. 'This is *amaaazing.*'

'And an awesome location for late night drinks.' Mac ducked inside and returned with two cans of gin and soda.

We opened them.

'Cheers!'

'Sunsets are the best, they're spectacular here,' she said.

'I bet.'

There was tinkling from below.

'What's that?' I bent, prepared to run.

'There's non-stop noise, just building site stuff. Ignore it.'

I remained tense. 'This view is amazing 'n' all, Mac, but it's also *bloody scary*.'

'You have to admit, though, it's cool. Relax, we're fine.'

'I guess . . .'

We sat with our backs against the building's warm wall and I began to feel better. It was like old times, me and Mac drinking and chatting late at night, except we were perched on a remote balcony with a brilliant view all to ourselves. Clearly, she was happy. I should support her.

We discussed the resort and why Barren Cape wasn't popular.

'It's not exactly easy to find,' she said. 'You can't see it from the road, not like other beaches where you drive by and see the water. Plus, the resort signs make it seem secured and out of bounds, you know?'

'Yeah, you're right – people might assume there's builders here, that it's off limits. Not *you* though!'

We clunked our cans together again.

'So, you found out where I'm staying, mystery solved,' Mac said. 'Happy now?'

'Look, I'm sorry I followed you like a stalker, but I'm not sorry I found out about this. We're mates, we shouldn't keep things from each other. And what if something bad happened? I'd never know to look for you here. You need me. I'm your backup, your insurance.'

'Let's talk about you for a change. What's happening with Theo?'

She'd deliberately changed the subject but I didn't mind, because Theo *was* my favourite subject. Mac hadn't met him, she stopped going to Horizon ages ago. She went a few times when I first moved into the flat, but eventually admitted it wasn't her scene. 'Too many fake tans and fake brands', apparently. She preferred the more rundown, cheaper pub in the next suburb.

'Theo's uploaded some new photos, wanna see?' I took out my phone.

'I suppose . . .' Mac grumbled, then laughed.

We shuffled closer together, me scrolling through Theo's Instagram account, pausing on the photos of him. 'Isn't he cute?'

'When do you see him next?' Mac said.

'This weekend at the club.'

'Ask him out then. Seriously. Do it before I go to London.'

'Mmm, maybe.'

She finished her gin and plonked the empty can onto the ground. 'C'mon, I'll walk you back to your car.'

I put my phone away. 'Do you have to?'

'Huh?'

I grinned. 'I've got an idea. How about I spend the night?'

22

MAC

It wasn't what I expected to hear. It was nice having Erika with me, but I'd devised the resort room for me, and me alone.

'You want to stay? You said this place frightens you.'

'I'm used to it now. I reckon it'll be fun,' she said.

'It won't be comfortable.'

'I'm tough, I don't mind.'

Tough. It wasn't a word I'd use to describe Erika.

She persisted. 'Won't it be nice to have company?'

I stared at the distant sparkle of Adelaide. I didn't really fancy trekking out of the resort and back to the layby and Erika's car. And she was already here, she knew my secret – what harm could it do?

'I guess we could share the bed . . .'

Erika clapped. 'Yay! Let's do it!'

We opened another can of gin and returned to the balcony. Erika told me more about Theo. I sat, half-listening, half-thinking about this strange point of life I'd reached. My last relationship was more than a year ago, with Peter, who I met through mutual friends. Theoretically, he ticked all the boxes for a great boyfriend, but after a while I realised I was trying my hardest to be attracted to him and truthfully, I wasn't. He was pissed off when I ended things, and it was an awkward confrontation because I hadn't expected him to shout at me. I completely disconnected from him online, but did see him at a bar once. I turned my back and hoped he hadn't spotted me. The last I heard, he'd moved to Sydney. If I was in a relationship now, would I be living with that person? Would a partner help out, as Sandy had said? I hated to think she could be right, but a boyfriend would likely have accommodation, and surely they'd let me stay as long as I needed.

When our drinks were finished, Erika and I went inside. I kicked the rubber wedge beneath the door.

'Does that work?' she asked.

'Try it.'

She tugged, couldn't get the door wide enough for her fingers to wriggle through. 'You're so clever.'

It was nice to hear compliments. I wasn't delusional: this room was a valid living option. Maybe not legit, but logical under the circumstances. I removed my shoes and set them by the door, then dug through my bag for my toothbrush.

'Getting ready for bed already?' Erika said.

'I've got work in the morning, it's already past eleven.'

'I don't have a toothbrush.'

I boggled my eyes. 'I draw the line at sharing mine.'

We settled on the inflatable mattress, giggling like schoolkids as our elbows and legs collided. I switched off the lantern.

'Shit, it's properly dark,' Erika said.

'Mmm,' I murmured.

She squirmed about for a bit, trying to get comfortable. 'What do you think is gonna happen to this joint? Will a developer finish it or will they tear it down?'

'Dunno. I guess it'll sell eventually.'

'Can you imagine returning in a year or so, when the resort is actually finished and full of guests? We could book this room. How hilarious would that be?'

'I can barely think a week into the future, let alone a year.'

'Is it better, having me here? Less scary?'

'It's definitely noisier.'

'Ha ha, very funny.'

I felt her moving again, then a glow lit the room like a tiny television. I frowned. 'What are you doing?'

'Checking messages. And getting one last look at Theo before I go to sleep. Those lips. Yum, it should be illegal to be so perfect.'

Five minutes later, she was still scrolling.

'Erika!'

'Okay, *okay.*' She closed the phone, the room went dark. She fidgeted some more.

I tried to subdue my irritation, to focus on the lulling wind and waves. Further away, a metallic jingling. After a week here, that backdrop had become my windchime.

'Are you awake?' Erika whispered. 'I'm scared.'

I propped myself up onto one elbow. 'I *knew* I shouldn't have let you stay.'

'I'm sorry, babe, it's majorly creepy here! It'd be okay if there were more people . . .'

'The whole point is the lack of people. *I don't want people.*'

'I'm sharing how I feel. I'm not as brave as you. Don't you feel exposed? Anything could happen.'

My face burned. 'Well, what do you want to do? Shall I walk you to your car?'

'No, I'm only venting. Sorry. I'll shut up and let you sleep, you won't hear another peep.'

True to her word, she went quiet.

But now my brain wouldn't stop ticking. I stared at the ceiling, listened to the sea, the sporadic clinking of the construction site. After a while, Erika was breathing steadily, a hiss escaping between her teeth.

My senses stayed buzzing. It was like waiting for a visitor – I couldn't relax until they arrived.

23

ERIKA

Peachy light seeped into the room. My arms and legs ached; all night I'd tried not to infringe on Mac too much as we shared the unstable mattress. She was crouched by her mini stove, her hair in a tight, pristine bun. She wore workout clothes: loose shorts, a spaghetti-strap tank top showing off her broad upper back.

I reached for my phone. It was 6.07 am. 'Jesus, it's so early!'

'I've got stuff to do. And I make a point of not being here during daylight,' Mac said.

'You're a machine.' I sat up. My teeth were furry, my skin dry. Staying overnight without toiletries was ick. 'The coffee smells good.'

She gave the swiftest of smiles, maybe fuming over my chatter last night. It wasn't my fault I was spooked, even more so when the lantern was switched off. I felt better now, having survived it, and seeing how she'd set everything up so comfortably. It wasn't like squatting in an abandoned house with rotting ceilings and sleeping druggos. As she said, it was private and contained, secluded and somehow relaxing. This was . . . industrial glamping.

Mac went to the balcony and I hopped up to join her. 'I wanna see the sunrise!'

'It rises in the east, we're facing west.'

We laughed. We had a running joke about me and directions. We drove to a music festival in Victoria last year. I was navigating and we took a totally wrong turn. We didn't realise until we hit the next town, when Mac had squinted at the entry sign: 'Timboon? I didn't know we were coming this way.'

The sky was layered in hues of blue, the water sparkled, there were no roofs blocking the outlook. I breathed in the salty air and snaked an arm around Mac's waist. 'Ah-*mazing*!'

'Yeah,' she said. 'I still can't believe I have this to myself.'

I raised my phone to take a photo.

Mac swiped at it. 'Don't share this on the socials!'

'It's okay, babe, I've got my location switched off.'

'People will ask where this is.'

'I won't tell them. It's so speccy, I've *got* to share.'

'Please don't.'

My shoulders slumped. 'Fine, you're the boss.'

Behind us, the coffee pot bubbled. Mac rushed indoors and I whipped my phone up and snapped three sneaky pics. She was pouring coffee into a plastic cup when I joined her and she offered it to me.

'You're the best,' I said. 'Actually, it was fun sneaking in. Like, escape room stuff, but in reverse.'

'That's not what you said last night.'

'I know, I was lame.' I drank the coffee too quickly, sting-ing my tongue. 'I was thinking . . . I could stay again tonight, bring my own sleeping bag and mattress? Flatmates again!'

Mac stared.

'What?' I said. 'You don't think it's a good idea?'

'This isn't a game for me, Erika, this is serious.'

'I am serious!'

Mac shoved her feet into her sneakers. 'I'm here because I'm desperate. You've got a place to live, parents who adore you, free meals, there's no reason for you to be here.'

'That applies to you, too. You could pack up and come to my house now.'

She glowered at me. 'You know it's not the same thing.'

'I don't wanna sit at home when you're here,' I grumbled. 'Please. I'll bring the drinks this time. My shout. It'll be fun.'

'It's too risky. I don't want any noise. I don't want to get caught, do you? How would you feel if a guard found us and marched us away? Or the police? This needs to stay low key.'

'Fine.'

When we finished our coffees, Mac went to the balcony and scoured the area, acting all vigilante before we went downstairs. I pulled a face when her back was turned. I didn't get it; surely two people was safer than one? And I wasn't a child, I could stay quiet.

She led the way outside, her head on a swivel. At least the sun was up and I could see where I was stepping. There were Bird of Paradise plants, several palms, wildflowers with white petals. The air was warm and I wanted to run to the water and throw myself in.

124

'I didn't get to visit the beach,' I said.

Mac kept walking. 'Trust me, it's not that great.'

'Then why'd they put the resort here?'

'Does it look like a roaring success to you?'

'Come on, let's go see it real quick—'

She spun around. 'Ssh!'

She ducked beside a shrub and I instantly copied. Her eyes were wide as she put a finger to her lips.

SCREEK!

Something steel was being dragged.

'What is it?' I whispered.

'The gates,' she whispered back.

We made ourselves smaller. I was so scrunched, my nose almost touched the earth. A couple of ants scurried around Mac's knee. We listened until, far off, a door slammed. An engine fired up. We locked eyes as we tracked the noise, until finally the vehicle disappeared.

'Shit,' she muttered.

'Who was it?'

'Probably a security guard.'

We got to our feet, wiping soil from our clothes.

'Can you imagine if they caught us hiding? How majorly awkward,' I said.

Mac grinned. 'I'd blame it on you.'

I slapped her shoulder and we continued to the fence. She wriggled under and I went next, then we trudged to the layby. The passing high-speed traffic made me nervous. I'd left my sunglasses in the glovebox and the daylight was blinding. Neither of us spoke and that was fine, because I was thinking.

When we reached the cars, my T-shirt was damp and flies buzzed my face.

'So, what are you up to today?' Mac said. Trying to make things normal.

'I've got a uni assignment to work on.'

She sighed. 'Hey, sorry I was snappy earlier. I'm protective of this place, but I'm glad you stayed last night, I'm glad I got to show you.'

'Me, too.'

I got into my car, lowered the windows and started the engine. Mac lingered, pretending to organise items in her boot, but I knew she was waiting to make sure I left.

24

MAC

Our cars more or less kept pace until we reached the expressway and when I lost sight of Erika, it was like a weight had been lifted. I was glad to have shared my whereabouts – at least one other person should know where I was living. And now that she knew, she'd stop nagging me for information.

I yawned. I'd only had four or five hours' sleep. It'd be nice to have the resort to myself again.

I was rostered on for the breakfast shift at Clover's. I parked in my usual spot in the street behind the café and checked my emails before leaving the car.

My passport had been approved! I'd paid extra for faster processing, but it meant I had to collect it from the passports office in the city. I let out a *yip!* of delight. However, there was no update on my visa. I hoped it wouldn't be rejected. Maybe I wasn't deemed skilful enough? I'd checked flight times and ticket prices earlier in the week, but didn't dare book anything until my papers were in place.

The café was louder and brighter than ever. I tied my sage green apron around my waist and got to work, greeting people, chuckling at their jokes, taking orders and clearing tables. I overheard a conversation by the windows, two older men in business shirts chatting.

'The thing is . . . the housing shortage is a myth.'

'Mate, you don't have to tell me, I drive past an empty block near my office every day.'

'People are fussy, that's the problem, their expectations are sky high.'

I rolled my dishtowel into a coil, tight enough to make a ropey weapon. The two corporates didn't have a clue what they talking about. I couldn't wait to get onto a plane and leave this all behind. Sure, maybe things wouldn't be perfect in London. Maybe Georgia and I would get on each other's nerves, maybe it'd take me a while to get a job. But it had to be better than my situation here. At least share housing was a way of life in London, and there'd be hundreds more job opportunities.

A familiar figure walked across the courtyard. Impeccably styled hair, a spring in his step, eyes shining – at me. My heart jolted, but not in a good way. He chose a chair, lifted his sunglasses and watched me approach.

'Beautiful day,' Anton said.

I'd never seen him out of gym clothes before. He wore tailored shorts and a short-sleeved shirt buttoned to his throat. I held a stack of menus against my chest. 'Did you know I worked here?'

He smiled. 'I saw you here one day when I was driving past.'

'Just randomly, just a coincidence?'

'It was very lucky.'

I dropped a menu on his table and marched off. Ten minutes later, I returned to take his order.

'What do you recommend, Mac?' he said.

I didn't like my name on his lips. I stared at a shop across the street. 'Everything here is good.'

'What's your favourite dish?'

'The salad of the day,' I said, to shut him up.

'Done. Hey, when do you knock off?'

'Are you serious?'

Without waiting for a response, I took his order to the kitchen and focused on the other tables, pretending I wasn't livid. Chatted with customers, pasted a smile on my face, all while feeling Anton track me. When his salad was ready, I delivered it without a word, rushing back to the kitchen.

He took his time eating, paying more attention to me than his bowl, while others came and went. To the outsider, he was a pleasant, polite customer, but I knew him as a persistent creep. I considered asking a colleague to take over his table, but I didn't want to get into the reasons why. I wouldn't be working at the café much longer. Ha. Imagine Anton's face when he learned I'd quit.

When I eventually checked his table again, I was surprised to see it empty. Although it was a relief, it took an effort to unclench my jaw and enjoy the fact I didn't have another awkward inter-action waiting for me.

After my shift, I refreshed my emails, and once again there was no visa update. There were no notifications from friends, either. Not a single person had reached out, including Erika, and that was fine with me because I didn't need her pressuring me to leave Barren Cape. In the café bathroom, I pulled on bathers before re-dressing. The day was so blistering that I was fixated on swimming. I took one of Clover's famous jaffles and a packed salad, buoyed at the thought of a tranquil swim followed by delicious food. My temporary lifestyle was incredible! I'd brag, if it wasn't so imperative to keep it confidential.

I was houses away from my car when I jerked to a stop.

Anton was leaning on the hood.

25

ERIKA

The red bikini or the floral one? I decided to bring both.

I was in my bedroom, steadily working through my packing and ignoring any guilt over Mac. She'd understand later. She'd forgive me. I tried the red bikini on, jiggling to get everything in place. I looked hot, even if I did say so myself. Then I donned my slothing outfit again, and shoved both sets of bathers into my overnight bag. Crammed more clothes in: denim shorts, T-shirts and a short kimono for when I was roaming the resort. Damn, I was gonna be sexy. Then it was practical things: a towel, pillow, I even plucked a toilet roll from the bathroom cupboard. There was an air mattress and pump in the garage; I made a mental note to collect those on the way out.

I knocked on Josh's door and when there was no answer, I walked in. The curtains were closed as usual, his bed a mound of sheets and clothes, and it stank of man farts. I rummaged through the mess on his desk and found the wireless speaker under a tank top. Nabbed a bottle of sunscreen, too. Back in my room, I sat cross-legged on my bed and scrolled through the message thread I'd started with Theo. Mac wanted me to ask him out? Well, I had, in a way. Only, I wasn't sure she'd appreciate my tactics.

The idea came after spending the night at Mac's resort.

Accommodation plan for Theo? Check.

Sexy, sunny location? Check.

Theo all to myself? Check.

I had messaged him: *Hey, ru still 'homeless'?*

He wrote: *sadly, yes. Know anyone looking for a housemate?*

Funny bout that.
I know a place with heaps of spare rooms.

Tell me more!

First . . . it's top secret.

You can trust me

I mean TOP SECRET

Swear I won't say a word

Ok
It's better if I show you

We had arranged to meet in the carpark outside Horizon at 1 pm and I told him to bring overnight stuff.

I threw food into a picnic cooler while simultaneously eating breakfast. When I was done, I stared at my phone, wondering how and when to tell Mac. She was fierce about keeping the resort a secret and she'd throttle me if she knew what I was planning. This was a betrayal, yet surely she'd soon forgive me. It was greedy to keep that enormous place to herself, and she'd understand when she realised Theo was an evictee. I'd explain it to her later. She'd see my point of view.

When everything was packed inside the boot it looked like I was going to be away for weeks. I'd begun to reverse down our driveway when Mum's Kia rolled in.

'Move!' I called out.

Mum threw her hands up like: *What's going on*?

She reversed, got out and stood in my way as I was trying to ease past the letterbox. 'Erika, can you stick around a minute and unpack the shopping?'

'No, I'm already late.'

'Late for what?'

'I'm meeting a friend, Mum, I've gotta go!'

'Will you be home tonight?'

'No. I'm going camping.'

'I thought you hated camping. You never want to go with us. What about your uni assignment?'

And Mac thought I had it easy, living at home again. I sighed. 'It's under control.'

'All right . . .' Mum finally moved and I was free to go.

I cranked up Dua Lipa and set the air conditioner to high. Nine minutes later I was entering Horizon's carpark. My stomach flipped when I spotted Theo leaning against an old grey sedan. I parked alongside, quickly checking my reflection in the mirror. Theo reached into his car and removed a gym bag, opened my passenger door and threw it onto the back seat.

He gave a huge grin. 'Hey.'

'Hey,' I said, trying to be chill.

Theo ratcheted the seat to make room for his long, tanned legs. He wore board shorts and a tiger tattoo trailed his right shin. 'Thanks for doing this. You sure it's okay?'

'Of course! There's heaps of rooms, it's not a bother.'

'I'm intrigued. Also a bit embarrassed . . . I'm not usually this destitute.'

'Don't be, I get it. We were kicked out ages ago and still can't get a lease.'

'Well, I appreciate this, you're a champion.'

He tilted towards me as he clicked his seatbelt into place. I wanted to pull him closer and smell his hair but instead, I checked my blind spot and shifted into drive. I could hardly believe Theo was in my car. Theo! It was the first time I'd seen him outside the nightclub.

'Mind if I change the music?' he said.

'Go for it,' I said.

He synced his phone with the stereo and I saw the digital words on the dash: THEO'S SAMSUNG. *His* name in my car. Electronic dance music swelled and I swayed with it. We reached South Road, then the expressway, the same route I'd taken when following Mac, only this time there was sunshine and sexual tension. I tried to focus on the traffic, intensely aware of Theo sitting just across the console.

'So what is this place and why is it so secret?' he said.

'I told you – it's better if I show you.'

'It's not a cult or something?'

'Ha, yeah, I'm going to kidnap and brainwash you!'

'How many other people are there?'

'Just me and Mac. Don't tell anyone please, Mac would kill me.'

'Who's Mac? Your boyfriend?'

A laugh burst from me. 'She's my mate. We shared a flat before the landlord decided to turn it into a holiday rental.'

'Jeez. Lots of that going round.' Theo smiled. 'Is she gonna be there?'

My nerves pinged at the thought of Mac seeing us arrive at the resort. 'I'm not sure.'

26

MAC

'Dude, what the hell?'

Anton grinned and adjusted his collar. 'You were busy in the café, so I thought I'd catch you out here instead.'

I was so angry and stunned I could barely string sentences together. 'That was ages ago . . . have you been waiting here since then? And how did you know this was my car?'

'I've seen it at the gym.'

'You know what, never mind, I'm not interested.' I moved towards the Fiesta.

'Mac, why do you have to act like such a stuck-up bitch?'

I stiffened. 'What did you call me?'

'I'm doing my best here.'

'Leave me alone!'

I unlocked my car and climbed in, fumbling with my dinner. The passenger door opened and Anton landed beside me, the food containers tipping between us.

'Get out!'

He lurched across the console, wide eyed, face shining in the heat. 'I don't understand what your problem is. I know you're into me, you watch me at the gym.'

'No, *you're* watching me!'

'You don't have to play coy.'

'I'm not!' I slapped his reaching hand away.

'Don't be so frigid.'

I elbowed my door ajar and stumbled onto the verge. The street was empty. 'I'm calling the police!'

'What for, I haven't done anything.'

'You're harassing me!' I opened my phone.

Anton slithered out of the car. 'Okay, I'm out! Fuck's sake, are you happy now?'

Dunk! He kicked the door.

'Don't come near me, EVER AGAIN!' I roared.

I climbed in, pressed the locks, gunned the engine and drove. When I checked my mirrors, he hadn't moved from the kerb. I continued for a couple of minutes before parking and draping myself over the steering wheel, gulping in air.

Anton was unhinged and had a completely skewed view of us. The way he'd leapt into the passenger seat, the things he'd called me! Beyond belief. I glanced around, wary that he might be cruising by. I had no idea what type of car he had – unlike all the details he'd collected on me.

When my heart rate had returned to normal, I phoned Sabina.

'Hey, Mac, what's up?' She was brusque. We weren't close, we rarely saw one another because we operated with a skeleton crew at the gym. I heard people in the background. I hadn't rehearsed what to say, and took a beat to organise my thoughts.

'You there?' Sabina asked.

'Sorry, yes, I'm here,' I said. 'I want to talk about one of our members, a guy called Anton.'

'What about him?'

'He's been pestering me, asking me out. He won't take no for an answer.'

'That sucks, but it happens, it's a gym, you know that,' Sabina said. 'It's full of people working on their bodies, feeling good about themselves. Skimpy outfits, mirrors, you know the drill—'

'That's no excuse! Anyway, it's much more than that. He's been following me. He turned up at my second workplace, he forced his way into my car.' I explained what had happened, giving Anton's full name, while Sabina made occasional murmurs on the other end.

'Well, that's totally unacceptable. I'll have to ban him.'

'Thank you. And can you please warn the staff?'

There were more voices on the other end; Sabina was conducting several conversations at once. 'Okay, leave it with me. He's not going to be happy, but it can't be helped. Are you okay?'

I let out a long breath. 'Yeah, I think so. But there's something else.'

'What?'

'I'm . . . quitting.'

'You're quitting because of this Anton guy?!'

'No, I already had plans to leave. I'm going to London.'

'When?'

'Soon, it all depends on my visa—'

'You *sure* it's not because of what just happened?'

'I'm sure.'

'All right, send me an email, I need all the details in writing.'

'Thanks, Sabina. I'm sorry for the short notice—'

The call disconnected. I sat staring at the screen. I hadn't expected Sabina to cry over my resignation, but her bluntness stung. So much for the gym being a second family. I scooped up the café food and used tissues to mop spilt salad dressing. As I cleaned, I kept surveying my surroundings. My hands were still shaking.

27

ERIKA

We were getting closer to Barren Cape when I realised I didn't know exactly where the turn-off was. I pulled over and consulted my phone, acutely aware of Theo's proximity in the passenger seat. I wanted everything to go absolutely perfectly.

'I'm gonna double-check the location.' If I couldn't find it, I wasn't about to call Mac for directions and have my magical plan collapse.

'I thought you knew the spot,' Theo said.

'I do, I was there last night.'

'Is there an address? Want me to look it up?' He waggled his phone.

'Hang on . . .' My fingers enlarged the map on the screen. 'Got it.'

We began driving again, his leg bouncing in sync with the music. I watched the road carefully until I finally spotted the blue sign for the tourist stop. 'I remember now!'

Theo smacked his hands together. 'Excellent.'

Rather than park at the layby, I continued onto the thin resort road. I didn't want to make Theo walk too far, wanted everything to be easy and comfortable. Scraggly trees and brown bushes crowded either side.

'This is different,' he said. 'I should've told my friends where I was going. All this hush-hush – you're actually a serial killer, aren't you?'

I laughed. 'You're gonna have to trust me.'

A minute later, we rounded a bend and the resort was there: two giant concrete blocks behind a high fence. It wasn't as ominous as the other night with Mac, when it was dark, when I was waiting for a ghostly hand to grab me. This right now – the sun shining, Theo alongside me – it was uplifting, like being on holiday.

'What is this?' he said. 'Looks like a ghetto.'

'Ha ha! It's nothing like that. You remember the resort they started building? Barren Cape? It was going to be luxury accommodation. There's heaps of rooms, a day spa, swimming pool . . . all unfinished, obviously. The owners ran out of cash.'

'They just left it here?'

'Yeah, isn't it amazing?'

His eyes narrowed. 'We can't just walk in.'

'We did. There's nobody here, no security, nobody cares.'

'And you slept here? Wow.'

I beamed. He was impressed.

We parked and got out of the car.

'It's bloody hot.' He fanned his face. 'Where do we go?'

I pointed. 'Down there, it's not far. Let's leave the gear in the car for now.'

I was afraid Theo would change his mind at any minute, baulking at the weird surroundings, so I hurried towards the fence. Dust kicked up through my toes. We followed the wire, me searching for the entry that Mac had dug. I hoped Theo wouldn't laugh when he saw it.

There was a '*WHOOP!*' behind me.

He was pointing at the ocean. 'You didn't mention that.' He hustled past.

'I thought we were gonna check out the resort,' I said.

'Later!'

The path turned soft, crumbling at the edges. In seconds, we could see a tiny beach with a rocky outcrop at the far end – the beach that Mac couldn't be bothered showing me. Theo kicked off his thongs and stripped off his T-shirt. A tattoo of musical notes stretched from one shoulder blade to the other. He jogged past mounds of seaweed and dipped his toes to suss the temperature before striding in. I removed my clothes, trying not to let the bikini be drawn away, too. It was a struggle and one of my boobs popped out. I shrieked and laughed, tucked it in, but Theo wasn't watching, he was head down and swimming.

Slimy weed tickled my ankles as I waded through, willing myself to acclimatise to the relative frostiness. When I was thigh deep, I swam, aiming determinedly towards my future boyfriend. Theo was floating with arms and legs stretched out, lifting and dipping with the sea.

'This is epic,' he said.

'Glad you like it,' I said, as if welcoming him to my regular haunt.

He twisted in the water. 'So Adelaide would be over there . . . Mistle Bay is next, Carnaby would be down there.'

'I guess.'

'Wicked. We have this to ourselves.' He duck-dived, emerged and shook water from his hair.

We paddled lazily for five minutes, circling, floating. It was like a dream. I couldn't believe I had him all to myself.

He drifted closer, jerked his chin towards land. 'So you and Mac found this joint?'

'Mac did, then she brought me.'

'She has a key? She knows someone?'

'We snuck under the fence.'

'Get outta here! That's breaking and entering, you little crim.'

I giggled. 'It wasn't as if she smashed a window or broke the locks, she just dug under the fence. She's already spent a few nights here. She has everything sorted, even a stove.'

'No shit? She sounds full-on.'

'She's been couch surfing for so long, she even slept in her car. It's been rough.'

'Jeez, sounds like she needs friends. Why didn't you help her out, Erika?'

'I did! She stayed with me for a while, and I made it very clear she was welcome—'

Theo laughed. 'Ha, you should see your face! I'm messing with you.'

I splashed water in his direction. 'You dick.'

He dodged the spray, laughing again, then swam towards me. 'So where exactly did you sleep?'

'The top floor of that building on the left. It was going to be hotel rooms.'

'What's it like inside?'

'It's . . . empty.'

'Nothing at all?'

'Nope, only private space and that's all we need. We're not spending all day indoors. And Mac says the isolation is awesome, far away from any creeps.'

'How do you know *I'm* not a creep?'

I nudged him with my toe. 'Theo!'

The gap between us closed. He looked great when wet, skin glistening, hair slick. He dipped low, chin in the water, considering me with those sexy eyes.

'Shall we go inside the resort now?' he said.

I would've agreed to anything. 'Yeah,' I said, 'let's do it.'

28

MAC

I drove into the CBD to collect my passport. I wanted to stay busy, focus on London, to forget Anton and my awful afternoon. I replayed what he'd said. The callous, disgusting words. He was delusional, he thought somehow I'd been *interested in him*? I'd shown him the ropes when he joined the gym but that was far from flirting. In fact, I'd outright refused when he asked me out. Several times. How could he have interpreted that as a positive sign?

I coasted in, the traffic relatively light outside of rush hour, and found a park a few blocks away from the pillared building that housed the passports office.

My photo wasn't too terrible, considering I wasn't permitted to smile. Somehow, my serious face had an optimistic lift, a certain gleam in my eyes. I snapped a pic of it and sent it to Georgia. Then I went to a health foods café, messaged Dad to tell him about my pending travel as I sat drinking a green smoothie. There was only a 90-minute difference between Adelaide and Bali, but running the dog shelter took up most hours of the day. I didn't expect to hear back from him instantly, but I had a feeling he'd be happy for me. Unlike Sandy.

I was eight years old when my parents broke up; had never really understood what happened, except they weren't getting along. I could vaguely recall the tension in the house, a sensation of tiptoeing between two prickly adults. There was no shouting, but plenty of vicious bickering. And then one day, Dad packed his bags. He knelt by me on the kitchen floor, sobbing and apologising as he said goodbye and I was so stunned by his tears – the first I'd ever seen from him – that I became completely numb. I'd often wondered, if I was older, would I have tried to reason with them? Would I have asked questions? I'd never fully discussed it with Georgia, couldn't recall her being in the kitchen when Dad was leaving. Maybe we could talk in London. There was nothing to be repaired in the family, but it was important to check my memories, to perhaps understand what had gone wrong.

I checked the gym staff intranet. Sabina had posted a note letting everyone know I'd resigned and my shifts were available. I hastily added a sentence, saying I didn't want to give away my hours *just yet*, I was still waiting on my visa. The vague nature of my resignation might annoy Sabina, but I had to keep earning money for as long as possible.

How would Anton react to being banned? I couldn't imagine he'd take it very well, but hoped he'd learn a lesson and would behave better around women in the future. I wondered about the workout photos he'd taken of me; did he really delete them? Fuck him, he could look, but he'd never, ever be able to touch me.

I flicked through social media. Police were still searching for the missing prisoner, Curtis Burbank. I studied his mug shot. He had dark brows, close-cropped hair, a symmetrical face, the hint of a sneer – or was that my morbid imagination? There were thousands of comments, the public was outraged.

You should be sacked

How did u let this happen

Incompetent!!!

Burbank is a stone cold killer. So much for keeping us safe

My phone pinged with a message from Vikki: *Hey sorry about the other day. Things are less hectic now, wanna stay over?*

I sat, considering the offer. Vikki shared a townhouse with her boyfriend Mason. He was nice enough, but his overt spirituality began to grate on me when I spent a couple of nights with them. He was fond of sharing wanky quotes like: 'When you visualise, you materialise.'

'I see you, Mac. I understand, I empathise. You crave a home,' he told me one morning.

'I don't crave one, I bloody well need one,' I'd said. 'Everybody does.'

'Focus on that need.'

'Mason, praying for a lease won't make a lease appear.'

He'd spread his hands out. 'Keep an open mind.'

His Zen attitude was almost as bad as Sandy's irritating idea that I wasn't trying hard enough.

I texted back: *Thanks Vik, I'm sorted. Appreciate u, tho!*

My private room at Barren Cape, the sea views, the solitude – it beat Vikki's invitation, hands down. Even my inflatable mattress was more comfortable than her sofa.

Until my visa arrived and I booked my flight, there was no better place to wait.

29

ERIKA

'You sure there's no cameras?' Theo said.

I gestured around me. 'Can you see any? Come on!'

I led him to the gap beneath the fence. Removed the hoodie from my waist and pulled it on for protection before slithering under.

Theo laughed. 'Holy shit, you're a ninja.'

He followed my instructions, first shoving our bags and my food cooler under the wire. Then he lay down, twisting to get his wide shoulders through. 'Shit. I can't fit.' He retreated.

'Let's dig.' I started clawing and Theo burrowed from his side, both of us giggling. It was tough and my nails soon filled with grit, but we made the depression deeper. When Theo tried again, he scraped through and knelt beside me.

He winked. 'Thanks, bub.'

His soiled T-shirt clung to his abs, still damp from the swim. Before I knew what was happening, he pitched forward and put his lips to mine. My heart caught, and I leaned in. His lips were soft and warm. When we parted, we stared at each other with goofy smiles on our faces.

'That was nice,' he said. 'I've been wanting to do that for a long time.'

I couldn't string two words together.

He offered a hand and pulled me to my feet, which was just as well, because I was electrified and numb at the same time.

'All right, I'm ready for the tour.'

'Cool.' I could still feel the imprint of his kiss as we set off.

The resort was almost alluring, bathed in sunshine and scattered with palm trees, yuccas, a line of drooping agapanthus. Even the rambling weeds looked tropical. The perfect spot for our relationship to begin, and I had Mac to thank for it.

Recovering my power of speech, I pointed things out. 'That was going to be a day spa. And over there – that huge building was going to be double-storey suites. Very swish.'

'What's inside?'

'Dunno, I guess it's empty.'

'You haven't gone in?'

'Nah, I haven't explored from top to bottom, I haven't had a chance.'

We passed the empty pool. 'That would be a wicked skating bowl,' Theo said.

'Ha, you're right!'

We arrived at the furthest courtyard, the entry that Mac and I had used. 'This is where we go in,' I said. 'Help me lift this section.'

While Theo watched, I climbed through the opening with none of the fear and trembling of my earlier visit. I was on a high, thinking about our kiss and dreaming of the next one. I bet no other girl had taken Theo on a first date like this. It was pretty clear, now, that this was a date, that he was definitely interested in me. I could not stop smiling.

I pointed down the corridor. 'There's rooms all the way to the end.'

Theo entered the first one and I hurried after him. Sunshine framed the boarded-up window. 'Not much happening here.'

'We want the fourth floor, follow me.'

We entered the stairwell and I climbed first, wondering if Theo was checking out my butt. At the top level I estimated which door we needed, there being no numbers. The first two I tried revealed empty rooms. 'I swear I know what I'm doing,' I said, and Theo laughed.

The next door was correct. 'This is it,' I said.

We put our gear down and Theo's eyes swept the room. Mac's mattress, the stove with coffee pot, the lantern.

'You've got everything, you're all set up.' Theo peered into the en suite. 'No toilet though?'

'Nah, they didn't put them in.' I slapped the board covering the balcony. 'Here, let's move this.'

'Holy shit!' Theo said when the view was revealed. The sunshine was dazzling, and the sea sparkled beyond the resort's fence. We were royalty on a castle balcony, except that my hair was blowing into my face. As I gathered it in one hand, Theo stepped close. Chest to chest, we kissed again. He smelled like salt water and sunscreen and browned skin. I draped my arms around his neck and pressed closer. It was dizzying.

When we pulled apart, Theo shifted behind me, arms around my waist, chin resting on my shoulder. I closed my eyes for a second, relishing the moment.

'This spot is awesome,' he whispered. 'Where do I sign?'

We both chuckled.

'There's heaps of rooms, take your pick.' Mac would hate me saying that.

We remained on the balcony, me hardly daring to breathe in case Theo stopped holding me. Had he been waiting for an opportunity like this, too? How long had he been interested in me? I imagined being here with the resort completed, lights strung across the gardens, the pool full of water, music playing. A gigantic bed behind us, luxurious cotton sheets. Making love. Sleeping in. Ordering room service. Making love again . . .

'I gotta tell the boys about this,' he murmured.

'Sorry?'

He dropped his arms and I turned to face him. 'AJ and Kingy, my housemates. They will *lose their minds* when I tell 'em. You don't mind, do ya?'

'Um, we need to keep this small, remember? It's a secret.'

'Sure, it'll be small. Us three boys . . . you and Mac. We have, what, hundreds of rooms?'

We left the balcony and Theo opened the neighbouring room and looked in. 'Exactly the same.' He tried the next door.

'I should message Mac, tell her what's going on,' I said.

'Go for it.'

I typed on my phone: *Hi Mac. Surprise, I'm at The Place! It's so nice here, had a swim*

I couldn't think what to say next, so I just hit send. Theo moved on and I trotted after him. I hadn't ventured this far with Mac last night.

At the end of the corridor, he stepped into the second stairwell and leaned over the railing. 'COOEE!'

The shout bounced and echoed.

'Theo, we're s'posed to be quiet.'

'Relax, there's nobody here except us.'

'Let's keep it down in case people are walking by.'

'Okay, whatever you say.' He removed his phone from his pocket. 'I'll share my location with the boys. They're at work but they can join us after knock-off.'

'Maybe we should wait, run it by Mac first.'

'She's your best mate, she won't mind.' Theo was texting. 'I'll tell them to bring bedding, booze too.'

I messaged Mac again: *Pls don't be mad. I brought a friend. You know who!!!*

The fact that Theo was also bringing friends? I decided to share that news later.

Theo rubbed his hands together. 'All right! They'll get here around six. Let's go back to the beach.'

We returned to Mac's room. I put my Roxy straw hat on, Theo donned a baseball cap and we grabbed our towels. I took the mini wireless speaker from my backpack, too.

'Good one!' Theo said.

I glowed inside: me, perfect girlfriend material.

We returned to the sand, I wrapped my phone in my towel and tried not to worry that Mac hadn't responded to my texts. I was here with Theo – she'd forgive me. We ran into the water again. When he reached waist-high depth, Theo stopped and held out a hand for me. Our fingers weaved together, he drew me to him, and I finally got to wrap my legs around him. With his arms circling my back, we were as close as could be. I blinked the seawater from my eyelashes, and the waves buffeted us as we kissed. I wanted to remain locked together, but Theo eventually lifted me off.

He chuckled. 'Woah, we better take it easy.' He back-pedalled in the water, eyes on me.

'Glad I brought you here?' I said.

'Bloody oath. If you hadn't asked me, I was going to ask you out.'

'Really?'

'I've had my eye on you for a while.'

'Glad to hear it.' My cheeks ached from all the smiling.

Suddenly, he splashed me.

'Hey!' I spun, my back to him. If he wanted to break the mood, he had, but that was okay. I liked playing, too. I freestyled for a few metres, putting space between us. When I came up for air, I was closer to the shore and Theo was doing duck dives.

I glanced at the resort. Wondered about his mates; hoped they weren't dickheads, that they wouldn't ruin the day. Mostly, I wished Theo hadn't called them at all, that we could stay here alone and pretend to be stranded on a desert island. But Theo was a very sociable guy. It's one of the things that had first drawn my attention.

Then something moved inside the compound. I trod water, shook droplets from my face and tried to focus. My pulse skipped as a shadow moved between the buildings.

30

BREX

I stayed in the basement for a few nights, with Flynn and Cindi coming and going. When they first told me they were returning home and to school, I was pissed off. 'You're leaving me here alone!'

'We have to act normal, we don't want anyone to be suss about us,' Cindi said.

I snorted. 'All right, CSI.'

'Do you want our parents to come looking?'

'We need to grab more food and water,' Flynn said. 'We've gotta charge our phones, too. We'll come back with supplies every night.'

They were both right, but I refused to smile about it. 'Well, I guess that's okay.'

Flynn still wanted to leave Adelaide, but Cindi said that was crazy. I knew I'd figure something out eventually, but in the meantime I had the basement bunker. It wasn't so bad. Better than being in class. Sometimes I snuck down to the beach. I didn't go in the water, I sat on the shore and mucked around with the damp sand. Started making a small castle, but by the time I'd decorated it with seaweed it looked more like a mermaid's head. A dead, dried-out mermaid. I found two black stones for her eyes.

When I was too hot from the sun, I had a shower in the public toilet block. The water was cold, in a good way. I let it wash the sweat away; even opened my mouth to drink.

I slept a lot, too. And I began decorating the basement wall with a felt-tip marker I found in the desk. At first I didn't know what to draw. I'd only ever done tagging before, but I wanted to do something more creative. In art class last year we had a project to paint 'everyday moments'. That meant we didn't have to paint anything fancy, or paint a person, we could focus on any ol' boring thing nearby.

I chose the empty popcorn tin. It was decorated with green Christmas leaves and the label said 'Happy Holidays'. I was going to change that as soon as I could think of better words. 'Happy Homicide', maybe.

Mum phoned. When I didn't answer, she texted: *Michael says you haven't been home! Where ru?*

I couldn't come up with a reply. It was hard to think about Mum and the boys, it was like they belonged to the past. Was it possible to go back to the house? I wasn't sure where I belonged, and it gave me a queasy feeling.

There was something else on my mind, while I was drawing. The old dude on the roof.

I wondered what he looked like now. Did he smell? Were birds pecking at him?

I knew I should stay away, but the marker was drying out and my arm was tired. It'd be hours before Flynn and Cindi turned up.

So I left the room and let my feet lead me to the stairs.

I climbed slowly at first, *thud, thud,* wondering if I might change my mind. Then I got excited, wanting to get to the roof as fast as possible. I wondered why I'd left it so long, and started running, as if the body would disappear if I didn't get there soon.

When I reached the door, I was out of breath. I walked onto the roof and crept around the airducts.

He was lying where we left him, but seemed different in the bright daytime. His arms were neatly by his sides, his feet slanted away from each other. Sunlight gleamed on the bag covering his head, and I couldn't see past the plastic. I inched closer. If Flynn or Cindi were here, they'd shout at me to stop. When I was about a metre away, I could finally make out his eyes. I'd wondered if they were open or closed but they were neither. They were partially shut, like he was squinting, trying to figure out what went wrong.

31

ERIKA

'What's up?' Theo swam to my side.

'I thought I saw someone moving.' I pointed.

'Mac?'

'Uh, maybe. Or your friends could've rocked up?'

'Nah, they wouldn't have gone inside without us.' Theo squinted into the distance. 'I can't see anything.'

I couldn't see anything, either. 'Could be a trick of the light.'

'I've had enough swimming anyway. Let's go check out the rocks.'

'Okay.'

We walked hand in hand on the beach, Theo swinging our arms exaggeratedly, making me laugh loudly. We weaved about, avoiding the disgusting seaweed and crunchy shells, and the ocean droplets soon evaporated from my skin. When we reached the rocks they were larger than I expected, many of them more than a metre wide. Theo dropped my hand and clambered around, while I sat wriggling my toes in a calming tidal pool.

'Hey, there's a cave here.' He pointed.

He disappeared. Next thing, I heard the 'Oo-oo who-oo-oo whooo-oo oo-oo' of Duck Sauce's 'Barbra Streisand' coming from the cave. Theo, having fun with acoustics.

'Nice singing,' I said when he re-emerged.

He perched beside me. 'There's graffiti in there and blackened rocks. Someone's been lighting fires.' He stared at the sea and I watched him from behind my sunglasses.

'I'm so glad you're here,' I said.

He smiled with all his teeth. 'Me too. It's gonna be a good night.'

As we went back to our spot, we could see two men in the distance.

'Hey!' Theo waved. 'It's the boys.'

He jogged towards his mates while I meandered behind. When I caught up with them on the sand, they were standing around an esky. Theo introduced AJ first. I recognised him from Horizon – he was a flirt, often leaning over the bar, trying to chat us up. He was a shorter, paler version of Theo, with shaggy hair cut to chin length. Kingy I'd seen before too. He had brown hair, a thin moustache over thick lips. He was more laidback than AJ, but the pair of them usually shoved to the front of the crowd during Theo's sets.

AJ gave me a huge smile, while Kingy looked unsure he wanted to be here.

'This is sick, man,' AJ said. 'A resort, hell yeah.'

'Settle down, you haven't seen it yet,' Theo said.

'You didn't tell anyone else, right?' I said.

'Not yet.' AJ grinned.

'Please don't. This is supposed to be low key.'

'Fine, I'll keep it zipped.' AJ dragged two pinched fingers across his lips.

Theo pointed to three pizza boxes stacked on the esky. 'Let's eat!'

The sun was lower, the air was cooling, and we still had the cove to ourselves. I couldn't quite recall what day it was, when my next uni assignment was due, anything of the normal world. It was like we were on an island where the usual rules didn't apply. We sat, passed food and drink cans around the circle. It reminded me of hanging out with my brothers, only nobody was waiting to pounce on my leftovers. The pizza was delicious and I munched gratefully, listening to Theo answering AJ's questions – pretty much the same questions Theo had asked me earlier. Kingy studied the distant buildings while he ate.

'Where were you last night?' Theo asked.

I remembered that his mates had been evicted from their share house, too.

'Yvette's,' AJ said.

Theo laughed.

'What's funny?' I said.

'She's my ex,' AJ said. 'You know – desperate times, desperate measures.'

Disgusting.

'How about you, Kingy?' Theo said.

'At the oldies' place.' Kingy flicked a pizza crust towards a prowling seagull. The bird beaked it, then soared a few metres away.

'I was looking at places online today,' AJ said. 'There's a three-bedroom at Hamley that could be good. It's got a two-door carport too.'

'Bit out of the way, mate,' Theo said.

'Everything else is too expensive, we're running out of choices.' AJ reached for his beer.

'If we move to Hamley we'll be spending more on petrol.'

'All right, grandpa.'

We ate and drank, watching the sunset. Just when I thought it was beautiful, it became more and more spectacular: swathes of orange and yellow turning brighter and brighter amid the purple.

'Very speccy,' AJ said.

I took photos. There was no reply from Mac yet. Had she seen my messages or not? As the air chilled further, I pulled my hoodie on.

'We should make a fire,' Theo said.

'What with?' AJ said.

'We walked past plenty of kindling,' Kingy said.

'Right, mate, you've dobbed yourself in,' AJ said. 'I'll dig a pit, you start collecting.'

'I'll go, too,' Theo stood.

'I'll come with you,' I said.

'Nah, that's okay, we've got it covered.'

I watched Theo and Kingy disappear down the track. AJ knelt and began carving out sand like an eight-year-old.

'What can I do?' I said.

'Sit and look cute,' he said.

'Piss off.'

'Ha ha!'

I walked to the water and snapped a few selfies, draping my hair over one shoulder, changing the angles. Held the screen closer and wiped the mascara that had smeared. Theo and Kingy returned with armfuls of sticks and dried brush, dropping them beside AJ's pit. Then the guys crouched, talking and laughing, arranging sticks, while I remained by the shoreline, alternating between watching them or the water.

When Theo scooped something from the sand and came hurtling towards me, I didn't know what to do. His hand trailed gunk and seaweed. 'Stay there!' he warned.

I ran. 'Noo!' My bare feet pounded the wet sand, Theo's laughter metres behind me in the growing dark.

He waved the squiggly mass. 'It's nature's beauty treatment.'

'Noo!' I screamed again.

A current ran through me – I didn't want to be caught, yet I badly wanted to be caught. I spun away from Theo, both of us in hysterics.

And saw Mac's outline on the dunes.

32

MAC

Erika stopped running, but the DJ was still in flight. I recognised him from the Instagram photos she'd shown me. A dirty blond, with a string of musical notes tattooed over his sloping traps. He threw a handful of sea gunk and it landed on Erika's calf. She shrieked. It would've been funny if I wasn't so livid.

'Sorry, you stopped so suddenly.' Theo was laughing and puffing.

Erika wasn't laughing, she was gawping at me.

I didn't shift position, staring her down. After I watched the ute arrive, I'd stormed back towards my car, intending to leave the place. But why should I leave? I was here first. Erika had acted all anxious about my welfare, when in truth I was far down her priority list. She was here to party. As well as Theo and Erika, two guys stood by a flickering firepit on the sand. One of them was blond like the DJ, with no biceps or pectorals to speak of. The third was the tallest of everyone. He had the best arms, although his waist looked spongy.

Erika raised a cautious hand and waved at me. 'Hi.'

I maintained a numb mask. She muttered to Theo before walking over to join me. I left the sand and waited on the footpath; didn't speak until she was by my side.

'What's going on?'

'Did you get my texts?' she asked.

I nodded towards the guys on the beach. 'Who are they? Are they working at the resort? I saw their truck.'

'Oh, ha ha! No, that's Kingy's car, he's a friend of Theo's. They're vineyard workers.'

'So you brought a DJ and his mates here. Fucking great, now *everyone* will come. What the hell, Erika? I showed you this place in confidence.'

'I'm sorry, babe, I really am, I only told Theo and—'

'You've got the hots for him and can't help yourself!'

Erika flinched. 'Mac, please, they're Theo's housemates. Well, ex-housemates, since the landlord chucked them out. They're like us, they've got nowhere to stay.'

I couldn't believe what I was hearing. 'Oh, *now* the truth comes out! You've already told them it's okay sleep here, have you? *You* weren't even supposed to come back, let alone bring people.'

'They need somewhere to crash.'

'This isn't a real fucking hotel, Erika! Where are they living now? Tell them to go there!' The others were watching us. I hated this. Curious strangers. Judgement. Fighting to maintain dignity in the presence of random idiots. 'Have they been inside the resort already?'

Erika picked at her fingernails. 'Theo has.'

'Do they know this was my idea, that I broke in?'

She nodded.

'Oh, great, they know I've committed a crime,' I said. 'Now they can dob me in.'

'Why would they? They think it's cool.'

'Huh. Yeah. I bet they do.'

'They won't be a hassle. There's plenty of rooms – I don't understand what the problem is.'

'You weren't supposed to tell anyone, now I arrive and there's a party going on!'

'It's not a party, it's a few friends hanging out.'

'Secret. *See-cret.*' I enunciated the word as if Erika was a child who didn't understand the language.

Her eyes glistened. 'I'm sorry, okay? I feel terrible.'

'And I feel furious! I wanted this for myself. I'm tired of begging friends for a bed, of not getting a single second alone.'

'They won't invade your space, I promise. Come over and I'll introduce you—'

'Fuck introductions, I want all of you to go. *Now.* You included.'

'You're kidding.'

'I'm not.'

Erika lifted her chin. 'I am *not* going to ask them to leave. You don't own the resort.'

'I was here first.'

'Seriously? That's your argument?' She walked away. 'Come join us if you want, it's up to you.'

She reached the fire circle and the guys moved apart to let her in. Theo draped an arm around her. She was queen of the harem, any regard for my situation forgotten.

I marched to the entry ditch. Earlier, I'd seen my camouflage branch flung aside; Erika, the treacherous cow. I paced there, thinking. I could pack my things right now and go to Vikki's after all. But I'd already turned her down and it was early evening – it'd be awkward.

After I'd slithered under the wire, I kicked soil into the gap. Let them dig through that! I wanted Erika gone; the DJ and his mates too – all gone before the party grew any larger, which it surely would. I threw a handful stones on the pile for good measure. Hustled to the top floor and, as expected, there was strange gear dumped in my room. My room! Erika's backpack, a food cooler, a gym bag. Another bloody air mattress! Sunscreen and a half-empty bottle of water. I kicked the tube; it slid across the floor and struck the opposite wall.

Only then did I realise the balcony board had been removed. I always closed it before leaving. Those fuckers! I stepped outside. The sky had shifted into brooding blue and purple, normally picturesque, but now an irritation. I supposed the gang on the beach was lapping it up. While the dunes blocked my view of the firepit, I could see dark figures standing near the sea. Erika would be sharing her side of the story: *Mac's uptight, don't worry about her, she'll come round.*

I held the balustrade so tightly I could've ripped it away.

Fuming, I gathered their belongings and returned to the balcony. At the last second, I stopped myself from flinging the stuff over. I already had an argument on my hands, I didn't want the fight to become bigger than it had to be.

I ditched their stuff in the corridor instead, and wedged my door closed.

How long before everyone came inside? Would they knock and try to say hello? God, it was awful. I slumped on my mattress and checked my email. No news on the visa application. I opened Instagram, my feed full of friends eating, drinking, trying on new outfits, cuddling with their dog/cat/fiancé. Vikki had shared a photo of Mason painting their veranda: #dreamhome, #renovating #lifegoals. How would my friends react if I took a selfie in this bare room? #Squatting #CrimLyfe #BreakAndEnter

I checked Erika's Instagram. She'd shared a photo of herself beaming on the beach with the early sunset behind her.

'No!' I shrieked. I'd explicitly asked her not to share Barren Cape on social media.

Instead of a caption, Erika had added a series of beach-related hashtags. I supposed that was her idea of being secretive. A few friends had commented, '*Where is this?*' but Erika hadn't responded. Yet.

Her giggling invaded my thoughts. They were nearing the building. She laughed again – the happy hostess – and I flushed with fury. She was being too loud, reckless, had completely forgotten about the security patrols. I tracked the voices until they reached the fourth floor. The additional dirt and rocks hadn't deterred them.

Outside my door, Erika said, 'Oh, here's our stuff.'

Knock, knock.

I ignored it.

'Mac?' Erika's voice.

'Go. Away.'

There was murmuring, then footsteps clumping. I stood with an ear against my door like a lonely neighbour, trying to decipher what was happening. Heard bits of conversation.

'How about this?'

'Check it out, man.'

I was frustrated at not knowing what was going on. My bladder was bursting too, but I refused to go out there, so I went to the en suite and examined the drains. There was no choice. I squatted over a hole. If the smell of urine lingered, there were plenty of other rooms I could switch to.

Knock, knock.

The noise nearly made me yelp.

'Mac?' Erika had returned.

'What do you want?'

'Can I come in?'

'No!' I hustled from the en suite in time to see the door catch on the wedge. I braced against the wood. 'Go away!'

'Oh, come on, babe, it's only me here. I wanna talk.'

'What do you want to say?'

'Please, open up.'

I removed the stopper and opened the door a fraction. Erika's face was in shadow but still, I could see a groggy smile. 'The guys wanna meet you,' she said.

'Tell them to *get the fuck out.*'

'Please don't make this weird. I want us all to get along.'

'Erika, do you have any idea what you've done?'

The DJ appeared beside her, wearing shorts and no top, exposing his sunken chest.

Erika looped an arm through his. 'This is Theo.'

'Hey.' Theo oozed relaxation, only making me more tense.

The shorter blond dude with the clownish face shoved his way forward. Laughing eyes, cheeky sneer, bushy brows. He had a beer bottle in each hand and a toolbelt hung on his waist.

'This is AJ,' Erika said.

'What are the tools for?' I said.

AJ grinned. 'We made some improvements.'

'You did *what*?'

'We opened the fence panel near the public toilet. Now we have easier access.'

Erika looked proud. 'Isn't it great? We don't have to use the ditch anymore. And the guys are gonna open their balcony, like yours.'

'You shouldn't be tampering with anything!'

'You did.'

'That's different.'

AJ offered one of his bottles. 'Drink?'

'No, I'd rather you pissed off completely.'

'Mac . . .' Erika protested.

'It's all good,' AJ said. 'Erika explained everything, we'll keep it on the down-low.'

I glared. 'Messing around with the fence isn't keeping it on the down-low.'

'Nobody will notice, it's just an adjustment to the bolts.'

The third guy skulked in the background, towering behind everyone else.

'This is Kingy,' Erika said.

Kingy nodded, fleshy lips pursed, his gaze not landing on anyone in particular.

'Hi,' I ground out reluctantly. 'Look, if you guys think this is gonna be a party—'

'We're chill, we won't get in your way, promise,' Theo said.

They all exchanged glances. I hated this, me against them like some cranky tenant. It was my fault for trusting Erika.

They didn't deserve an explanation, but I wanted to try. If I could get them onside, they might be persuaded to leave. They'd had their beach party. 'I'm sorry if I seem harsh, but you've gotta appreciate my situation,' I began. 'You've just been kicked out of your rental, right?'

The three guys bobbed their heads in agreement.

'Yeah,' Theo said.

'We've been flat hunting for months, and put in more tenant applications than we can remember, every single one unsuccessful.'

'Woah, that sucks,' AJ said.

'I'm not here for a laugh, it's more than that to me. I've pestered and annoyed all my friends, slept on spare mattresses and couches. For all that time, I've been packing my bag every morning, getting into my car, trying to work out where I'll sleep, and it's *draining*. Hopefully I'm only here for another couple of days, because I'm waiting for a visa to go to London.'

'We get it,' Kingy said, unsmiling. He took me seriously.

'Thank you. This is my quiet spot, so I'd really appreciate if you could all—'

'We'll stay out of your way,' AJ said.

'That's not the point, the more people here, the more chance we'll get spotted.'

'We'll only stay one night.' He grinned. 'Or two . . .'

'Aw, piss off,' I snapped.

'Mac, you're being unreasonable,' Erika whined. 'You don't need this entire place to yourself! Can you reconsider, please? There's no need to be selfish.'

'I'm going to bloody strangle you,' I said.

Theo frowned. 'Hey, relax.'

'We should bail,' Kingy said.

AJ elbowed him. 'Don't be like that, mate.'

Kingy stepped back. 'Hanging out on the beach is fair enough, but I don't wanna sleep in a building site and I don't want any hassle.'

'Just one night, mate, what's the harm?' AJ said.

'Yeah, we may as well stay now,' Theo said.

'We're here, we've already started partying,' Erika said.

'All right . . . I guess I'll stay,' Kingy said, not looking at me.

'Gee, *thanks for understanding*.' I shut the door in their faces and leaned against the wood.

On the other side, Erika mumbled: 'Sorry, guys.'

Footsteps clomped down the corridor, the conversation faded. I let out a silent scream. What an awful day, beginning with the run-in with Anton. I didn't even get a chance to tell Erika about it, because she'd led this invasion of my territory. Traitor! When push came to shove, she'd tossed me aside for her latest crush.

The wind picked up, the room cooled, and I realised how hungry I was. I heated noodles and ate quickly, waiting for another knock, for loud music or laughter. But it was quiet, and that was worse, because I had no idea what Erika and the guys were up to.

33

ERIKA

We stayed on the same floor as Mac, setting up at the other end of the corridor. Theo and I had our stuff in one room and, without even having to discuss it, AJ and Kingy had settled diplomatically two rooms down. As Theo had suggested, they'd brought sleeping gear: a rolled-up swag, long sunlounge cushion, sleeping bags and pillows. Plus the esky.

Theo sat beside me on the floor while AJ and Kingy got to work removing the balcony covers. I removed a few of my favourite crystals from my bag and lined them along one wall; smooth, shining talismans that always travelled with me.

'I didn't know you were into crystals,' Theo said.

'There's lots you don't know about me.' I laughed. 'Almost everything.'

'Fair enough. What are they for?'

'The moonstone is for balance and harmony, this bloodstone calms the mind . . .'

'And you believe in this stuff?'

I looked at him. 'You think it's weird? Mac teases me about them.'

'Nah, they're cool.'

I didn't tell him about the rose quartz, meant to attract love, but it seemed to be working, because we threaded our sand-covered feet together. My cheeks were flushed, my brain fuzzy. The sun, the booze, the bud we'd shared on the beach – I was feeling the effects.

'I'm sorry for all the drama,' I said. 'Mac isn't normally like that.'

'It's not your fault,' Theo said. 'You told her I was coming, right?'

I nodded, even though it wasn't strictly correct. I texted Mac once Theo and I were already here, and hadn't said a word about the other two. I leaned into Theo's solidness, instantly feeling better.

'She'll calm down,' he said. 'I bet she hangs with us later.'

'I hope so.'

AJ gulped his beer. 'Where's the tunes?'

Theo set up the portable speaker and fiddled with his phone.

'Not too loud,' I said.

'That's no fun,' AJ said.

'We can do mellow,' Theo said.

As the music started, AJ slowly removed his toolbelt in a striptease motion.

Kingy rolled his eyes. 'Give it a rest.'

I opened the esky; the ice had melted and bottles were bobbing inside. There was nothing left apart from beer. For once, I was thirsty enough to drink it.

'Hey, hey, she appreciates the ale,' AJ said, snatching another for himself.

We crammed onto the balcony together. Now that the sun had completely disappeared, the city lights were the main attraction.

'This is sick,' AJ said.

Theo nodded. 'Yeah, sweet.'

'Reminds me of New Year's at Glenelg, remember that?'

The boys laughed hard. AJ bent over the railing, his top half disappearing.

'Be careful,' I said.

Kingy pointed at the ground. 'Who's that?'

'Who's what?' AJ said.

We looked down. I saw the curving cavity of the swimming pool, stretching from the Callista building and ending halfway along ours. There was enough moonlight to see the weeds and wildflowers, the hills of soil and gravel. Tropical trees cast shadows.

'I can't see anyone,' Theo said.

Kingy was still pointing. 'There was a person near that tree, maybe it was a security guard.'

'At this hour?' I said.

'Could be the late shift.'

'You're hallucinating, mate,' Theo said.

'It's a ghost,' AJ said. 'A bogeyman. The beast of Barren Cape.'

'Fuck you,' Kingy said mildly, pushing him.

'Hey, let's go up on the roof,' AJ said.

'Can't, I checked the door earlier, it's all locked up,' Theo said.

'Boring.' AJ drank more beer. 'Fine, forget the roof, I've got an idea. Let's play a game.'

My senses sharpened. One girl, three guys. 'What kind of game?'

'Well, it's not a game for pussies,' AJ said.

'Just tell us,' Theo said.

'It's still forming in my mind, but I've got a name for it. Night Hunt.'

Night Hunt. I didn't know what the game was and I already disliked it.

'How do you play it?' Theo said.

AJ laid out his game plan, if you could call it a plan.

He wanted to play hide and seek. Only, *everyone* would be hiding and *everyone* would be seeking. All throughout the resort, in the dark.

I waited for Theo or Kingy to say it was a stupid idea, we weren't in primary school anymore. But they laughed, and Theo began workshopping it.

'We could set a time limit. No, wait – we play until one person's left standing, no matter how long it takes.'

'I dunno,' I said. 'You do remember we're trespassing? If we're running around the resort playing games, we're bound to be seen.'

'Out here, now? Nobody gives a shit,' AJ said. 'Dudes, we can do whatever we want! Tame nights are for the suburbs.'

'It could be dangerous, we could get hurt.' The game concept was creepy. I wasn't sure I could keep up with the guys – and I was certain I'd be the first one picked off. I recalled that figure I'd seen inside the resort, back when Theo and I were first swimming. Had it been a security guard or another intruder? Probably just an illusion.

'It'll be harmless fun. Live a little, Erika,' AJ said.

'Ah, leave her alone.' Theo hugged me and I nestled into him. Wished we could retreat to our room, be alone.

I peered at Kingy. 'Do you wanna play this hunting game?'

'Dunno.' He shrugged. 'I'm too old for chasey.'

'It's not chasey, just hide somewhere,' AJ said. 'Hang out and be a sniper, dude.'

'Pfft. If everyone's playing, I guess I will,' Kingy relented. 'But don't cry when I win.'

AJ laughed. 'Onya, buddy!'

'Here, I've got some motivation.' Theo dug in his pocket and withdrew a packet of pills.

AJ bounced on his feet. 'Ooh, nice.'

The boys took a tab each.

'Babe?' Theo offered his palm.

I glanced around the circle. I wanted Theo to know how fun I could be and, as AJ said, we weren't in the suburbs anymore. Besides, it might give me the courage I needed.

With all eyes on me, I swallowed a pill. 'All right, let's do it.'

AJ howled with victory.

'Are there any more rules?' I said.

'What sort of rules were you thinking?' Theo said.

'Well, no physical stuff, no grabbing or pushing,' I offered. What I meant was: *Keep your paws off me. Unless you're Theo.*

'Fair enough.'

'Let's keep the rest of the game fluid,' AJ said. 'Remember, it ends when the last person is hunted down.'

'That means we can be strategic and play the long game,' Kingy said.

'And pounce when we're ready!' AJ said.

Long game, hey? Strategic? I had a rush of confidence. The boys thought I'd be the first person caught but they were wrong. I'd be way more patient and stealthy than them, more subtle, harder to pinpoint. I was fit, light on my feet. I'd kick ass.

'Right, the game begins outside,' AJ said.

We finished our beers, Theo switched the music off and we dashed along the corridor, snickering like naughty children. I thought about going to Mac's room and inviting her, but she'd refuse. What's more, she'd tell us to knock it off, put a stop to the game.

We gathered by a palm tree, our faces lit under the massive moon. Theo pulled me close and kissed me. 'Good luck.'

My body zinged with enough energy to run laps of the resort. He was smiling with those luminous eyes, and I decided to let him catch me early. We could snog in a hiding spot – or do more – while AJ and Kingy were creeping around without a clue.

Tucked in with Theo on one side, Kingy on the other, I joined in with their ludicrous whooping. Would we wake Mac? Who cared? We were a tribe.

AJ said: 'Ready? Go!'

We scattered like dice.

34

MAC

'*WHOO!*'

'Shut up,' I growled, dragged from sleep.

'*Ha ha!*'

Laughter and footsteps thundered. I reached for my phone. It was 1:14 am.

'Shit.' I rubbed my eyes, blinked to achieve focus in the dim room.

THUD! THUD!

What was going on?

I sat up. Moonlight shone through the open balcony. I struggled to my feet and padded across the room. Wind lashed at me as I checked the area below. I'd heard people, but couldn't see anyone among the shifting leaves and branches.

Then, out of nowhere, a ghostly call: 'Whoo!'

'Oh, grow up!' I yelled. 'I was sleeping!'

'*I was sleeping!*' someone mimicked in a high voice. Impossible to tell who.

Incensed, I pulled a hoodie and sneakers on. Removed the door stopper and checked the corridor. 'Erika, are you there?'

Only a tunnel of darkness. I phoned her and it went straight to voicemail.

Noise erupted outside again. Cackling. Then: '*BOOOO!*'

'Boo it up your arse!' I yelled.

'Ha ha ha!'

I marched from the room. 'Erika, where are you?' I opened doors, one after the other, finding no one but eventually spotting abandoned sleeping gear and an esky.

Then: *tink-tink!* Stones hitting a balcony.

I phoned Erika again. 'You better stop doing this!' Punched out a text message: *Call me right now!!!* I ran to the stairwell on light feet. At the top landing, I leaned over the handrail and pointed my phone torch downwards. 'You guys, stop mucking around!'

'*Whoo-hoo!*'

An angry pulse beat in my wrists. I raced downstairs, the temperature dipping as I went. Tucked my hair into the hoodie and slipped outside. The full moon cast everything in an eerie blue. I made my way carefully to a tree and backed against the trunk, watching. If nobody would talk to me, I'd figure this out for myself. Waking me up, booing and throwing pebbles – it was so childish. And if there was an evening security patrol, they'd soon hear the macabre noises. I was going to throttle someone. Theo and his mates were morons.

I tensed as I heard scraping nearby. Bending branches or approaching feet?

Ten metres away, a form emerged from a row of yuccas. Looked to be taller than Erika. Silently, carefully, I raised my phone and shone the light.

35

ERIKA

I crashed past trees and plants, the branches reaching for me, a jungle that wanted to munch me up. I had an intense desire to laugh. Clamped my teeth to keep my weird sniggering to myself.

The closer I got to the beach, the louder everything was. The waves boomed in my ears, my pulse pumped, the leaves rustled; it was impossible to hear if anyone was nearby. I stumbled when the ground dipped, and then the garden petered out and the wire fence loomed. Sea and sky blended together in a wall of navy blue. End of the road. I needed to turn back, needed a hidey hole.

A mound of gravel stood a few metres away, almost taller than me. I circled it, tucked in my T-shirt and lay on the stones. Scrambled up to peer over the top; a soldier in a trench. Palm trees danced, reminding me of giant inflatable tube men. Ha ha.

Ssh, Erika.

What was this game? I forgot the name.

Night Hunt.

Nighty-night, hunt-hunt.

Night, cunt.

My body shook with laughter.

What were the rules? I forgot the rules.

Fluid, AJ said. Like lazy ocean waves, the sweat trickling from my hairline.

Where was everyone?

Here, girlie, girlie.

Did I hear that or remember it? Growing up, I played a lot of games with my brothers: hide and seek, chasey; eventually they'd all turn on me. My terror was their fun.

Here, girlie, girlie.

Or was it Theo and his mates I could hear?

Theo, AJ and Kingy banded together.

A boy band. In matching outfits. I giggled.

A sneaky crew, coming for me.

I stopped laughing. Rolled over and watched the moon. Could it be used to tell the time, like the sun? Make predictions, see the future? *Hello, Mrs Moon. What's going to happen to me? Does Theo love me? Do I love Theo?*

I rolled over again. *Pay attention, Erika!*

Important to be serious, watchful, to protect myself.

I stretched taut feet and legs, imagined my tendons as elastic that could snap. Gravel carved my forearms and thighs. I needed a new hideaway, somewhere mellow, indoors. Back to my room? Too obvious. *Miss Obvious. Disobvious. Obliviousness.* My brain was a thesaurus, unlocking and creating words. My mind was amazing, I should tell everyone! That would be a better game, they could quiz me all night and I'd rattle off new words. *Machine-gun mind. Rat-a-tat! Deal with that.*

I eased myself up, walk-walked, fast-fast, quiet-quiet. Me, a power walker.

Where was Theo? I wanted Theo. Wanted just us two, in our little camp room. Stupid game had separated us. Why did I say yes?

Where was I? Mind mushy. I might survive this game if I hadn't dropped an E-bomb.

DUNK.

Noise nearby.

A door closing.

'Who's there?'

I found a skinny door I'd never seen before. How did I get here? I grabbed the handle. *Voila!* It twisted in my magical hands. Ha ha, predict this, stalkers! Gonna win this game.

And then, *ouch.* It pulled shut, my arm whipping with it. Not so magic.

'Who's there?' I pouted. 'Theo? Let me in.'

The night was huge at my back. Windy. Darkening. Too dark.

I turned and huddled by the wall. Closed my eyes tight like a child because, if I couldn't see the hunters, they couldn't see me.

36

MAC

'Aah!' A cry, and the nearby silhouette staggered.

I sprang over. 'Theo? What the fuck?'

He raised a hand to shield his eyes. 'Ha, you got me.' He crouched and massaged his ankle.

'Are you okay?'

'I twisted something, hurts like a mofo.'

'What's going on?'

'Night Hunt.' Theo widened his eyes dramatically.

'Never heard of it.'

'It's a game, we just made it up.'

'Are you for real? Do you have any idea how late it is? I was sleeping!'

A shower of stones landed nearby, then somebody ran, giggling.

'Ha, piss off!' Theo laughed. 'Is that supposed to be scary?'

'Who was that? Why are they throwing things?'

'I told you, it's Night Hunt. Rules are fluid, AJ said. But you can't grab anyone, no wrestling, that's Erika's rule.'

'Where is Erika?'

'I don't know. That's the point. She's hiding.'

'Alone in the dark?' I couldn't reconcile that with the Erika who had clung to me timidly when I'd brought her here. There was no limit to what she'd do to impress Theo. 'So, how do you play . . . Night Hunt?'

'Well, you've gotta hide, not let anybody see you, and try to find them first.'

'You mean *hide and seek*? Are you kidding me right now?'

'Nah, nah, not like that. We're hunting each other, we're all looking.'

'That doesn't make sense. Is there a time limit?'

'As long as it takes.'

'It could go on for hours.'

Theo stuck a hand in his pocket and withdrew a clear bag of pills. 'This should help.'

They were wasted. That explained a lot. I waved him away. 'Can you tell everyone to quit? Please. Someone's gonna hear you and report it.'

'The others aren't gonna listen, they're having too much fun. Just find them, like you did me.' He reached for me. 'Help me up.'

I bent, Theo slung an arm over, and we rose like partners in a three-legged race. He groaned.

'Do you need a doctor?' I said.

'Nah, I just need to elevate my leg.'

'You won't be able to get up the stairs. Maybe you shouldn't stay tonight.'

'I'll give it a go.'

We shuffled to the courtyard until Theo called for a halt. He leaned against the wall and wriggled his foot tentatively. 'She'll be right.'

'Are you sure?'

'Yeah, thanks, man. Enjoy the game.'

'What about Erika?'

'Dunno. She's having fun, I guess.'

He disappeared inside and I slunk away another 20 metres to stand alongside a palm. My sight had adapted and the environment wasn't so intimidating. I wondered where Erika was and if she was quietly freaking out. This might actually be an opportunity to frighten her and get payback after she'd spilled my secret. Could be fun. I tied my hoodie tighter. The days might be hot, but the night brought a swirling sea chill. A gust stirred the leaves. Where could Erika be? I became a statue, watching and waiting for movement.

In another couple of minutes, I was rewarded. A shadow moved nearby. A shorter, female shape. I darted over, reaching.

'Gotcha!'

'Fuck!'

But it wasn't Erika who smacked my hand.

It was Brex, the high schooler.

37

BREX

Star towered over me with her wide shoulders, her head hooded, fists bunched, like some kinda gaming warrior. 'What are you doing here?' she said.

'I could ask you the same thing,' I said.

'How did you get in? It's two in the morning, you should be home in bed!'

'Well, I'm not.'

'You can't be running around, this is no place for kids.' She stepped forward.

I stepped back. 'You shouldn't be here, either.'

'That's different, I'm a grown-up.'

'A grown-up lurking in the dark?'

'I wasn't . . . never mind. Your parents must be frantic. I'll get my keys and then I'll drive you home.'

'No way, I'm not going anywhere. You can't tell me what to do.'

'Brex, don't be silly—'

Star reached for me and I skipped away. 'Don't touch me!'

'I'm sorry.' She held her hands up. 'That wasn't cool. Can you just let me help you? What's going on, why aren't you at home?'

'Like you give a shit.'

'I do! I do care. I know what it's like to . . . drift.'

'You don't know anything about me.'

'Well, if you let me drive you home, we can talk some more. Or, I could drive you someplace else. Is there any family I could take you to? Please.'

I didn't wait another second. I ran, threading between the trees.

'Brex!' she called.

I zigzagged through the patchy garden, before diving low and crawling between two shrubs.

'Brex!'

Fuck Star, telling the universe that I was here. Trying to take care of me when I didn't need it.

I'd left Flynn and Cindi in the basement while I ducked outside to pee. On the way back, I heard voices. I hid and watched as a bunch of adults ran in different directions, giggling and hooting. They weren't supposed to be there. They were intruders, just like us.

And now I knew Star was one of them. What was her deal? How long had she been here? Had she seen the three of us?

She crashed about nearby, kept calling me, but I stayed tucked.

'You'll hurt yourself!' she warned.

I'll hurt you if you don't shut up.

After a few minutes she called out again. 'Okay, fine! I'm not chasing you any longer, the game's over.'

A man shouted: 'Will you shut up?'

Took the words right out of my mouth.

Star argued with him. I lay listening, plucking pebbles from my skin, wondering if he was her boyfriend and hoping Flynn and Cindi wouldn't come looking for me.

The argument stopped and things fell quiet. Moving carefully, I eased up and peered around. When I was sure they'd gone, I slunk back to our building. I sprinted along the basement corridor and tried the door. It was blocked by the desk.

'Let me in!'

I heard furniture scraping, then Flynn appeared. 'You all right?'

I shoved past. 'There's more people out there.'

'We know! One of them tried to get in.'

'*Get into this room?*'

'No, the building.'

'We were waiting for you by the exit,' Cindi said. 'Some woman tried the door. Flynn caught it in time.'

'Oh my god, did she see you?'

'Nuh, we kept quiet. She gave up and wandered off.'

'Well, I bumped into someone too.'

Flynn frowned. 'Who?'

'A woman I met on the beach. She gave me fifty bucks.'

'Why would she—'

'Listen. She's out there now, arguing with a guy. There's a few of them, playing some kinda game.'

'Game? Fuck. How many are there?' Cindi said.

'It's hard to tell.'

'What if they find . . . what if they go onto the roof?'

'I don't know!' The room was warm, too warm. I pulled my T-shirt away from my skin. 'Let's go up there now.'

Cindi shuddered. 'Do we have to?'

'He can't hurt us.'

'But he's . . . ick.'

Flynn stood up. 'Brex is right. C'mon, we can see what's going on from up there.'

'That's right,' I said. 'We'll keep watch and be ready for anything.'

38

MAC

'Brex!' I bolted after her, blindly thrashing past trees and bushes. She'd disappeared in an instant.

The pool emerged alongside me, a deathly pit, and I changed direction. 'Brex, come out, this isn't funny. Be careful, you could hurt yourself!'

I halted, listened, trying to swallow my loud panting.

I'd lost her.

I couldn't stand the thought of her lost in the dark. Even worse if she bumped into one of the guys, high on pills, playing their hunting game. It'd be terrifying. Did her parents have a clue she wasn't home in bed? They might be anxiously searching . . . or oblivious. For all I knew, Brex snuck out regularly.

'Okay, fine!' I said. 'You can keep hiding, I'm not chasing you anymore. Everybody, the game's over!'

Then, a male shout: 'Will you shut up?'

'Who's that?' I snapped.

'You're fucking up the game.' It was AJ.

'Good! Get over it,' I said.

I tramped about a bit, but eventually gave up. Inside Semira, I took the stairs one slow step at a time, the heat growing more oppressive as I rose. I felt deflated, seeing Brex and then losing her. I should've been calmer, set her at ease. Maybe I could've pretended to play Night Hunt with her and get her to open up. She needed a friend, not a crazed woman yelling at her.

I was on the first landing and looking forward to bed, when I heard whimpering. It sent an icy wave through my overheated body.

'Anyone there?'

I followed the sound.

'Erika!'

She was a few metres along the corridor, alone on the floor, clasping her knees.

I crouched and touched her shoulder. 'Are you okay?'

She assessed me through slitted eyes. 'Mac. There's too many doors.'

'Everything's all right, I'm here now.'

'Mac attack, my friend is back.'

Oh boy, she was high. I sat with my leg against hers, feeling her body's vibration.

'Where is he?' she said. 'Where's Theo?'

'He went to his room. Your room.'

'The game's over?'

'That's right.'

'Did you win?'

'Nobody did.'

Erika leaned on me. 'Let's be friends again.'

'We didn't stop being friends.'

'I love you, babe, I don't wanna be mad. Remember when we were living together, I was sick and you looked after me?'

'I remember. You were in bed for days.'

'You brought me medicine and OJ – not from a bottle, you squeezed it from real oranges. I asked you to tickle my forehead like Mum used to when I was a kid, and you did it, even though you didn't want to.'

It was true, I hadn't wanted to tickle her, but she'd pleaded and I opted for peace.

'You're so lovely, Mac. Look at your muscles, your strong muscles, you're a beautiful stallion, a sleek, shining horse.'

'Please don't pat me like that.'

'You're my mighty queen.'

'My god, Erika, you need hydration.' I stood, took her hands and pulled her up. 'Come on.'

We made painstaking progress upstairs, Erika's fingers digging into my bicep. I toed my door ajar and settled her onto my mattress. 'Here.' I passed her a bottle of water.

She gulped. 'Woah, this is delicious.'

I searched the food box and found a chocolate-flavoured protein ball. 'Eat this.'

Erika stared as if I'd handed her a magical orb. 'What is it?'

'Oatmeal, butter, protein powder . . . 160 calories,' I said.

'It'll give me superpowers.'

'Sure.' I watched her taking appreciative nibbles.

'Hey, have you seen a schoolkid here?' I said.

'A schoolkid?' Erika stared at the ceiling as if the kid would be floating up there.

'Yeah, I saw her a few minutes ago, she can't be more than sixteen years old.'

'I was sixteen, so long ago. I had an Ed Sheeran T-shirt. Where is it, did I lose it?'

I sighed. 'Forget it. I'll take you to your room.'

'No!' Erika's eyes bulged. 'They'll get me!'

'I already told you, the game's finished. Theo will be there.'

'Yay, Theo. I love him.' She took my hand and we shuffled along the hallway until we reached an open door.

'Theo?' I said.

No answer. I fished out my phone and the light revealed a sleeping Theo – torso on the mattress, legs spilling on the floor, as if he'd flopped in exhaustion. I steered Erika beside him.

'Macky-Mac, got-my-back,' she chanted.

Theo moaned but didn't wake. I removed Erika's shoes and she lay down.

'My bloodstone, gimme my bloodstone,' she said.

I grabbed a random crystal from the floor and put it in her hand.

She clutched it without checking which one it was. 'Kiss me goodnight.'

I planted one on her forehead and she smiled with her eyes closed.

'I was brave at first, I was so fast,' she mumbled. 'I was Black Widow.'

'Ssh,' I said.

'A magic door opened and closed.'

'Go to sleep.'

I watched over her for a while, her hands folded flat under her cheek, then went to my room. Stood on the balcony, waiting to catch sight of Brex. It was unsettling. I'd failed her. I wondered about her home life, who she lived with. I hoped her parents realised she was missing from her bed; they needed to step up and take better care of her.

I had a bad feeling.

I secured the wedge beneath my door.

39

ERIKA

When my eyes edged open, I couldn't make out where I was. I lay blinking in a fog, waiting for my brain to catch up. My skin was tacky and I kicked off the sleeping bag.

Barren Cape.

Theo.

He wasn't lying beside me. Our stuff was strewn around the room and the boards were propped against the balcony, subduing the hot sunlight. Did he do that for me? Aw, nice.

I reached for my phone. Theo had texted: *In Kingy's room*

When I arrived, beach towels were spread out like picnic blankets.

'Hello, beautiful!' Theo patted the space beside him. He was wearing the same shorts as yesterday with a fresh T-shirt. There was nobody else in the room. It smelled of coffee, there were takeaway cups and an almost-demolished box of donuts.

I rubbed my bleary face and sat beside him. 'Where is everyone?'

'The boys went to work – not before we did a breakfast run.' He handed me a cup.

'Thank god.' It was lukewarm but I craved the caffeine.

Theo scratched his head. 'What a night, hey? Bloody AJ, he's always coming up with wild ideas.'

'I can barely remember a thing . . .' As I said it, fragments floated back to me. I'd been lying on a hill of gravel. My hand went to my midriff, as if I'd find shards there.

'I crashed early,' Theo said. 'I think I was the first one out.'

'Huh? You left the game? Why didn't you come get me?'

'You were still playing. I didn't wanna spoil your fun.'

Mac entered the room wearing gym clothes, hair tied up and sneakers carefully laced. She was carrying her green keep cup.

'Morning,' Theo said, all sunshine.

I smiled, but Mac didn't smile back. 'Hi, did you sleep okay?'

'Is that a trick question?' she said.

'Donut?' Theo offered the box and Mac shook her head. 'That was a laugh last night, hey?'

'If you say so.' She stood at the open balcony. 'I found you all alone, Erika, stoned out of your brain.'

I giggled nervously.

'It's not funny, you were terrified, babbling,' she said. 'And Theo, you hurt your ankle.'

'I'm fine,' he said.

'See, we survived, we're all in one piece.' My temples had begun throbbing and I downed more coffee.

'What about Brex?' Mac said.

'What about what?'

'The schoolkid – I told you about her last night. She was here.'

Theo frowned. 'What schoolkid?'

'I met her on the beach the other day, then last night I bumped into her – inside the fence! She's a child, she should've been home in bed. For all we know, she's sleeping here too. I was wondering if you two would come help me check that she's gone.'

'What, *now*?' I said.

'Yes, now! I'm leaving for work soon.'

'And if we find her, then what?' Theo asked.

'We make sure she leaves.'

'You're gonna tell her to get lost?'

'Not in those words, of course not. I'll offer to drive her home.'

'What if she doesn't want to go?'

'She doesn't have a choice, she's not allowed to be here.'

'Neither are we, to be fair.'

I nodded. 'Theo's right. And we don't know anything about this kid, I wouldn't feel comfortable forcing her out.'

'It wouldn't be *forcing*. Her family must be worried, we can't ignore it.' Mac was getting worked up. Drops of coffee erupted from her cup.

'How old is she?' I asked.

'It's hard to tell. Fourteen, fifteen.'

'So, she's not a baby, she knows what she's doing.'

'She's pretty bloody young!'

I covered my ears. 'Can you please stop shouting?'

Mac stared. 'You were all perfectly fine about waking me up last night.'

'Sorry, babe. I'll look for this kid . . . but can we do it later? My head's not straight.'

'You're pathetic. You're so self-centred.' She left the room.

I struggled to my feet. 'Mac!'

'Leave her,' Theo said.

'I can't.'

I stopped in her doorway; she was slinging a gym bag over her shoulder. 'Don't be mad.'

She pushed past me into the corridor. 'I'm not mad, I'm frustrated and confused. Brex is a vulnerable kid, and neither of you give two shits.'

'I wouldn't know what to say to her, it's all so awkward. Teens scare me.'

'Teens need us. I bet lots of people have let her down, and I know how that feels.'

I felt a spike of anger, which only added to my growing headache. 'You're not gonna forgive me for bringing Theo here, are you? The truth is, we've made it safer, it's better if there's more of us.'

'Safer? You were running around like lunatics. I was happy on my own. I wasn't afraid.'

'You think you're so tough, but you're not. If you let people help you, Mac, if you told your family anything, you wouldn't be forced to camp out here alone.'

'You bitch . . . Forget it, I'll search for Brex on my own. You can go back to your fuckboy.'

'Excuse me?'

'You heard me!'

Theo arrived and inserted himself between us. 'Hey, hey, what's going on?'

'Fuck off,' Mac said. 'I don't understand why you're here at all.'

'We're just chilling,' he said.

'Chill somewhere else, dickhead!'

'Come on, let's go.' I took Theo's hand and led him back to our room as Mac's footfall faded towards the stairs.

40

MAC

As I descended, I paused at each level to hiss: 'Brex?' I walked the corridors from end to end. It was hard to focus on my search while I was simmering about Erika and Theo. How could they be so self-centred? Maybe Erika had always been like that, I just hadn't noticed before.

'Brex?'

I reached the courtyard exit. The sky had a rosy tinge and branches bent in the wind. I was running out of time, was due at the gym soon. Reluctantly, I gave up the search and walked to the layby, feeling the heat-lamp sun on my head. Got into the Fiesta and drove, keeping a lookout for any wayward teens walking alongside the road.

As I went through my workday motions, I couldn't shake the sense that Anton would reappear, even though he'd been banned. He'd left an uneasy imprint on me. My argument with Erika stung, too. When I added in my vexing relationship with Sandy, the idea of London shone brighter and brighter. It would be a new beginning.

After my shift, I went to the café on the ground floor, ordered food and opened my phone for some sleuthing. I wished I had Brex's surname, but surely her first was unusual enough to leave a trail. The problem was, I couldn't remember the entire name: Brex-*something*. I searched 'Brex', receiving results mostly related to an international basketball team and an IT company.

I visited the SA Police Facebook page and entered her name there. Zero results. I scanned the most recent stories. Police were looking for a missing 71-year-old Norwood woman who suffered from dementia; a motorcyclist had been killed after colliding with a tree overnight; and they were still hunting Curtis Burbank. There was no post about a missing teenage girl.

My food arrived and I began eating, opening my inbox so I could flick through emails at the same time.

And there it was.

A British government message: *Your visa application has been approved.*

'Yes!' I slapped the table, my feet did a little jig. The barista stared and I gave a sunny smile. I wanted to shout and share my win with everyone in the café. As my pal Mason had told me, *when you visualise, you materialise.* Ha ha. I messaged Georgia with the good news.

Grinning madly, I finished my meal and drove to the resort. The world was brighter, the suburbs basking in golden sunshine, smiling people sipping iced lattes, birds flitting between the trees.

Unexpectedly, my mask crumbled. I let the relieved tears flow. Until then, I hadn't realised how much anxiety I'd balled up.

If my visa had been rejected, I don't know what I would've done. There was no way I could continue my ridiculous squatting, I would've been back to applying for rentals and begging friends for accommodation. Thank god it'd worked out. I mopped my eyes, sniffed and tried to relish the positive outcome.

I used the car's Bluetooth to phone Sandy. 'Hey. I wanted to let you know – I got my visa.'

'Oh. So you're still going ahead with it.' Her tone chipped at my happiness.

'Yes, I'm still going. And don't worry, I won't stay with Georgia for long, I plan to be self-sufficient.'

'I should hope so.'

'Can I come over tomorrow? I need to get my winter gear organised.'

'What time?'

'After twelve?'

'That should be fine, though if you want lunch—'

'I won't be long, I just want to grab clothes. See you then.'

I disconnected before another argument could take hold. If all my cold weather gear wasn't stored at Sandy's flat, I'd be tempted to leave the country without saying goodbye.

I visited a liquor drive-thru. 'One bottle of Prosecco, please!'

When I arrived at the resort on foot, the chilled bottle stashed in my backpack, Erika's car was still parked alongside the fence, the pink frangipani sticker on its bumper. The same ute was alongside it. She hadn't heeded my advice about less obvious parking, but at least they were keeping quiet. I couldn't hear a peep until I was passing the Callista block. Music, not too loud.

Erika, Theo and Kingy were arranged around the swimming pool, dangling their feet as if it was full of water.

'Hi!' She jumped up and trotted towards me.

I stiffened when she pulled me into a brief hug, but then relented. A ceasefire would be good.

'I'm sorry about before,' she said.

'Me too,' I said. 'Guess what, good news – I got my visa.'

'Mac!' She hugged me again. 'Congrats, that's amazing.'

I pulled the bottle of sparkling wine from my bag. 'Want to help me celebrate?'

'All right, but just one drink. I'm working tonight. Theo has a set, too. You should come with us. Kingy and AJ are coming.'

'Nah, I'll be fine here alone.' I was delighted they were leaving; today just got better and better. 'Where's AJ?'

Erika giggled. 'Passed out inside.'

'You haven't seen that schoolkid, by any chance?'

'Nope, nobody but us.'

She held out two plastic cups. I poured, then sat between her and Kingy. His shorts bore faded paint stains and 'EAT THE RICH' was printed across his T-shirt.

'This is a great spot,' he said. 'Sorry we gatecrashed, it wasn't cool.'

'Thanks for saying that.'

'I heard you got a visa, where are you going?'

'London – as soon as I book a flight.'

'In a hurry, hey?'

We chuckled.

'So – Erika said you and the guys were evicted?' I said.

205

'Yep. I was renting a house in Eden Hills for four years, with mates coming and going. The place felt like my own, you know?'

'I won't ever have enough money to buy a house.'

'None of us will. My parents reckon I should live at home for a few years while I save up.'

'Oh, so you *do* have somewhere to stay?' I raised an eyebrow.

A grin split Kingy's face. 'C'mon, you know the drill. Once you've moved out it's hard to go back and live with the folks. They want to eat at the table together every night, Mum's always worried I'm not dressed properly for the weather. It's like being eight again – I wouldn't be surprised if she dragged out the ol' Lego boxes.'

We laughed again, sipped our drinks. Erika was chatting with Theo, the relaxed playlist our backdrop. While I was beginning to see the merits of having people here, my eyes roved constantly and I listened for any vehicles approaching. If the security guard turned up, we'd have to run, and quickly.

'What about friends?' I said. 'You must have other options than . . . here.'

'I could ask you the same thing,' Kingy said.

'Ha, fair enough.'

He looked at me. 'It took guts to break in, it's a ballsy move.'

'Or crazy.'

'It's not crazy. Why should these buildings go to waste? International investors think they can grab a piece of Australia and then when things turn to shit, they leave local contractors in the lurch.'

'Hey, hey!' A shout interrupted us.

It was AJ, arriving from Semira, already bobbing to Theo's music and wrecking our relaxed vibe.

'I'm here! When are we eating? I'm starving.'

'He's right, we should grab dinner now, then head to the club.' Erika got to her feet. 'Sure you won't come, Mac?'

'No thanks, I'm fine.' I rose with them, the Prosecco tucked under one arm. 'Well, it was nice to meet you all, if you're ever in London—'

'Oh, we'll see you again tonight,' AJ said. 'We'll have Night Hunt, part two. I've got ideas and new twists, we're gonna dial it up!'

My body tensed. 'You're all coming back here?'

'Yeah,' he said.

Irritation bloomed. 'You're practically spending the night at Horizon, why don't you go straight home afterwards?'

'We already planned to sleep here,' Erika said.

'Plans can be changed.'

'Oh please, Mac, don't start this again, I thought we were cool.'

'It doesn't make sense. Just go home to your own beds, for fuck's sake.'

'All our gear's here,' AJ said.

'Take it away with you now. I'll help you pack.'

'Chill, be cool.'

'Do you even care about getting caught?' I barked. 'Your cars are parked right outside! It's idiotic.'

'It's no biggie, the cars could belong to any rando at the beach,' Erika said.

'And what happens when there's nobody on the beach? Where would security go looking then, genius?'

We glared at each other until she wheeled away, muttering under her breath. I didn't care enough to ask her to repeat it. The boys filed after her.

Kingy gave a weak smile. 'Have a nice night.'

Theo put an arm around Erika as they walked away and she leaned in. For Theo, she was the whole package: accommodation; chauffeur; sex partner. I hoped he wasn't using her. She was dazzled by him and no longer gave a fuck about anyone else.

I gulped the rest of my cup and stormed to my room, the bitter bubbles swelling in my chest. It was dim, and I opened the balcony to let in the muted evening sun. Sat on the mattress and opened a flight website on my phone. Scrolled through columns of prices and dates.

The phoned dinged in my hand.

A message from Georgia: *Yay, visa!!*

I replied.

> *I'm about to book the flight*
> *Still time to change your mind, haha*

No change of mind x

> *Is the fifth too soon?*
> *That's four days away*

Sounds great to me!!
Can't wait to see ya

I returned to the flight website. It felt odd to choose 'one way' rather than 'return', yet I truly didn't know when I'd come back. This wasn't a short holiday, this was me embarking on what could be a new life. I read over the details once more, made careful selections and filled out the passenger information. 'Okay, here goes,' I whispered.

And hey presto, I had a booking number.

The confirmation landed in my inbox, and I forwarded the schedule to Georgia. She responded with a love emoji.

It was happening, it was really happening. I was leaving Australia in just a few days.

I brimmed with energy. Thought about going for a swim but then thought of Brex again. For all I knew, she was still at the resort. If I could find her, we could talk. It wasn't too late for me to try to connect with her, to check if she was all right. Maybe I could offer some meaningful support.

And there was another enticement. Semira was the only building I'd entered. It could be fun to explore another one. Who knew what I might find?

I put my pliers in my back pocket and left the room.

41

MAC

After just a short time at Barren Cape I felt a sense of ownership, but still I moved cautiously, sticking close to cover and being watchful. I stayed attuned to engine noises but heard the rushing tide instead; waves bursting into foam when they hit the shore. I realised I'd been so focused on maintaining privacy that I hadn't taken any beach photos. I made a mental note to do that before I left. Despite an unnerving few days, I didn't want to forget this place. The secluded cove, the distant cliff, even the mounds of seaweed. Hopefully in a few years' time I'd be settled into my own house, with my own mortgage, and I'd look back on this time as a weird yet wonderful adventure.

My plan was to enter the so-called luxury building, Callista. Wouldn't I be annoyed if it contained better rooms? But when I reached the reception block, I realised Brex could just as easily be inside it. If I was searching for her, I better do it properly.

Sheets of newspaper had been pasted all over the entryway. It was a miracle the glass was intact, and spoke to how isolated this spot was. I peered between the yellowed pages but could see only dark emptiness. I kept moving, entering a short, shaded walkway. Tried the door at the end. When the handle turned, I let out a short laugh. Too easy. How long had it been open? Zero rating for the security staff!

When the door closed behind me, my heart rate unexpectedly kicked up. I'd kidded myself that I was more confident among these abandoned buildings, but once I entered an unknown zone, my senses prickled from pure instinct. Someone could be hiding here, we'd proven that during Night Hunt. I bet Brex hadn't expected to see all of us; I certainly hadn't expected her.

'Brex? Hello?'

I took a right. As with all things resort, the ceiling was high and the walls and floors were bare, making the setting deceptively cavernous. Metres away, a blockish, three-sided reception desk rose from the centre of the floor. I padded over, my fingers tracing the cold slab. Too bad if they wanted to change the décor later – this piece wouldn't be easily budged.

I slipped behind the counter.

'Welcome to Barren Cape, how are you this evening?'

The joke fell flat when my voice echoed eerily. I froze, waiting for my imaginary customer to respond.

Returning to the corridor, I entered the stairwell and jogged up. The first two levels were expansive, empty and boarded up. There was no point removing a window panel and checking the view.

'Brex?' I tried.

No sign of her, nor anyone else.

I returned to the stairs and ran up, relishing the exercise. Reached the very top, blocked by a door covered in warning signs. If the lower door was open, why wouldn't this one be?

Bingo.

The door gave way and I stepped onto the breezy roof.

The setting sun was just at the right angle to be blinding. I threw up an arm to shield my eyes.

'Brex? You up here?'

There was a maze of air-conditioning ducts, a compact brick structure and various other industrial detritus. No teenager sitting and watching the view. Good. Hopefully she was home now, enjoying dinner, watching YouTube, whatever it was that kids did these days.

I approached the roof's edge, took out my phone and snapped a few aerial pictures. The colours were stunning. I certainly wouldn't see a wide horizon like this in London. I wondered if Georgia's house had a garden. I didn't really know much about the place at all.

The air was cool. I tucked my phone away and headed for the door. Then something caught my eye. It looked like a sleeping bag but as I drew nearer, the material became clothing.

I leapt back, clapping a hand over my mouth.

A person was lying alongside one of the air ducts, and something was very wrong. They weren't hiding and they weren't sleeping, because a plastic shopping bag was tied over their head.

It was a corpse.

'Fuck!' I yelped.

'You shouldn't have come up here.'

I whirled around. Brex.

'Oh my god, are you okay?' I moved position to block her view of the body behind me. 'Did you see . . .'

'Yeah.' She stood like an apparition, staring blankly at me.

I drew the phone from my pocket, trying to keep it steady between two trembling hands. 'I have to call the police. I think you should wait downstairs.'

Before I realised what was happening, she rushed me, knocking the phone from my hands.

'Hey!' I protested.

Then two more people appeared.

42

BREX

Flynn and Cindi stood either side of me. We should've acted sooner, should've hidden the body in a better spot. Now Star had found it and everything was so much messier.

Her eyes were bugging. 'What's going on? Who are they?'

'They're with me,' I said.

Flynn collected Star's phone from the ground and handed it to me.

'Hey, that's mine, give it here,' she said.

I checked the screen. No call had been made.

'Look, I don't know what's happening, but we have to call the police,' she said. 'Unless you already have?'

'This is nothing to do with you.'

'Excuse me? There's a dead man. This isn't some game, this is real!'

Cindi snorted. 'Of course it's real, you stupid bitch.'

Something changed in Star's eyes. She was coming to

understand her situation. I saw her trying to hide the panic, judging her next move.

She ran.

'Get her!'

We spread out. Star was heading for the stair door but Flynn blocked her way. I was ready when she veered left, arching her back and just staying out of reach. She leapt over one of the silvery ducts and I slid after her. She was nearing the roof's edge and swerved, aiming for the opposite corner. Cindi appeared, her arms wide like a basketball defender. Star turned around, but I'd closed the gap. Flynn joined us.

'There's nowhere to go,' I said.

'Unless you're gonna jump,' Cindi said.

Star glanced behind her.

In that split second, we all dived forward.

It was mayhem. I grabbed one arm, Cindi a leg, Flynn got Star in a headlock. Even folded over, she didn't give up easily. Grunting, she forced us right and left. I lost my grip and she backhanded me, knuckles slamming my forehead. Pain exploded. 'Fuck!'

She twisted and punched Flynn in the ribs but he didn't let go, just wrestled harder. She was almost bent double, Cindi coiled around her leg, and when I joined in to hang off her other arm, Star couldn't stay standing. We brought her to the ground like lions with a deer.

'Get off!' she screamed.

We were a squirming heap on the concrete. Flynn lay across her torso, keeping her down. She wriggled and raised her knees but Cindi and I pressed with all our weight.

My blood was fizzing. 'Stop fighting!'

But Star kept struggling. 'Let me go right now!'

'No.'

'My friends are here.'

'Liar! We saw them leave.'

'They went to get food, they'll be back in a minute.'

'Your story keeps changing, you're full of shit,' Cindi said.

Star raised a knee, I pushed it back down. 'Brex,' she said, 'I thought we were friends. This isn't right.'

Flynn twisted to look at me. His face was red, there was a scratch on his cheek. 'What do you wanna do?'

'I . . . I . .' My brain was fried. Star had seen the body – we couldn't let her go. But I had no idea what to do with her.

Her eyes drilled into mine. 'This is crazy! You know me, you can trust me. Whatever's happened, let me help.'

'Don't listen to her,' Cindi said.

Star stayed focused on me. 'Who is the dead man? Did he hurt you?'

'Shut up!' Cindi screeched.

'We can't let her go,' Flynn said. 'She'll run straight to the cops.'

Star began writhing again. She was so strong that the three of us struggled to hold onto her.

'Keep still!' I said. But she tried to coil and roll onto one side. I felt my grip loosening again. 'Flynn!'

He put his hands around Star's throat.

Her legs flapped. I heard a guttural groan.

Finally, she stopped moving.

43

MAC

When I came to, there was a bear on my chest and anchors on my legs. Panic flooded me. It was like being trapped in a bench press, and almost impossible to breathe.

The tall boy was still pinning me, his knees on my biceps, pinching my skin. I could see my horror reflected in his round eyes. Smelled his body odour, his bare legs inches from my face. I tried to turn away but couldn't. My neck burned. The tinted orange sky hadn't changed, yet it felt like I'd been out for hours. I began struggling, but the force field remained. Brex weighed down my legs, while the girl in the red singlet was looping a plastic tie at my ankles. I tried kicking and bucking. The girl swore and shrank away as my legs flailed.

'Lie still!' The boy's spit flecked my face. He put hands on my neck and didn't have to apply any pressure before I went limp and compliant. I'd already blacked out and didn't want to re-enter that darkness. Tears of terror and anger slid down my cheeks.

'Don't do this.' My voice was a squeak from my sore throat.

'Shut up.'

Red Singlet resumed tying my ankles, then the boy shifted aside so she could do the same to my wrists.

'No!' I said.

They ignored me and continued their work. The cuffs were tight and painful.

Brex stood, the trio surrounding me. 'Stand her up.'

Her friends grabbed my armpits and forced me to my wobbly feet. My shorts slipped down and I yanked them up, moving awkwardly. They'd used four cable ties: two strands on my wrists, two on the ankles, crossed over to reinforce them. I twisted my hands. There was little give. I tried to scream. All that came out was a painful cough.

'Stop that!' Brex was breathing fast, her eyes wild. I wondered if she was on drugs. She patted my pockets and removed my wallet. Then she tugged me towards the door.

'Where are we going?' I whispered.

'Shut up.' Red Singlet shoved me.

We entered the dark stairwell. I sat on my butt, terrified of falling head first.

'Move! Hurry up,' Brex said.

'I can't . . .' I nodded at my bound ankles.

She groaned. 'Fuck's sake.'

'Take the ankle ties off, we can put new ones on when we get downstairs,' the boy suggested.

'We don't have anything to cut them with,' Red Singlet said.

Brex chuckled and put a hand over her eyes. 'All right, you'll have to go down on your arse, Star.'

The boy prodded my back and I inched along. I couldn't believe this was happening to me. Who was the dead person? Did the kids stumble on the body, like me, or were they involved? If they could do that to someone, what was stopping them from doing the same to me?

At least they hadn't tossed me from the roof. That was something, right?

Brex got bored watching my slow progress; she trotted on and disappeared below. The other two were also impatient, toeing my shoulder blades. If I wasn't perched so low and defenceless, I would've turned and tried to upend them.

Down, down, we went. Past the ground floor and towards a basement I didn't know existed. Brex was waiting with her phone light. The other two pulled me to my feet again. We were in a dank corridor with pipes in the ceiling. It had an unnerving submarine vibe. I was being stowed; removed far from any help. I was so bound up, I couldn't try walking away, much less running. Were they going to kill me here? Put a bag over my face, too?

Ahead of us, Brex waved towards an open doorway. 'In you go.'

'Please,' I rasped. Tried to communicate with my eyes. *Stop this. I was nice to you . . .*

The others shunted me inside. It was more like a large storage cupboard than an actual room. The floor was bare and shelves ran along two sides, not quite reaching the low ceiling.

'Sit.' Brex nodded at the ground.

I shook my head.

'Flynn,' she said.

The boy punched me in the stomach.

Oof! I bent over. I'd never experienced anything so sharply agonising. While I gasped, they jostled me to the floor beside a shelf, their legs crowding me. The boy, Flynn, yanked my feet into position and Red Singlet passed him more cable ties.

'No!' I rolled away.

Someone kicked my thigh. I curled up, chin tucked in.

'Are you gonna behave?' Brex growled.

I nodded, my eyes shut. They pushed and positioned me so Flynn could tie one ankle to a shelf leg, which was bolted to the concrete. He tested the cable – there was no give. Now my hands and feet were bound together, while one ankle tethered me in place.

'Don't do this,' I said, voice hoarse.

'Behave yourself, we'll be back soon,' Brex said.

They filed out, shutting me in. My larynx wouldn't allow me to call after them.

I strained at the ties, achieving nothing except drawing the plastic into my skin. It was useless – the strands were far too strong. I tried sitting, raising my arms high and slamming the cable onto one knee. It produced a dagger of agony; nothing broke except for skin. Tears spilled as I nursed my wrists. When I recovered, I tried unpicking the ankle restraints instead, even though I knew it was impossible: cable ties didn't work that way.

Then the door opened. It was Brex.

'You look bummed to see me.'

A shape came flying; my pillow landed at my feet. Next, she rolled two bottles of water towards me. They were from my own supply. They'd found my room.

'See, I'm looking after you, Star,' she said.

'Did you do it?' I asked.

She paused in the doorway. I couldn't see her friends.

'Did you hurt that man?' I said.

'Shut up,' she said.

'Wait, please don't—' I began, before the door slammed again.

I hung my head and listened to sneakered feet running away. Shut my eyes, pressed my lips together and willed myself not to freak out.

Erika and the guys, they'd be at Horizon by now. It'd be hours before they returned. And when they did, who's to say they'd come looking for me? I sure as hell couldn't shout for them.

I opened my eyes and drew the pillow closer. Rather than being comforting, the new items unsettled me. How long did they plan to hold me here?

44

BREX

We caught a train into the city to shop at the mall, moving through the crowds without anyone knowing who we truly were. Who we'd become. I was proud of Flynn and Cindi, proud of myself. When we shoved through a group of Aldgate College kids, I deliberately stuck my elbow out. Boujee fuckers better not mess with us.

We used Star's credit card at the mall, her real name staring at me in tiny raised letters. I bought a pair of half-price Nikes with the back tabs and mud guards. Everything we chose had to be under a hundred bucks because we didn't have the card's code. I used payWave at the register, body firing, ready to run if something went wrong. When the card worked without a hitch, we really got going. We moved from store to stove, grabbing clothes and accessories. We were watching Cindi try on sunnies when Mum phoned me.

'Where are you, *where have you been*?' she screamed.

'I'm hanging out with Cindi,' I said.

222

'I need you home. Right. Now.'

'Is he there?'

'Who, Michael?'

'Shithead.'

'Don't call him that. Michael's staying here and you better get used to it.'

'Then you better get used to me not coming home!'

Two women by the counter turned to stare at me.

'You're the kid, I'm the mother and you'll do what I say.'

I shook my head. She just wouldn't listen. 'You know he tries to sneak into my room at night? I hear him rattling the door.'

Mum was quiet for a beat. 'He's checking on you – he checks on the boys, too. Stop inventing drama. He warned me about this. You want to ruin everything for me, but I need a man in my life. It's not easy. When you're older, you'll get it.'

'I'll never get why you like *him*.' I ended the call.

'You all right?' Cindi was standing close by.

I was breathing hard. Everyone was an audience, the shop music was too loud.

Cindi grabbed my arm. 'Let's get out of here.'

In the James Lane toilets, I slammed the cubicle door behind me and sat for a while. Why couldn't Mum take my side? Shithead was gross around me, practically drooling, how could she not notice? I pressed my fists against the cold walls hemming me in.

Cindi tapped on the door. 'Brex?'

'What?'

'Wanna wear our new clothes?'

I felt better when we'd changed outfits. I loved the clean smell and soft fabric of my new shorts and top. We posed in front of the mucky mirrors for a while, taking photos. Cindi painted liquid colour onto my lips. It was gentle and ticklish and I didn't want it to stop.

'This colour's called Carnivore,' she said.

'Do I look okay?'

'You look amazing.'

Next, we went to a trendy café and bought proper food for dinner, not burgers. It was way better than what Mum and the boys would be eating at home. I kept the credit card safe, fingers constantly checking its position in my pocket.

'*We rich*,' Cindi said.

'You know it,' I said.

Flynn tried to order ciders and when the staff refused, we cackled. We didn't mind too much. We took turns recharging our phones in a power outlet beside the table. People sat eating around us, the lights were low, RnB was playing, and it was hard to believe we had Star – I mean *Mackenzie* – tied up at Barren Cape and a dead man on the roof. I always thought I was badass, now I knew for sure. I had my friends, money, new clothes, dinner. I didn't need Mum, didn't need her house. I could take care of myself. This was the real beginning of my life.

'What are we gonna do with her?' Cindi said.

'Ssh.' I glanced at the diners around us.

'What? Nobody's listening, they're too busy jabbering.'

Flynn pushed a slice of tomato around on his plate. 'I reckon we leave her there and never go back.'

'What . . . forever? So, she starves to death?'

I nudged Cindi hard. 'Shut. Up.'

'Ow!' She rubbed her elbow. 'We have to talk about it.'

'Someone will find her eventually,' Flynn continued quietly.

'And then she dobs us in, and we wait for the cops to knock on our door. Great idea!' Cindi scowled, the point of her nose literally turning up. She'd throw her food at Flynn if he wasn't careful.

He wouldn't look at either of us. 'I was thinking, we should get a bus ticket. Maybe even a plane, we could go to Melbourne or Sydney. We shouldn't stay here, we should use this chance to get away.'

'Get away?' I said. 'You mean *run away*? What would we do, where would we live? Our families would come looking, everyone would.'

'It doesn't feel right to stick around and wait to see what happens.'

Cindi and I exchanged a glance but I couldn't tell what she was thinking.

'We'd need a lot of money for that,' I said. 'I wonder how much money she's got.'

'Probably nothing,' Cindi said. 'She's homeless, she's on the bones of her arse.'

'She had enough money for this.' Flynn waved at our shopping.

'If we had her PIN, we could see into all her accounts, and we could take more too.' My legs bounced under the table.

When we left the café we still hadn't agreed on a plan. None of our ideas seemed right.

Outside, it was properly nighttime, and cars and buses had headlights on. People rushed past with shopping bags or business satchels. Despite everything, I yawned. We'd been awake for ages.

'What now?' Cindi said.

'I'm not going home,' I said.

'I'm not either,' Flynn said.

'Well, I'm not sleeping at The Cave,' Cindi said.

Flynn pointed at a glitzy building across the street. There were lights strung around its doorway and carpet over the footpath. 'We've got money.'

Cindi clapped. 'Yes! I've never stayed in a hotel. Can we? Please?'

'I don't reckon they'd let a bunch of kids in,' I said.

Flynn opened his phone. 'We could try a less flash place – the motel on the road near school?'

'The one behind the pub?' I could picture the long building with its mural of seagulls. 'Okay, let's try.'

We crowded around as Flynn booked a room online; a family option with a queen bed and single bed. I recited the credit card's number and he typed them in. 'Done.' We jumped in a cab, Flynn sitting up front, me in the back with Cindi. She reached across the seat, threaded her fingers through mine. I watched the busy city through my own window. I couldn't wait to see our motel room, to spend a night away from home. *Suck it, Shithead.*

Flynn went to the reception desk while we waited in the carpark.

'Any problems?' I said.

'Nope.' He flashed the keycard.

In our very own hotel room, Cindi and I whooped and danced. Flynn howled too, but his eyes were wet. I knew he was worried, he was thinking about what we'd done and what might come.

There was a stack of thick towels on the bed. I threw them in the air. 'Whee! Two towels each!'

Flynn rubbed his sleeve over his face and managed to smile. We fell onto the mattresses. They were firm and the sheets tucked in tighter than I'd ever seen before. The pillows were oddly long, but super soft.

Cindi ducked into the bathroom 'Check it out! Shampoo, conditioner, moisturiser!'

'Gimme one.' I caught the mini tube that she threw, rubbed lotion over my arms. I hadn't thought about buying makeup with Star's credit card; I decided I'd do it the next day.

I scanned through the TV channels until I found music clips. Cindi upended her shopping bags and laid her new gear over the bed. Flynn filled the bathtub. We ordered pizza and sat eating on the bed together.

'This is the best night ever,' Cindi said.

I smiled. 'I don't want to change a single thing.'

45

ERIKA

'This here, this is all you need.' AJ chewed loudly. 'A hot feed, somewhere to put your head at night. No rent, no landlord, no power bills. No mortgage, no capitalist lifestyle—'

'Oh jeez, he's getting political,' Theo said.

We were crammed into my car on the way back from Horizon, Theo beside me, AJ and Kingy in the rear, all the boys eating burgers. The Barren Cape turn-off wasn't far, and there was no other traffic on the road – not surprising, after 2 am. The moon was full and round, and I slumped in my seat, exhausted after my shift. My head throbbed and my feet ached; I must've poured hundreds of drinks. AJ had nagged me for freebies but I ignored him, he wasn't worth getting fired over. I would've liked to just stare at Theo behind the decks, but the club had been packed and the bar didn't let up. I had to be content with glancing from afar, recalling the taste of Theo's neck from earlier that day. Was it sea salt or sunshiny sweat I'd tasted? I'd given him a small hickey and wished that everyone at the club knew it was me.

'We've been brainwashed, man,' AJ continued. 'Caught in the machine. I'm not interested in mowing the lawn every weekend, I'm not interested in IKEA shelves.'

'Yeah, you're onto something.' Theo shoved fries into his gob. 'This is a legit lifestyle.'

That made me twitch. The resort was fun for a few days but I wouldn't want to stay any longer. The sex with Theo was exciting, it was fire, not only because our relationship was new, but because of the threat of being caught. But now I wanted to be back in a proper, soft bed. I'd mentioned it to Theo earlier. 'You could come to my place,' I said, as we snuggled.

'I thought you lived with your parents,' he said.

'I do, but they're cool, they wouldn't mind at all.'

'No thanks, I'm not into it.'

It was disappointing, but I'd come up with another scheme since then, and it made a lot of sense, especially now Mac was leaving me for London. I decided to share it with the car.

'Listen, I was thinking, we could get an amazing share house together. Imagine! There's four of us, we could afford a really nice place, a massive one, with plenty of bedrooms. Maybe a few bathrooms, even a pool!'

'Those kinds of places cost heaps,' Kingy said.

'That's my point,' I said. 'If we combine our incomes it won't be out of our league. And fewer people apply for huge houses, it's actually less competitive than looking for a flat.'

'Meh. I like the resort,' AJ said. 'We should stick it out longer, at least while it's summer.'

'But that's no solution. What about security patrols? We could get kicked out any day now.'

'If that happens, we move on.'

'Yeah, I mean, you can't beat the location,' Theo said.

'Or the price!'

The boys laughed.

My hands tightened on the wheel. 'I dunno . . . peeing in the bushes isn't fun. And I'm telling you, we should seriously look at renting together.'

The boys were hushed, no doubt thinking the same thing: they barely knew me; it was far too early to add me to their housemate list. But I was convinced it'd work; I was ready. They were fun and we got along so well. And I was developing feelings for Theo. It'd be a dream to share a house.

Theo broke the silence. 'I was thinking – the resort is the perfect place for a rave.'

AJ high-fived him. 'Mate, you're right. We could put on a show. People would go ape over it!'

'There's no electricity,' Kingy said.

'We can work something out.'

'No!' I interrupted. 'Are you forgetting it's illegal for us to be there?'

Theo chuckled. 'Raves usually are illegal.'

'But we'd spoil the place for Mac. We promised not to tell anyone.'

'I didn't promise,' AJ said.

'And *you* already broke the promise.' Theo raised an eyebrow at me.

'I was doing you a favour!'

The sign for Barren Cape appeared. I slowed the car, we hit the dirt road and in another minute my headlights found

Kingy's ute. The resort seemed subdued and placid behind the fence, but that changed as I exited the car. My hair flew into my face, the crashing of waves was louder than ever, the air was biting. I rubbed my arms, glancing at the inky scrub beside us. 'Hurry up, I wanna get inside. I am so tired, I'm gonna drop.'

Kingy and AJ spilled from the car, AJ stretching for the stars. We trooped down the track, Theo first, me next, Kingy and AJ last. AJ's yawns were like a wounded animal and I wanted to tell him to shut up. We slid beneath the fence and I didn't bother dusting the grime from my clothes. Our phones lit the route to our courtyard. It took all my energy to climb the stairs.

'So, what's happening now?' AJ said when we arrived at the top floor.

'Bed,' I said.

'Woah there.'

The boys laughed.

'Very funny,' I said.

As we neared Mac's closed door, I put a finger to my lips. Ssh.

I felt bad about our argument; I'd said horrible things. I'd apologise in the morning.

I entered my room with Theo in tow, nothing to break the darkness apart from our phones. AJ and Kingy continued on. The air mattress slid as I sank onto it.

'Sure you won't hang out with us?' Theo said.

I blinked up at him. His face was carved by shadow. 'Aren't you staying with me?'

'I'm gonna hang with the boys for a while. We're all still buzzed.'

I tried to hide my disappointment. 'Fine, close the door on the way out.'

'Do you want me to open up the balcony, let some air in?'

'No, actually, keep them closed.'

Theo kissed the top of my head before he left. I undressed and lay down. When I switched my phone off, it was like being in a tomb.

46

MAC

Clutching a shelf pole, I pulled myself to a standing position. Everything ached, especially my throat, as if I'd drunk steam. My limbs stung with bruises and scrapes. I shook the steel frame, trying to find a weakness or some way to whack it against the floor and make a racket. Nothing loosened, it was all welded too firmly.

'Help! I'm in here . . .' My voice was muted in my burning throat.

In the dim light from under the door, I saw that most of the shelves were empty. There were a few items – plastic bottles, some with spray nozzles. A bucket. Two slim cardboard boxes. There wasn't enough light to read any labels. Brooms and mops leaned in a corner. This was a cleaner's space, the only resort room I'd seen that actually contained something.

My mind flashed to the body on the roof. A man lying facing the sky, dressed head to toe in green with a bag over his head, like he was something that could be stored for later. Did someone suffocate him? I wondered how long the body had been at Barren Cape. The same time period as me? Feeling woozy, I sipped the water Brex had tossed in. It sloshed in my belly. I breathed carefully, worried I might throw up, but the feeling passed. It was horrifying to think of sleeping in the building next door to a corpse, oblivious. What about during Night Hunt? Any of one us could've stumbled upon him.

And then, anyone could be responsible. Theo and the guys? I barely knew them.

Not Erika. No way, it was nothing to do with her.

It had to be Brex. She and her mates weren't rattled by the corpse at all. They stopped me phoning the police. But why? Who was the man, and what motivated the kids to kill him?

Time went on. My mind and body were exhausted, the room was too warm. I needed to conserve energy. I rested against the bars, manoeuvring the pillow behind me, trying to find a comfortable position. With one foot anchored, the options were limited. I had some success lying with the pillow lengthways under my head and shoulders. My limbs went numb, my wrists and ankles were stinging. I wondered when Brex would return.

'Aargh!'

My moan was part fear, part anger. The groaning didn't last long, my vocal cords too sore and swollen. I flexed my toes and fingers to get the circulation going.

Not knowing the time was incredibly frustrating. Had Erika and the boys returned from Horizon? Even if they had, they wouldn't necessarily expect to see me, they'd assume I was sleeping. Actually, Erika probably wanted to avoid me – we were on tense terms.

Even worse, she might've taken my advice and gone directly home after the nightclub. It's what I had shouted at all of them to do. Fuck!

And my café shift? I was rostered on to work at breakfast. Clover might phone me when I was late arriving, but she wouldn't exactly send a search party. She could even assume that I wasn't going to come to the café again – after all, I'd quit. Sandy expected me to visit at lunch and collect winter clothes but if I didn't show, she wouldn't fret too much. Not immediately. Not for a few days at least.

I ignored my bladder for as long as I could. The kids hadn't thought about me needing the toilet, and to be honest, I hadn't either. I fixed on the bucket as my solution, but it was out of range on a middle shelf. I drank the remainder of one water bottle, then threw it. Missed the bucket completely. I removed one of my sneakers, held it between two hands like a netballer prepping for a three-pointer. The shoe struck, sending the bucket to the floor. It was still rocking as I lay flat and reached for it. The cable ties were excruciating as my fingers strained for the plastic rim. Finally I snatched the bucket up. I wrangled the bucket between my legs, pulled my shorts aside and crouched.

I was going to get Brex for this, make her pay. From the moment I'd met her and she'd asked me for money for the bus, I should never have trusted her. To think I'd worried about her welfare, when all this time she was a shark. She'd had no qualms beating me up. They choked me unconscious! How did a bunch of children get to be so evil? When they came back for me, I'd fight for my life, I'd knock every one of their skulls against this shelf.

Because I could literally be fighting for my life. They wouldn't free me after all this; it didn't make sense. I knew Brex's and Flynn's names and I'd seen all their faces.

Or was it possible they didn't care or didn't think too far ahead?

Even simply sitting, not moving, I was drained. Sore, thirsty and hungry. I pressed my fingers against my eyes, happier to see stars rather than let myself cry.

I had to be prepared for whatever happened when Brex returned. *If* she returned.

47

ERIKA

The sun was up when Kingy burst into the room.

'We gotta move – there's a security patrol here,' he announced.

I clung to the sleeping bag. I'd only had a few hours' sleep. 'Huh?'

'There's a security patrol! I was walking to my ute and saw a Toyota parked outside the gate.'

'Did they see you?'

'I don't think so, but they would've seen our cars. They're probably looking for us.'

'Shit.' I tumbled from the bed, pushed my feet into my sneakers. 'How am I supposed to move all this stuff?'

'You grab what you can, I'll be back in a sec.'

He disappeared. I checked my phone – it was almost 7 am.

Theo rushed in, barefoot and bare-chested, hair sticking out crazily. 'Fuck. I can't get into trouble, I can't have a criminal record.'

'I don't want a record either, none of us do.' I unplugged my air mattress and lay on it, trying to force out the air as quickly as possible.

He flung things into his gym bag. 'I've got a daughter. I should never have come here.'

'Excuse me? Theo! You loved every second.'

'Yeah, well, it was a dumb idea . . .'

'You didn't question it, not once. And you dragged AJ and Kingy here, that was all you.' I folded the mattress into as small a square as I could, then started packing clothes. 'Has anyone told Mac?'

'How should I know?'

I stared. Who was this man? Sure, I was alarmed, but Theo had become unrecognisable. Wild eyed, pale. You'd think the place was on fire. Maybe he was still high.

'I'll go see her,' I said.

A security patrol – would they call the police? Just how much trouble would we be in? Mac would be livid, she'd definitely blame it on our cars being parked so close.

I ran to her room and rapped on the door. 'Hey, you awake?'

When she didn't respond, I turned the handle. I expected her door wedge to keep me out; instead, the door swung open. The room was empty. 'Shit, wrong room.' I moved to the next one and knocked again. 'Mac, we gotta go.'

I was surprised when that door opened smoothly, too. Apparently I'd completely miscounted which room Mac was in. Or had I? The balcony boards were removed, propped against the wall as she always had them. There was an empty water bottle in the far corner. Yet she wasn't there – nor her bed, her stove, her food box.

Theo arrived. 'Hurry, let's move.'

'Hang on a sec, I can't find Mac.'

'She must be downstairs already.'

Kingy and AJ entered the corridor laden with bags, esky and pillows. AJ was grinning like this was just another game. 'Oh, man,' he said, 'how funny is this?'

'I'm not laughing, mate,' Theo said.

'Let's go,' Kingy said.

'What about Mac?' I repeated. 'I can't find her, her room is empty.'

AJ managed to curl his lip and grin knowingly at the same time. 'She left already.'

'That can't be right.'

'You sure you got the right room?' Kingy said.

'I think so, yeah, let me keep checking the others . . .' I ducked into the next few rooms, knowing that I was moving progressively away from where Mac had been holed up. Kingy ran in the other direction, inspecting more rooms. Theo and AJ didn't even pretend to help; instead, they hurried for the exit.

'She's not there,' Kingy told me when we reunited. 'Did you see her last night?'

'You mean after the club? I didn't look in on her, there was no reason to.'

'There's nothing we can do now, we've gotta leave.' Although Kingy looked sorry to say it, it didn't make me feel any better. 'Where's your stuff?'

We raced back to my room. I stuffed my crystals in my pockets, flung my backpack over one shoulder.

'Need a hand?'

'Yes, please.' I gave Kingy the mattress, he threw it onto his pile and we hustled to the stairs. Theo and AJ were already several levels below. When we reached the courtyard, they were waiting for us.

'Where do you reckon the guard is?' Theo asked.

'How should we know?' I said.

'Hang on, let me check it out.' Kingy put his load on the ground and crept away.

'Where the hell is Mac?' I whispered.

'I'm telling you – she's already packed up,' AJ said. 'She probably dobbed us in to the security company, that's why they're here.'

'No way, Mac wouldn't do that.'

'We can talk about it later,' Theo said.

Could AJ be right – could Mac have left already? She'd been angry, sure, but she would never be so spiteful. She wouldn't want me to get in trouble with security and, potentially, the police.

Kingy returned. 'The Toyota's still there but I can't see anyone.'

Theo swore. 'The guard could be anywhere.'

'Or guards – there might be two of them.'

'So what do we do?' I said.

'We get the fuck out of here,' Kingy said.

'Yeah, let's move,' Theo said.

We hurried for the fence, scanning for the guards. I braced myself, expecting shouted commands to *STOP!* Seagulls circled over us, there were wisps of early morning clouds. I fumbled with my gear. Kingy helped me to adjust, but Theo charged on without a word. We reached the wire and shoved our things under or threw them over, working in a production line.

'See anyone?' Theo hissed.

'Nuh, they might be on the beach,' Kingy said.

'Bloody hope so.'

Kingy led the way down the trail. At the carpark, his ute and my hatchback waited like the reckless, obvious clues they were. I stole a look at Kingy; he grimaced in return. Mac had warned us.

There was also a dust-covered Toyota with a rack of orange lights mounted on the roof.

'Uh,' AJ said, 'that's not a security truck.'

We stared at the colourful pastel logo: *Department for Environment and Water.*

'It's a bloody coastal patrol,' Theo said.

'Mate!' AJ wailed. 'Are you blind?'

Kingy's eyes were round. 'Sorry, guys. I was sure—'

'Dumbass.'

'We panicked for nothing,' I said.

'We got dragged out of bed for nothing,' AJ said.

Kingy placed my mattress by one of my tyres. 'I'm still leaving. I've had enough, I wanna sleep in a real bed.'

'Sounds good to me,' AJ said. He and Kingy dumped their things into the ute tray.

I opened my boot and slung my things inside. Instead of joining me, Theo tossed his gear into the ute, too.

'You're not coming with me?' I said.

'I'll stay in Kingy's rumpus room.'

'You can stay with me.'

'We already talked about this. You live with your parents.'

'So does Kingy!'

Theo scratched his chest. 'Babe, that's different.'

'Oh, *fine.*'

I don't know why I was debating his choice, because truthfully, Theo had annoyed me so much during our evacuation that I didn't want to be around him. He'd been selfish, flustered, hadn't offered me any assistance or shown concern over Mac's whereabouts.

I got into my car and buzzed the windows down to release the muggy air. As I clipped my seatbelt, I checked the resort over my shoulder. The faceless buildings, the pitiful palms. It'd been fun for a while, but I wasn't sorry to be leaving. I'd had enough of cement floors and unlockable doors, no running water, no cold fridge. And I definitely didn't want to wait until an actual security patrol found us.

Kingy's ute pulled out and I drove the dusty road after it.

48

ERIKA

As soon as I parked outside my parents' house, I texted Mac: *We moved out. Kingy thought he saw a security patrol, but it was a beach patrol. We got spooked!! Ha ha oops*

I expected an instant, gasping reply, but there was nothing.

I texted again: *I looked for you, your room is empty, where'd you go?*

No response.

Maybe she was at work. Maybe she was in whatever new space she'd found. I was hurt that she hadn't told me she was leaving, yet given our bickering, it was understandable. I lugged my belongings from the car to the front door and was struggling with my keys when Mum opened it.

'Hello stranger.' She stepped aside to let me pass.

I was so glad to see her, to be in the normal world and away from the drama of the resort, that I hugged her.

'Oh, this is nice.' She squeezed back. 'So you've finished camping?'

Josh was in the lounge doorway. '*Camping*. As if.'

'Shut up,' I said. 'Yes, I've finished camping. Forever.'

I showered and changed into clean clothes, then ventured into the kitchen for food. Mum was sitting with an iced tea, playing a game on her iPad. Josh was cracking eggs into a bowl.

'How's Mac doing?' Mum asked. 'Where's she staying these days?'

'She's doing great – didn't I tell you? She's going to the UK, her working visa came through just yesterday. She reckons she might go backpacking for a while.'

'Wow, good for her.'

'You should go backpacking, since you love camping so much,' Josh said.

I shot him a look.

'How long will she be away?' Mum asked.

'Ages, she says. Maybe a year.'

'I thought you two were looking for a place together,' Josh said.

I shrugged. 'Yeah, well, that's not happening.'

'Great, so we're stuck with you.'

'Oh, leave me alone—'

'For god's sake, stop fighting,' Mum snapped. 'I want a peaceful morning.'

Josh switched the blender on and the high-pitched roaring filled the room. So much for peace.

In my bedroom, I opened my laptop. One of my tutors had emailed to say they were concerned about my 'lack of engagement'. I couldn't disagree with that: I'd failed to attend a mandatory Zoom and hadn't completed an online test.

In another subject, an essay was due in three days and I hadn't even read the topic. I sat on my bed, laptop on my legs, and began playing with ChatGPT. But the words blurred together. I opened my phone to text Theo and ask whether he'd settled into Kingy's okay. Then I decided against it. He hadn't messaged to ask about me. I checked his Insta instead. The latest photo was from Horizon the previous night, a selfie, Theo beaming into the lens, the dancefloor crowd behind him with their worshipping arms in the air.

What would happen to us, now the resort was over? You couldn't call us a couple, it was sex and hanging out. I was a very convenient surprise in Theo's life – and isn't that exactly how I'd set things up? If I hadn't had the lure of Barren Cape, we might not have hooked up at all. Would Theo eventually get a share house with AJ and Kingy again? I wished they'd taken my idea seriously. I supposed Theo was terrified at the thought of being hitched to me. Still, even if he didn't want a relationship, a share house could still work. I wasn't a child, I wouldn't be devastated if we were friends with benefits. While it was comfy staying with Mum and Dad, I didn't want this to be long term.

The next time I saw Theo, I'd pitch the idea again, show him some rental listings to get him keen. I could mention separate rooms to reassure him.

I did my laundry, vacuumed my bedroom, and aimlessly scrolled social media. In the late afternoon, Mum knocked on my door. 'You should invite Mac for dinner before she leaves. I'd love to see her.'

'Okay,' I said. It was actually a good idea. Mac and I should patch things up before she left. I texted her.

Hey ru mad with me?

Where ru staying tonight?

Let's talk – also mum wants you around for dinner

I lay watching the screen for a bit, waiting for her reply. When there was none, I dropped the phone onto the mattress.

At 9 pm I undressed and switched off the light. My earliest night in years, and I needed it. I rolled myself in a sheet, relishing the sand-free bedding. Heard the murmur of the TV in the lounge, the hum of the dishwasher in the kitchen. One of my brothers bellowed – playing an online game with mates. The familiar lull of home. It wasn't long before I fell asleep.

I dreamed that a strange man arrived on our doorstep and Josh let him into my bedroom. The man wanted to snap photos of me, told me to stand against the wall. I resisted, saw a trap door and climbed through. It led to Horizon, music playing and lights flashing. Mac was on the dancefloor, springing up and down, laughing and surrounded by people. 'Mac! Mac!' I called, but she didn't hear me and the crowd swallowed her up.

49

BREX

We had pancakes for breakfast in the hotel room. We had Vevo playing on the TV, and Cindi and I sat in bed with the sheet over our legs, while Flynn ate at the tiny round table. We hadn't yet showered, and his hair stuck up on one side like a cocky's. He snored last night but I didn't mention it; it was awesome that he'd been able to sleep. I woke a lot, staring at a microscopic green light in the ceiling, all sorts of schemes crowding my mind.

Flynn said we should find Star's car. 'We can drive to Melbourne or maybe the Gold Coast or Byron Bay, somewhere chill like that. There'll be heaps of tourists and nobody noticing us.'

Flynn was on his Ls but he'd been learning since last year and I trusted his driving.

Cindi didn't want to leave, though. 'We'll run out of money in a few days, and I'm not gonna beg like a homeless person,' she said.

'And I'm not going to jail,' Flynn said.

'It was self-defence and the guy was bad! We murdered a murderer.'

'You didn't murder anyone, I did.'

I hadn't made up my mind what to do. Stay or go? I had nowhere *to* stay. 'Whatever we do, I want as much cash as possible,' I said. 'Let's go back to the beach and get her PIN number.'

We caught the beach bus, then ran from the bus stop into the scrub, so fast it was like flying over the sand. Maybe it was the fresh Nikes on my feet, maybe it was my new power and energy. Our backpacks were stuffed with swag. I wore pink Adidas shorts and T-shirt, the same as I'd seen on Insta last week. Cindi wore a flowery playsuit and sparkly *Eras* cap. Flynn was in a Miami Dolphins hoodie, even though he must've been stinking hot. We were prettier, fiercer and badder than ever.

The sun was shining, the waves were flat. 'Hey, we should've bought bathers,' Cindi said.

'There's no time for that anymore,' I said.

We hurried to the basement and I opened Star's door. 'We're back.'

She was on the floor by the shelf. Ducked her head, avoiding the new light. Hair fell from her pony, one of the water bottles was empty and the pillow was under her butt.

'Good, you've been making yourself comfy,' I said.

She squinted. 'Brex, let me go.'

'You should give up smoking,' I said, 'you sound terrible.'

Cindi laughed.

'This is serious,' Star said. 'Do you understand what you're actually doing? This is kidnapping, you're holding me against my will. You've gotta stop this before you get into more trouble.'

'You're the one in trouble,' Cindi said.

'Let me go. I promise not to say anything about you.'

I shifted closer. 'Speak up, I can hardly hear you.'

Star looked ready to cry.

'What's your PIN number?' Flynn said.

'I'm not giving you my PIN,' she said.

My breathing got quicker. 'Yeah, you are.'

'We'll make you,' Cindi said.

Star focused on me. 'Who's that man on the roof? Did you know him?'

I ignored her, opening Flynn's backpack. 'I brought orange juice, I figured you'd like that, being a health nut and everything. And an oat bar. It looks gross but it's probably your favourite. And here's more water.'

Star didn't say thank you, just glared, her lips pressed together. I wished she'd stop looking like that. There was no point in being a sook. A lot of things had happened but I couldn't change them now.

'You can have this food and drink after you tell me your PIN,' I said.

'Then what . . . you let me go?' Star said.

'We'll have to see if the PIN works first.'

'This is getting boring,' Cindi whined.

I swung the shopping bag and it hit her knee. 'Relax!'

She stroked her skin, giving me daggers.

'How about your car?' Flynn asked. 'Where'd you leave it?'

'I don't have a car,' Star said.

'Don't lie to us!' I yelled. All the nice mushy feelings I had from the hotel disappeared. Everything was gritty and nasty and tiring all over again.

Flynn dangled the car keys we'd found, holding them by their fluoro tag. It had name of a gym on it. 'It's not parked outside, so where is it?'

'They're not my keys,' Star said.

'Oh my god, I'm gonna lose it,' Cindi said.

Flynn shifted closer to me. 'We can search for the car, it can't be far.'

Star coughed again. It was all an act, she was fishing for sympathy. 'Let me help you,' she said. 'We can explain everything to the police. You're kids, they'll understand.'

I'd had enough. 'WHAT'S YOUR PIN?'

Flynn dived forward, then all three of us tried to grab a piece of her, like we could crush the information out of her. I pinched her at that sensitive point between the neck and shoulder.

'Tell us!'

She turned her head; sharp pain pierced my skin.

'She bit me!'

Flynn mashed her face into the shelf.

I clutched my sore hand, trying to press the pain away. 'For fuck's sake, tell us and we'll leave you alone.'

But Star thrust her legs out, slamming Cindi's shin.

'Ow!'

'Time out!' I said.

I snatched the orange juice and oat bar, and went to the door. Flynn and Cindi followed.

'Wait,' Star said. 'Don't do this.'

I shut the door. She needed to learn a lesson.

50

ERIKA

When I woke it was 8.23 am. I'd slept nearly twelve hours.

Theo hadn't messaged me and Mac hadn't either.

I texted her again: *Hey let's talk. Are you mad about the resort?*

The house was empty when I made breakfast. My parents had gone out, my brothers hadn't risen. I ate a slice of sourdough while staring through the lounge window. Two magpies pecked the front lawn, sunlight shone on the neighbour's white stone lion statues. It was set to be a scorching day and while I was grateful for the air conditioning and the comforts of home, I didn't feel a hundred per cent settled. A boring day of study stretched in front of me, and I was unsure about my relationship with Theo and annoyed that Mac was ghosting me. What – she was all set to travel and didn't need me as a friend anymore? Nice.

When I hadn't heard by 7 pm, I phoned her. It went straight to voicemail and I disconnected without leaving a message.

'Did you invite Mac for dinner?' Mum asked.

'I can't get hold of her. I think she's mad at me,' I said.

'Did you two fight?'

'No, not really . . . It's hard to explain.'

'Well, keep reaching out. Mac needs her friends.'

After dinner, I sat alone on the patio in the twilight. My phone hummed and I snatched it up. It wasn't Mac, it was Theo.

'Hey, babe,' he said.

I smiled. 'Oh, look who it is – the hardened criminal.'

He chuckled. 'I'm sorry I was a dick yesterday. I freaked out. Thing is, I can't have any custody issues with my daughter. My ex is okay, but her parents have it in for me. You understand, hey?'

'Your *face*, though! You should've seen it.'

'It wasn't just me, Kingy and AJ were hyped up too.'

'Sure.'

We discussed our day, neither of us with much to report. Theo was in Kingy's rumpus room waiting for a food delivery.

'So . . . I still haven't heard from Mac,' I said. 'It's weird.'

'She might want to be alone,' Theo said. 'I don't know her well, but she seems that type of chick. Self-sufficient, I mean. She wasn't very friendly at the resort, she didn't wanna hang out with us.'

'That was different, we invaded her space. Normally she's fun, she's not that stressed. It's my fault. I spoiled everything for her.'

'You were looking out for me and the boys. You did us a favour. Mac's pissed off and deliberately ignoring you, but she'll come around.'

'I guess . . .'

When we ended the call, I sat watching the sky turn a deeper blue. What was Mac's plan? Lay low until she left for London?

That didn't feel right. Mac could mope, sure – but she wouldn't hide and she'd never be shy to face me. I decided to keep reaching out. I'd ruined the resort; I didn't want to ruin our friendship. If Mac was sulking, I'd put in an extra effort and make it up to her. I searched my contacts and found Sandy's number.

'Erika, how are you?' Sandy sounded surprised.

'Good, thanks,' I said. 'I was wondering . . . is Mac there? Is she staying with you?'

'No, she's not here.'

'Oh. I haven't been able to get in touch with her.'

'I thought it was just me.'

'What do you mean?

'Mackenzie hasn't called me back. I was expecting her today. She said she'd be here to sort through her winter things before she leaves for London. And I don't even know what she has planned for her car. There's no space to park it here, she'll have to sell it—'

'Do you think she changed her mind about travelling? Did she buy her ticket yet?'

'Yes, according to Georgia. She's been trying to get hold of Mackenzie, too. She's planning to collect her at Heathrow.'

I rose from my seat and strolled onto the grass. 'Have you spoken to anyone at the café or gym?'

'Yes, I tried Clover's, they said she hadn't shown up. They didn't sound very happy with her.'

'That's strange, Mac wouldn't let them down. Are you worried?'

'There's no point worrying about Mackenzie, she's always done her own thing . . .'

I kept searching for answers. 'Could she have jumped on an earlier flight without telling anyone?'

'Without her suitcase?'

I looked at our house, TV glowing from the family room, Dad walking past the window with a red wine in his hand. 'Mac could be staying with someone else, I suppose. One of her other friends.'

'I don't know, Erika, she doesn't include me in anything.'

'I'll ask around and see if I can find her.'

'All right, love, you do that.'

I composed a mass message to Renata, Devin, Vikki and others who had accommodated Mac over the past few months.

Devin responded instantly: *haven't seen her mate*

Renata replied thirty minutes later: *Hi hon. Sorry, haven't heard from Mac in a while. Pls tell me she's found a flat and she's getting her shit together!!*

Interesting. Mac hadn't told everyone about her travel plans.

I called Theo and brought him up to speed. 'I'm worried, where could she be?'

'She's obviously found somewhere to hang out until her flight,' he said. 'Maybe another resort, ha ha!'

'Mac didn't show up for work and her mum hasn't heard from her. It doesn't make sense.'

'She's been drifting for a while, hasn't she? I reckon you're worrying over nothing.'

I shook my head, even though Theo couldn't see me. 'Something is off.'

He yawned, didn't even try to suppress it. 'Ah, well, she's a big girl, she knows what she's doing.'

We said goodbye. I phoned Mac again, left a voicemail: 'Hey, it's me. Nobody's heard from you and I'm trying not to overreact. When are you leaving for London? I'm sorry we argued, can you *please* message me? I really hope you're not avoiding me . . .'

By 10 pm, everyone in the house had closed themselves in their own rooms and I stood at the kitchen bench, nervously chewing almonds. A few more friends had responded to my message, all saying they didn't know where Mac was.

Vikki followed up with: *Is everything ok?*

I wrote: *I think so, just trying to locate her*

I scrolled Mac's social media. The last post was an Insta pic of the Mexican meal we'd had last week. The same night I'd followed her to the resort. I was the world's sneakiest, most unreliable friend.

I sat on a stool and tried to unravel the Mac puzzle.

Yesterday morning, I checked a few resort rooms and her stuff definitely wasn't there.

Her Fiesta wasn't in the carpark either . . . but she never left it there. She'd always been more cautious, parking in the layby fifteen minutes' walk away.

There was no point trying to sleep, I was too anxious. I had a hunch, and I'd be restless until I checked it out. Although it was probably ridiculous and a massive waste of time, I grabbed my keys and left the house.

51

MAC

I'd spent at least one night in the hellhole, maybe two. Alone in the dark, sore and terrified, my body clock had abandoned me. My stomach rang with hunger and I'd drunk all the water. I'd snatched only short periods of sleep.

I cried. There were tears of frustration at myself and how I'd gotten into this situation. Tears of fury at Brex and her friends, the vicious little turds. There were tears of regret and despair at this worst period of my life, the months of not knowing where I was going to sleep every night. Even worse, the wasted years of not studying or building any solid future. In my bleakest hours, I wondered if this was what I deserved.

There were fearful tears, too. A man was dead and I could be next. It was so hard to defend myself. I could feel the bruising on my arms and legs. Scratches, itchy bleeding. It was three against one – one of them being a hefty boy who was taller than me. They had no mercy. They wanted my PIN and my car's location. They must be planning to run away, could return any second and apply more pressure. Was it worth dying over money? I should've given them the code, but my instinct was to protect my savings. I didn't want to surrender another cent, I needed all I had for my trip – I had no idea how long it'd take to find a job in London. Yet this was serious, this went beyond my dreams of travel. Escape should be my priority. And once I did get out and I told the police everything, any stolen money would be returned. Wouldn't it?

I could give them the wrong PIN. But that might only delay things and make them even madder. It wouldn't speed my release.

I needed to be better prepared for their return. I struggled to my feet and reached for the nearest cleaner's bottle. Propped myself against the shelf as I undid the lid and sniffed. Disinfectant. After a minute of balancing and stretching, I nabbed a second, slimmer bottle. It had a child-safe lid that was difficult to unscrew. When I had it opened, there was an eye-watering chemical scent. I could try throwing it in the kids' faces or maybe pouring it over the floor, forming a slippery trap. But then I could fall over too.

The broom and mop were potential weapons, but out of reach.

My body was my real weapon. I'd been gaining strength for years, I had heaps more mass than the kids. I had to be prepared to fight harder. No more holding back. If I could get one of them in a chokehold, I wouldn't let go until they agreed to release me. Brex would be the best target: she was the ringleader; they wouldn't continue without her. But how would that work, and would I believe any of their promises? Would they believe mine?

I began working at the shelf again. Gripped one of its legs and braced myself for the sting of the cable ties. I wedged my shoulder underneath and lifted with my legs. *Push, push.* I was strong, I could do this.

Why did Sandy want to keep me away from Georgia?

Why did she have more faith in Georgia than me?

When I got out of here, I'd ask her. We needed a real discussion before I hopped onto a plane. I might not be back for months, years.

If I ever got onto the plane.

No, don't think like that.

I visualised showing my boarding pass to the flight attendants. Walking the narrow aisle, searching for my seat number. All the bustle and optimism and excitement of travelling. Clipping the belt around my waist. The mini wine bottles, the book I'd read, the movies I'd watch.

When you visualise, you materialise.

I was losing my mind.

What did I want to see in London? Big Ben, the Thames, Wembley Stadium. Most of all, I wanted to see Georgia. Her multi-level share house, the poky bathroom she'd complained about. Did the postie shove mail through a slot in the door, like I'd seen in the movies? I wanted to see the view from her kitchen windows while waiting for the kettle to boil. Wanted us to sit together with a comforting cup of tea. To walk to the pub arm in arm, sit at a scuffed wooden table and drink too much white wine.

It had to happen. It was going to happen, I was going to make it.

Push, lift.

The kids could be back soon. I refused to be at their mercy.

Push, lift.

The shelf budged. A spark flared inside me. I could do this.

Push.

Lift.

52

ERIKA

Finding the layby wasn't easy. The first turn-off I tried was wrong. I knew as soon as I took it, but had to keep to the straight road until I there was enough space to turn. The mistake added another layer of tension to my stomach.

The second turn-off curved almost immediately, and I knew I had found Mac's spot. Especially when my headlights shone on her red car. Bloody hell.

I parked close and climbed out. I half expected Mac to emerge, as if she'd been waiting for me the entire time.

'Mac.'

I peered through the glass, seeing the usual collection of gym shoes and water bottles. She'd wrapped a blanket around a pile of bags, probably to deter stickybeaks and thieves.

This was bad news. Mac couldn't get anywhere without her car. Unless someone collected her. She might have called a friend for a lift – but who? Nobody I asked had reported seeing her.

I returned to my car, shivering despite the warm air, and locked the doors. The moon was shining and although it provided light, it also enhanced the shadows. I called Theo.

'I found her car,' I said, voice low. 'In the same place she always parks, near the resort.'

'You drove out to Barren Cape again? Are you nuts?'

'I had to! And lucky I did. Where is she, Theo?'

'Maybe her car broke down. How does it look?'

'It looks . . . normal. I mean, there's no flat tyres. What am I supposed to look for? You want me to stick my head under the hood—'

'Erika, take a breath, it was just a question. I'm sure Mac is fine. She could've run out of petrol and phoned a friend.'

'That friend would've been me! She wouldn't want anyone asking questions about why she's parked out here. And why isn't she answering her phone? I don't get it.'

'I'm sorry, I've got no answers for you.'

I glanced around, the murkiness folding in on me. 'I think I should call the police.'

'They'll have heaps of questions. Don't let the cops know we broke in!'

'This is more serious than trespassing, Mac's pretty much a missing person.'

'C'mon, that's an exaggeration.'

'Nobody's seen her!'

'If you call the police, what would you tell them? Would you dob Mac in for staying at the resort? You could get her into trouble for nothing – she'll really fly off the handle then.'

'Well, I can't leave it like this! I can't go home pretending everything's normal.'

Theo gave a long sigh. I wasn't sure if he was sympathetic or growing irritated with me. 'I reckon you should leave. Sleep on it, call her mum again in the morning.'

I had a different idea. 'Mac might be inside the resort.'

'You said her things were gone.'

'Her *car's* still here. She could've shifted onto another floor or even another building. It's not unrealistic. Will you come into the resort with me?'

'Absolutely no way, that is a bad idea, a real bad idea.'

'Please, it's the only way to figure this out. What's Kingy's address? I'll pick you up.'

'I'm not going there ever again – and you shouldn't, either!' Theo was shouting. I heard others in the background – maybe Kingy asking what was going on. 'Drive home now, Erika. Let's talk in the morning. If you haven't heard from Mac, we'll come up with a plan.'

'Sure,' I said.

We said goodbye. I stared through the windscreen, headlights illuminating Mac's dusty car. Theo didn't understand – I couldn't ignore this. Nobody had heard from Mac, she wasn't answering her phone and she'd missed a shift at Clover's.

I reversed, exited the layby and turned in the direction of the resort.

53

ERIKA

The site stood desolate and still, the corners of the buildings stark against the moonlit sky. Branches bobbed in the wind and I heard the rush of distant waves. I hesitated to leave the safety of the car. This was my first time alone here and it was full of risk. I remembered the fear that nearly paralysed me on the night I joined Mac inside. Remembered Night Hunt, and being so high I couldn't think straight. It'd be easy to turn away, but going home would achieve nothing. I'd only sit in my bedroom, wondering and waiting for her to call. So I opened the door and put one foot on the ground.

I scampered to the fence, hearing Theo's words of warning. At least he knew I was here; he might never return to the resort but at least he'd raise the alarm if he didn't hear from me.

The ditch was closer than AJ's entry at the esplanade. Getting down onto my knees to slither beneath the fence was almost as daunting as exiting my car: I had a sensation that someone would appear and jump on me while I was on the ground.

My plan was to return to Semira and check all the rooms before venturing further. When I made it into our courtyard, its familiarity had me breathing more easily, yet I was far from comfortable. I climbed in before I could talk myself out of it, every inch of me tingling. Stood in the daunting dark. Was I brave enough to keep going?

I had to be.

I reached for my phone and switched on the torch function. Every gloomy corner was threatening.

'Come on, come on, come on,' I geed myself up.

Ground floor first. I walked the corridor with the light trained ahead of me. Found the same doorless, empty rooms. When I reached the stairwell, I climbed fast, didn't want to linger in that stifling vertical. On the second and third storeys, it was the same result. No trace of Mac, nor any of her belongings.

I thought the familiar top level, where we'd camped out, might feel welcoming. Reassuring, even. I'd had good times here with Theo. But I was wrong, I didn't feel any connection or comfort. I recalled that feeling of nervous humiliation when we fled yesterday morning. My words to Mac that night drinking gin on the balcony; my promises to keep my mouth shut. What a mess, what a bleak, awful mess.

'Mac?' I whispered loudly. 'You here?'

I counted down to her room. This was it, I was sure. A balcony board was against the wall. I checked the en suite. A packet of wipes and an empty water bottle lay on the floor, artefacts of a previous era. When I returned to the main room, my phone beam picked up an item by the door.

The rubber wedge Mac used for security.

I put it in my pocket; it didn't feel right to leave it, she'd been so proud of her nifty workaround. This proved it was her old room. But where was she? I switched off the phone and went onto the balcony, holding the rail and letting my eyesight adjust. The esplanade street light glowed; beyond that, the shining city. I leaned over to look at the Callista building, wondering if Mac's lantern might give her away. Then I realised – if she'd relocated, why hadn't she taken her doorstopper with her? It didn't add up.

Below, something flitted in the shadows.

I crouched, a startled reflex, keeping my eyes trained on the spot. It was near the centre building, the resort's reception area.

Could it have been Mac?

I wasn't game to call her name.

I left the room, jogged down the stairs and climbed outside. *Please, please be here, Mac.*

Without the many windows and courtyards of Semira, the small neighbouring building seemed impenetrable. I kept a hand on the brick exterior to guide me. Was excited when I discovered a nook I hadn't seen before and followed the murky passage, arriving at a door. It wasn't locked.

'Mac?' I whispered.

I entered a compact space, a doorway ahead, stairwell to my left. Couldn't hear footsteps or any movement. I shone the phone torch on empty food wrappers on the floor; the first garbage I'd seen at the resort. I eased towards the stairs. Unlike Semira, they led down as well as up. I decided to climb first – then I spotted the backpack. It was stuffed beneath the steps.

I bent to investigate. It was Mac's.

Her sleeping bag was there too, tossed over her food box. She must've stashed it all here while she decided where to go next. Seeing her things accumulated, shoved under a set of stairs, it hit me: she really was homeless. She'd told me often enough, and I'd always treated it as exaggeration, as humour mixed with self-deprecation. But it was real, Mac had nowhere to go. She was living on a knife's edge and nobody had provided meaningful help. Not me, not her other friends, not her parents. The guilt was too much, I needed to make this right.

BANG!

The detonation sent a convulsion through me.

BANG!

It was coming from below.

BANG!

'Shit, shit, shit.' My legs were shaking so badly it was a wonder I was still upright.

Was the wind causing that racket? I wondered about machinery, perhaps equipment to keep the resort running. But there was no electricity – it must be something else.

I took meek steps down until I reached the bottom and entered a thin, dark corridor. I wanted nothing more than to run away.

'Is anyone there?' I said.

Bang, bang, bang! Faster than before, and my heart rate kicked up, too.

Then, a strangled cry: 'Erika!'

'Mac? Is that you?'

BANG! BANG! BANG!

'Erika, let me out!'

Mac was here! I ran, tracking the sound. Flung a door open, revealing a dark room. 'Mac?'

I shone my light forward and she was there. Hunched into herself, avoiding the phone beam.

I ran to her. 'What happened?! What are you doing in here?'

'I'm tied up.' She yanked her wrists to show me. Then I saw she was connected to the steel shelving by the ankle.

I tested the plastic ties. 'Oh my god . . .'

'You need to cut them.'

'How? What with—'

'Quick, they'll come back!'

'Who? Was it a security guard—'

'It was Brex and two of her friends.'

'Brex . . . the girl you were looking for?'

Mac shook the steel she was tethered to. 'I swear to god, Erika!'

'I'm sorry . . .' I panned the phone light, searching for cutters, some sort of tools. This was a nightmare, discovering her like a caged animal. I fought to think straight, to control the fear.

'Try the shelves,' Mac said, her voice strained.

I pushed aside laundry containers, scoured from top to bottom. Nothing sharp, nothing useful.

'Hurry!' she said.

'I'm hurrying, there's nothing here!'

'Where's Kingy? He'll have cable cutters in the ute.'

There was no time to explain I was the only one left. 'Wait, I'll check next door.'

I raced to the corridor, on the hunt for something useful.

Then several things happened at once.

Footsteps echoed from the opposite stairwell.
Somebody yelled: 'Grab her!'
Bouncing lights impaled the darkness.
Behind the lights, snarling young faces.
And Mac shrieked: 'RUN!'

54

BREX

'Grab her!' I said.

We bowled along the corridor towards the stranger, another woman, about Star's age.

'Quick!'

Cindi jostled me and my shoulder hit the wall. 'Watch out!'

The chick disappeared at the far end.

I sped past an open doorway. Star was standing in place, staring. The woman had found her.

'Don't let her leave!'

We reached the stairs, me racing up first, our sneakers like drumbeats. I heard the *SLAM!* of the outer door. As I swung around the landing, Flynn barged past and reached the exit ahead of me. He held the door open, Cindi and I flew through. The moon shone but we were surrounded by dark shapes and no sign of the chick.

'Hold up.' I stopped. 'Wait, listen.'

Cindi and Flynn were either side of me, breathing too loudly.

'Where is she?' Flynn said.

'Shh!'

Nothing.

'She's hiding,' I said.

'Who is she?' Cindi said.

'What if she calls the cops?' Flynn said.

'Let's split up,' I said. 'When you find her, call out. Hurry.'

They disappeared to my left and right. I continued forward, jogging for the fence with the movable panel. One of my Nikes slid on a flat rock; I staggered but managed not to fall over.

Then I realised it wasn't a rock. It was a phone.

I scooped it up. The wallpaper was a young woman smiling. She had an arm around Star.

'Shit.'

She was one of Star's friends, she'd come back for her. Had the others come back, too?

I tucked the phone into my hoodie pocket. Thought about running, calling out for Flynn and Cindi, cutting our losses before things got worse. We'd searched for Star's car, walking around the entire site, but we didn't find it, though there were plenty of tyre tracks in the dry sand. We could hop onto an interstate bus instead. I should've listened to Flynn. We could've left days ago. This bitch was ruining everything. Why'd she have to come snooping?

Then, there was a yell.

'I called the cops!'

It was her and she was nearby.

'They're on their way,' she screeched, 'so you better fuck off!'

I kept a hand on her phone in my pocket. Wanted to laugh so hard. She was lying, no way did she make a call. I was pretty sure she was alone, too. If the guys had returned, she'd be talking to them, she'd be organising an attack. I tried to guess her position.

Flynn yelled: 'Bullshit!'

'It's true, I called triple zero, wait for the sirens!' she said.

I bit my lip, couldn't respond to Flynn without giving myself away. Edged forward, then I heard running. I stopped and listened. Maybe Flynn and Cindi were circling.

A twig snapped and I squatted like a monkey, staring and waiting. There she was, in three-quarter pants, dark hair pinned up, creeping away from a tree.

I was excited to scare her; felt the tingling power rise up from my groin.

'So, you called the police, hey?' I said.

She dropped blindly to the dirt. It was hilarious.

'How did you manage to call when I'm holding your phone?'

She didn't move a muscle.

'By the way – nice photo of you and Star. Are you besties?'

She sprang up and started running for the beach. I was after her like a shot, less careful of my steps now, hands itching to grab her. She reached the fence and was trapped. Dumb, humungous mistake. I threw myself forward, shoulder first.

BAM!

We collapsed against the wire. She was taller than me, but not by much, and I used my weight to crush her in place.

'Get off!' she screamed and squirmed.

'Flynn!' I called out. 'Over here!'

We grappled, shoes skidding in the dirt. She shoved me hard and I fell onto my arse. Then she threw herself over me, fumbling for my pockets. I pulled her hair, sank my teeth into her arm, just like Star had with me.

'Ow!'

She jumped off and ran. I lay for a second, getting my breath back.

Where were Flynn and Cindi? Was I meant to do this on my own?

I got to my feet and started sprinting again.

55

ERIKA

Branches flayed me as I ran.

This was like AJ's Night Hunt, except much, much worse. I couldn't believe I'd played that idiotic game, that we'd thought creeping through the resort was fun. There was nothing fun about this, it was the most terrifying moment of my life.

Who were those kids? What did they want? They had Mac tied up!

What would they do to me, now that I'd crashed the party?

I had tried to be smart, bluffing that I'd phoned the police. But in truth, my hands were empty. Somehow, somewhere, I'd dropped my phone. The ruse had worked with a couple of the kids – I'd seen them running towards the carpark. I thought I was safe, until that girl surprised me, her voice shattering the quiet. I wondered if it was Brex. I felt the sting of her teeth on my arm.

I was desperate to draw more breath into my lungs but terrified of making noise. Sipped air carefully, fighting my tremors. I couldn't stay hiding, Mac was relying on me. I had to make a move. My car seemed the best choice. I still had the keys. I'd slip under the fence, run and drive for help. It was devastating to think of leaving Mac behind, but it was for the greater good. I'd drive to the nearest house and plead for them to call the cops.

I forced myself to leave the safety of the wall.

I ran a few metres, then my right foot slid on the soil. I flung my arms out for balance but it was too late. I sank like a demolished skyscraper: one second I was upright, the next I was on my knees. '*OW!*'

'Ha!'

It was her. Closing in, enjoying this.

I scooped a handful of sand and threw it behind me. Heard a gasped '*Fuck*' as it rained down; hopefully it hit her in the face. The diversion bought me enough time to get to my feet and hobble away. I dodged a cluster of bushes.

And then the earth opened up in front of me.

56

MAC

'Erika?'

Just when I was thanking the universe for the miracle of her finding me, just when I thought I might be freed, Brex and her mates had returned. I was sick at the thought of them catching up to Erika.

'Don't you touch her!' I wailed.

There was nothing I could do; my pathetic voice barely made an impact. I raised the shelf that I'd finally loosened from one floor bolt, heaving it up and dropping it again.

BANG!

BANG!

I was trapped, and it was killing me that I couldn't help.

Please be all right, I thought, *please be all right*.

All light had left the corridor hours ago and I was folded in blackness. It must be night, which could enable Erika to dodge the kids – provided she ran fast enough. In any case, now she could alert Theo and the other guys. Then Brex would be done for. Let her try to take on people who weren't tied up. Fucking bitch. I bet she'd run, her and her mates.

Minutes passed.

Where was Erika? Where was everybody?

Perhaps they were struggling with the kids, still chasing one or two. Someone would've phoned the police by now. I raised and dropped the shelf again, the pressure too much to handle.

Then: 'Mac, I'm coming!'

My body went to jelly. 'Erika! Are you okay?'

A feverish beam danced into the room. Erika threw her arms around me, trembling and gasping. 'You all right?'

'Not exactly – help me get loose,' I said.

She put her phone on the shelf, its light shining into the ceiling. She had scissors. 'I'm gonna cut you free.'

'Scissors? Doesn't anyone have anything better?'

'Mac, let me do this!'

'Sorry. Do my ankles.'

Erika knelt, hands shaking violently. The tip of a blade dug into my skin. 'Shit, I'm sorry.'

'It's okay, keep trying.'

She repositioned the scissors, carefully slid a blade under a cable and got to work.

'What happened, where are the kids?' I asked.

'Dunno. Outside. I think they ran away.'

'What about Theo and Kingy? Did you call the police?'

'Mac, I need to focus!' A small cry. '*I'm doing my best!*'

I tamped down my burning questions, including whether Erika knew about the body on the roof. I didn't want to rattle her any more than she already was. I was taut with tension, feeling the pull and tug, my eyes flicking between her work and the beckoning doorway. Where was everyone, the rescue team?

Erika shifted closer, eyes hollow and grim in the faint light. She opened the scissors wider. 'Nearly there.' But it was obvious they weren't coping, the two halves loosening. She gripped tightly, wrangling back and forth.

Then the blades broke, sliding into two useless pieces.

'Shit!' she cried.

I strained at the cable. 'Get Theo, get help.'

'They're not here! They left, we all did.'

'What the actual? YOU GUYS LEFT?'

'We didn't have a choice, we thought we'd been found! I'm sorry, Mac, we assumed you'd already gone. Your room was cleared out.'

'Cleared out? That can't be right.'

'I saw your stuff under the stairs. That's where I got the scissors – from your food box.'

It was difficult to form words. The boys were gone, I was relying only on Erika. She began sawing with an open scissor blade, like it was a knife.

'*Please* let this work,' she whispered.

The plastic dented my skin, it was searing. I grimaced but didn't complain, alert for footsteps. If Brex returned now, I'd still be hampered, I wouldn't be able to attack her or defend Erica. I drew my legs apart, fighting to weaken the plastic. Erika sawed hard and I yelped as the cable dug in further.

'I'm sorry,' she choked.

'Keep going!' I said.

Ping!

The tie was severed.

I jumped away from the shelf, feeling so free I could've floated.

'Thank you!' I twisted a foot for circulation.

'Hurry, we have to move!' Erika grabbed her phone.

We ran beneath the low ceiling to the stairs, me moving awkwardly with my bound wrists. Erika scurried up and I followed, into the short corridor. Shapes formed as moonlight filtered in. Erika stopped, dragging a backpack from the shadows.

'What are you doing?' I said.

'This is yours.'

'Leave it.'

'No.'

She pulled the straps over her shoulders and we rushed on. She opened a door and we spilled into the night air.

'Quick,' she said.

The shadowy resort garden loomed like an obstacle course. As I ran, I waited for a shout, waited for pursuit. Prickles and gravel shredded my one socked foot. I ignored the stinging, running along the boundary. Erika was leading us towards the esplanade.

'Here!' She pointed.

I saw the gap in the fence; the one AJ had created. I'd been upset at the news, now I welcomed the easy exit. We dived through and tore along the path towards the carpark. When we were in sight of her car, Erika pressed her key fob and I fumbled the passenger door open and fell in. She dumped my bag in the back, then slipped behind the steering wheel. I slammed the lock with my elbow while she fiddled with the ignition.

'Hurry,' I said.

Erika whimpered. 'I'm trying!'

I waited for Brex to appear, for hands to pound the car. Erika finally inserted the key and the engine fired. We lurched forward. I twisted and peered out of the rear window, glimpsing the high fence and tall buildings we were leaving. We picked up speed, bouncing, and Erika began crying.

'It's okay, it's okay,' I said. 'We're leaving.'

She wiped her face, drove even faster. The tyres slid beneath us and the tail of the car swayed.

I braced my feet on the mat. 'We're going too fast—'

The wheels spun and we slammed into the soft edge of the road. My head snapped forward. We sat gasping, the car lights shining into the scrub.

'Oh my god, oh my god,' Erika chanted.

'Keep calm, we'll be fine.'

'What AM I DOING?'

I checked behind us: no figures running our way, not yet. 'Put the car in reverse.'

Erika's hand moved to the gearstick.

'Now slowly, carefully . . .' I said.

We reversed out of the powder and rumbled forward, Erika's sobs turning into quieter sniffing.

I exhaled. 'You're doing good,' I said. 'Keep moving.'

'Why are you still whispering?' Erika said.

I stroked my sore throat. 'They choked me until I passed out.'

'They're animals!' She was crying again.

'Hey, it's all right, I'll survive. You rescued me, you're a badass. God knows what they were planning, but you found me and I'm *so grateful.*'

We reached the bitumen and picked up speed.

'I've never been so scared in all my life.' Erika stared through the windscreen. 'Could hardly think straight, they were chasing me . . .'

'Did they hurt you?'

'No. I ran.'

'Where did they go?'

'It's all a blur.'

A set of headlights approached and passed on the opposite lane. When I caught a glimpse of a pedestrian, my head whipped around. Was it one of *them*? I couldn't tell. I nursed my sore wrists and watched the scrub flying by, fighting chilling images: Brex materialising on the roof; the kids piling on; the horror of being forced to the ground and unable to do anything to protect myself. The man dumped alongside the air duct like a piece of garbage. Who was he?

'I can't believe it,' I said. 'I was alone this whole time, you guys had gone . . . Still, you came back for me.'

'You weren't answering my texts or calls,' Erika said. 'Sandy hadn't heard from you, nobody had. I wondered where you were, never dreamed *this* was happening. It's been days, I didn't know what else to—'

'Wait, what day is it?'

'Sunday.'

'Shit, they've had me since *Friday.*' It'd been impossible to track the hours in the basement. I'd been tense for an age, hoping for sounds of rescue – or of Brex returning. Sleeping on and off. It'd messed with my memory and senses. 'My flight to London is in four days!'

Erika gasped. 'You booked? I had no idea.'

'I did it before the whole . . . basement thing. It all feels so unreal.' I spotted the turn-off and pointed. 'There.'

We entered the layby and Erika's car lit up mine. I was so relieved to see it, my breath hitched. We pulled up alongside.

'Got any water?' I asked.

Erika reached behind her and retrieved a red drink bottle. She had to hold it to my mouth, like bottle-feeding a baby. I took hasty gulps, droplets spilling past my chin.

I raised my tied wrists. 'I've got pliers in the boot.'

'How do we get in?'

'There's a spare key under the car. Help me out.'

Erika exited, ran around the bonnet and opened my door. 'Show me.'

I pointed to the right rear wheel. She lay on the dirt and explored under the chassis. When she sat up, she was holding a tiny magnetic box. She slid the lid open and pressed the fob.

We rummaged through my boot until I found the pliers. I offered my wrists and Erika used the small but sturdy pinchers to snip the plastic. I was properly freed.

'Thank you,' I said, 'thanks for coming back for me.'

'Of course.'

We leaned against the car for an introspective moment, gathering ourselves.

Then I said, 'There's something I need to tell you.'

57

ERIKA

I didn't think my heart could race any faster, but it did. 'What do you have to tell me? I don't know if I can take much more.'

Mac gripped my hand. 'You know I was looking for Brex?'

'You were worried about her.'

'Yes. I went into that middle building, and up onto the roof . . .'

'Tell me.'

'There was a dead man.'

I pulled my hand away. 'No.'

'I don't know who he was, he was lying there—'

'Are you sure he wasn't sleeping?'

'Erika. There was a plastic bag covering his face. It was all bloodied.'

I leaned away and vomited. Coughed a bit, then straightened. Still nauseous, quaking, it was a miracle I'd driven us here safely. Memories resurfaced, unwelcome images, but I shook them away.

'How long do you think he was there?' I asked.

'I don't know, I didn't get close before Brex and her mates arrived. I was going to call the police and they stopped me.'

'Fuck. Do you think . . .'

'That they were involved? They must've been.'

'But they're just kids.'

'Huh. You saw what they did to me.' Mac's fingers traced her neck.

'Was it a security guard?'

'He wasn't wearing a uniform.'

'Did you see any injuries?'

'I didn't get that close, then it was all over in a split second.' Mac started crying, choking out her words. 'I bet he was some poor homeless guy. It could've been me!'

I put an arm around her shoulder. There were no words. I couldn't make it better. And I was still processing everything myself.

Mac mopped her face on her arm. 'Where's your phone? We have to call the police.'

I'd been dreading this. 'Hang on, let's think for a second.'

'Think? Think about what?'

'What are we gonna say?'

'That there's a dead man! That a bunch of kids held me hostage!'

'Wait, we need to talk about it.'

'No, we need to call the cops while Brex is still in the area.'

'The police will ask a thousand questions, they'll want to know what we were doing at the resort. We could be suspects.'

'We didn't kill anyone! Those kids did.'

'We don't know that.'

'I didn't touch the body, you didn't go anywhere near it. You didn't even see it. C'mon, let's make the call.'

I shook my head. 'We broke in, Mac, we were there *illegally*. We'll look so suspicious.'

'That doesn't matter now, it pales in comparison to what's happened. Those kids beat me up, choked me, stole from me. The evidence is all over me. And they're murderers.'

'We don't know what happened to the man or how he died.'

'We can guess.'

'He could've fallen and—'

Mac thumped her car. 'Fallen headfirst into a plastic bag?'

'Listen . . . what we do next will affect everyone: you, me, Theo, AJ, Kingy. We were all staying at the resort – the full story will come out. Theo's petrified of getting a criminal record. He's a dad, remember, it could create custody problems.'

'Forget Theo, squatting isn't a serious offence. If he was here right now, he'd want to report the dead guy, too.'

'I'm not so sure of that.'

Her eyes rounded. 'Do you think one of the boys could be involved?'

'Theo and the others? No way! Never.'

'Well, we can't just say nothing. There's a dead man, probably with a family that's looking for him. I was held in that basement for two days. Those kids shouldn't have the chance to do this again. With Brex's name, it won't be hard to find her. We can explain, we can go to the nearest station—'

'Trust me, going to the police is a mistake.'

We were silent for a beat.

'What's going on, Erika? Have you told me everything?'

'Of course. What do you mean?'

'You want to keep a lid on this. It doesn't feel right.'

I put my hands in prayer mode. 'Think about it, Mac, for your own sake. The police will investigate, there'll be a court case and you definitely won't be leaving the country. You'll be charged with breaking in, you'll have a criminal record. The UK government won't like that, they might not let you in. Ever.'

'But I'm the victim.'

'Exactly, you don't deserve to be in trouble, not after everything you've gone through. You deserve to go to London, to see Georgia and put this all behind you. Do you want to be stuck here for another couple of years?'

'And the dead man? He doesn't deserve this, either.'

'I agree. But we had nothing to do with that. So, I'll phone the police when we're both far away from here. I'll do it anonymously, I'll keep us out of it.'

'Will you mention Brex?'

'Do you want me to?'

She kicked a tyre. 'Argh, what a mess. Like you said, there'll be an investigation. My gear's still there—'

'Not your backpack, that's why I grabbed it.'

'There's my lantern, the food supplies. They'll find my fingerprints.'

'You don't have fingerprints on file, do you?'

'No. I guess not.'

We rested quietly. If anyone had asked what I'd do in a situation like this, I would've imagined lots of frenzied activity. Phoning people for help, demanding action. In reality, I was disembodied, detached. There was also numb relief. We'd escaped. My skin still tingled with the girl's violent scrabbling, but we were free.

'Okay,' Mac murmured, 'we'll do it your way.'

'Really?'

'Yes, if you promise to phone the police about the body.'

'Yes, I'll call Crime Stoppers, don't worry.'

I scanned Mac, the bruises on her face, arms and legs. One of her shoes was gone. 'They really got stuck into you. Do you need a doctor?'

She shook her head. 'I don't want to be prodded under a spotlight or asked a million questions. I'm aching all over, but I think I'm okay.'

'We can at least put on a few bandaids.'

I opened my boot and retrieved the first aid kit. It wasn't professional grade, but it was better than nothing. Mac sat on her driver seat and I knelt by her legs, opened a swab and dabbed at a cut. Applied a few bandages, gently dressing her wounds.

'I'm gonna look ridiculous,' she said.

'At least you can joke about it.'

After I finished patching her up, we stood and embraced. She smelled the opposite of the usual Mac – instead of coconut lotion and pomegranate shampoo, there was muck and sweat. Remnants of fear. But she was whole, and she was safe. I wondered if she could feel my trembling.

'What are you going to do now? Do you want to stay at my place?'

'No, thanks, I'll go to Sandy's.'

Her answer was a relief. I was prepared to do anything to support Mac, but I needed privacy.

'Are you safe to drive?' I asked.

'Safer than with you driving.' She grinned.

I transferred her backpack.

'Thanks,' she said. 'I owe you. Big time.' We hugged once more.

As I drove from the layby, I felt a pang at leaving Mac. She shouldn't be alone, she was all shook up. But I assured myself she could handle it: she was so strong.

And I needed to focus on my immediate plans.

58

MAC

Erika looked tired and small in the driver's seat. Her hair was tucked behind her ears and she raised a hand as she coasted past.

I looked up. The stars spread as far as the eye could see. Breathed in the fresh night air. Wanted to bask in being outdoors, to reassure myself that I was free and I was okay. I'd been physically attacked, confined, denigrated. But I'd survived and I would do my best to put it behind me.

Yet, someone hadn't survived. Who was the dead man? When did Brex encounter him and how did he end up being killed? Perhaps he'd tried to assault her. What she did could be self-defence, which was all the more reason to alert the police. Thankfully, Erika was going to call Crime Stoppers, so he wouldn't be lying unclaimed. Let them investigate what had happened.

I rubbed my shoulder, parts of me still aching from being cable tied for so long. I found an old pair of jogging shoes in the boot. Pulled them on, then dug through the glovebox for a protein bar. I took cautious bites because of my sore larynx. I examined my bruises, scattered purple blossoms. Three of my fingernails were broken and my biceps were patterned with red scratches. I hadn't looked in a mirror to check my face yet. I wondered how much damage I'd inflicted on the kids. Probably very little in comparison. How would they explain any injuries to their parents? If their parents even noticed or cared . . .

I swapped my soiled T-shirt for a clean one. I'd like to burn the one I removed, I'd like to burn everything associated with Brex. Erika had the right idea, I should focus on my trip. I didn't want to be interrogated by the police and punished for living at the resort. Yet I did feel guilt over the dead man.

I started the car and cruised slowly to the exit.

———

I was exhausted when I knocked on Sandy's door. She opened after a few minutes, groggy, makeup free, in a nightie and socks.

'Hey, what's wrong?' Her voice was high pitched.

I'd already decided I wouldn't tell her anything. Not about Barren Cape, the body, Brex, none of it. How could I, where would I possibly begin? She'd have hysterics about the story. No, it was better to say nothing, to bundle it all away with me to London.

'I'm sorry to arrive out of the blue,' I said. 'I had . . . an argument with a friend. I had to leave.'

She stood back to let me in. 'Erika's been looking for you. And why haven't you returned my calls?'

'It's a long story. Can I borrow your phone?'

'Where's yours?'

'I lost it.'

'Oh my god, Mackenzie.'

She disappeared for a moment, then returned with her phone.

'Thanks,' I said. 'Sorry to wake you, let's talk in the morning.'

En route to the spare room, I ducked into the kitchen, grabbed a banana and wolfed it down so fast I almost choked. I made a cheese sandwich and chewed as I walked to the spare room, closing the door and sinking onto the mattress in relief.

When I was done eating, I cradled Sandy's phone in my hands. If I was going to go against Erika's wishes and call the police, now would be the time. This was my story, I was the victim – why should she dictate my actions? I ruminated over her argument that I had suffered enough, that there was no benefit in being further involved.

Head hurting, I looked up the 24-hour number for my bank. Made the call, reporting my credit card as lost. If I reported it stolen, I might have to make a police report. When the call was done, I kicked off my shoes and thrust a pile of clothes aside to make space to lie down. After two days in the basement I longed for a shower, but I didn't want to disturb Sandy further.

Even my tumultuous thoughts couldn't keep the tiredness at bay. I fell asleep instantly.

Later, I couldn't tell how long it had been, the mattress bounced and a gentle hand rested on my shoulder.

'Mackenzie?' Sandy was sitting alongside me.

I groaned and kicked at the sheet. 'What are you doing?'

'What *am I* doing?' Sandy said. 'You're shouting in your sleep.'

'No, I'm not.'

'You're having a nightmare, I don't want to argue about it. Are you okay?'

'Honestly? Probably not.' I rolled over.

59

ERIKA

Somehow I drove home, fighting the numbness that threatened to shut down my mind and body. I stayed well below the speed limit, barely trusting my weak hands to keep me between the white lines.

My mind flashed to the resort.

Mac's hoarse shout: 'Run!'

I could see the stampede of arms and legs coming for me.

'Hey!'

'Stop!'

'Fucking *bitch*!'

Running through the dark. Being chased.

Fighting, punching, clawing. I'd never been in a physical fight before.

Surprises in the shadows. A gaping hole.

I bit my lip, slapped my head.

No. No.

Stop thinking.

I'd rescued Mac, that's all that mattered. And I was going to keep protecting her.

When I reached my suburb, I pulled over and parked beneath a bottlebrush. All around me, ordinary houses sat peacefully in the night. Neighbours were tucked in their beds, and in the morning they'd rise for their usual routines. I envied them.

I had a few tasks to carry out.

First, I messaged the friends I'd contacted before: *Found Mac, all good x*

Hopefully, there wouldn't be any questions.

Next, I texted Theo: *Just wanted to let you know that I found Mac. She was still at the resort.*

Then I leaned on the steering wheel and closed my eyes.

Seconds later, they flew open. I couldn't stop the images. And if they were haunting me, what was Mac going through? I was distraught about everything that happened to her, but I hoped she would stick to the plan and leave the police to me.

My right elbow was aching. I took a closer look; it was so bruised, it seemed dipped in purple paint. I flipped the visor and examined my face in the slender mirror. Dirt and scratches, nothing too terrible.

Then I met my own eyes.

I couldn't stand to look at myself. I flipped the visor closed.

60

MAC

In the morning I showered, gingerly sponging my cuts and bruises. Lines on my wrists were glistening red, the aftermath of the cable ties. Again, I was in two minds about contacting the police and reporting what had happened. Brex and her friends should face the consequences. Where were they now? Hiding out someplace, laughing at what they'd done? Or back at home, pretending everything was normal? Planning for their next victim? Erika said she was going to call Crime Stoppers, but my firsthand account would add weight. What was the best move? If I reported what had happened, the police would detain Brex and her mates, they could prevent the kids from doing it again. At their tender age, having killed one man already, surely they were set on a path of violent crime. Though to be fair, I didn't know with absolute certainty that they were responsible.

Then I thought about Brex herself. Wily, charming, cunning. When we met, I saw a cheeky but vulnerable kid. I imagined detectives questioning both of us and comparing our stories.

Could Brex implicate me? For all I knew, the corpse was wrapped in one of my plastic bags. Who would the police believe? There was Brex: a chubby-cheeked high schooler; and me: a body-building, homeless twenty-something who had broken into the resort and squatted there.

Even worse, I had purchased a one-way ticket to England.

I replayed everything, wondering if I could've said or done things differently. Logically, I knew no amount of bodybuilding could've prepared me to battle three people at once. Still, I seethed that they'd got the best of me. I should've fought harder, fought smarter. When they surprised me on the roof, they'd seemed a bunch of clueless kids, and I was stunned after finding a dead man. I didn't realise how ruthless they were. How long had Brex been willing to keep me in the basement? What if Erika hadn't come searching?

I squeezed my eyes shut beneath the jets of water and willed myself not to crumble. If I went to the police, the resort saga would open up and I'd put all of us in the spotlight. It was decided. I'd keep my head down. It was only a matter of time before the cops found the killer, and if it was Brex, she deserved everything they flung at her. All attention would be focused there, and I'd be far away.

Stop, I told myself, *stop thinking, don't let her impact any more of your life.*

I dressed, pulling on track pants and a long-sleeved tee to hide my injuries. Leaned into the mirror to study my neck and recoiled when I recognised distinct finger marks. I felt tainted, like they'd branded me. I tore open a bottle of concealer and covered the marks, layer upon layer.

When I entered the kitchen, Sandy was on her laptop. I pulled my sleeves down as far as they'd go, pinning them with my fingers.

'That's some nightmare you were having,' she said. 'You're probably stressed about travelling.'

'Yeah,' I agreed instantly. 'It's pre-flight nerves.'

'I'm not surprised, you're doing it in such a rush. You're leaving in a few days!'

'Believe me, I'm aware.'

'What's going on, which friend kicked you out last night? That's pretty rough.'

'Please, let me have at least one coffee.'

My voice had almost recovered, now resembling the huskiness of a big night out. I made poached eggs and soft toast, struggling to swallow, but too hungry not to.

Sandy sipped from her mug, watching me over the rim. 'It's not Erika you're fighting with, is it?'

'No, Erika and I are fine.'

'Why have you been ignoring me? I was worried. Your flight's so close now.'

'I know. I'm sorry.'

Sandy must have sensed my flat mood because she fell silent, going back to her work. When I was done eating, I returned to the spare room and used her phone to call Erika.

'How are you feeling?' she asked after we'd said subdued hellos.

'Numb. Sore.'

'Same. Though I know I'm not as sore as you.'

'Did you call Crime Stoppers?'

'I said I was going to, didn't I?'

'What'll happen now?'

She sighed. 'I s'pose a story will break in the news. I haven't seen anything yet.'

'Shit. This will be huge. It'll be traced back to me, I just know it will.'

'We talked about that, there's nothing to link you.'

I pulled my feet up onto the mattress. 'I'm sorry, it's so bloody hard to pretend, to act like everything's normal. Where do you think the kids are? What are they doing now?'

'You should put them out of your mind. Don't think about them ever again.'

'Ha. Easily said, but I may need therapy.'

'You and me both.'

We were quiet for a moment. I chewed a nail.

'Have you started packing?' Erika said. 'You should get organised, focus on your plans.'

'That's impossible.'

'Babe, you have to. Take a breath, make a list and follow it, one item after the other. That's what I'm doing.'

I didn't know this version of Erika: so commanding, so focused. 'I'll try.'

'Do it, Mac. It's important.'

We disconnected. I stared at the wallpaper on Sandy's phone, a photo of me and Georgia. It was taken during a family birthday dinner at a restaurant two years ago. We were cheek to cheek and smiling, candles glowing nearby. I brought up Sandy's contact list, found my number and hit dial. It went straight to my voicemail. *'This is Mac, leave a—'*

I hung up. Where was my phone? At Barren Cape, in Brex's bedroom, or somewhere in between?

Then I did as Erika had suggested – I found a notepad and made a list. First action item, get a new phone. Then I groaned. Without a credit card, it'd be next to impossible to sign up for a new one. I returned to the kitchen.

'Do you still have your old phone?' I asked.

'Yes, it's in the box and everything,' Sandy said.

For the first time, I was grateful for Sandy's hoarding habits. She liked to keep packaging because it could be recycled for her online sales.

'Can I have it, please? I'll buy a replacement SIM, it'll be cheaper than getting a new phone. I'll pay you for it.'

'Don't be silly, I'll give it to you,' Sandy said.

She was being so agreeable, I wondered if I should share my story. She was my mother, she was meant to support me unequi-vocally. She'd be my shoulder to cry on as I related the trauma of finding a body, then being cable tied to a basement shelf. But then I thought of all the possible complications, including her deciding to tell the police.

I grabbed my keys. 'I'm gonna run a few errands.'

I drove to the bank. It was my first in-person visit since I'd opened the account years earlier. There were four other customers in front of me in the queue. One teller stood behind the counter, another staffer sat inside a glassed-in office. I had no idea what to expect, and marvelled at my ability to be calm. Only yesterday, I was wondering if I'd ever see daylight again. I tweaked my collar and hoped my makeup was still doing its job. Grew madder with Brex all over again, the shit she'd put me through, and what she was still putting me through. If I knew where she lived, I could've visited her parents and told them what a psycho their child was.

When I reached the teller, I told her about the lost card I'd reported.

She typed, focused on her screen. 'Your replacement card can take up to seven days.'

'I can't wait that long! I'm flying to London in a few days, I need money.'

She seemed genuinely sympathetic. 'That's terrible timing. Do you have any ID? You can still withdraw cash.'

'Great!' I showed my passport in its blue vinyl sleeve. My face stared back; if I had a mugshot taken, would it be similar?

The teller asked a few clarifying questions about when I'd opened the account. Then she was doling out hundred-dollar bills.

'How much is in my account?' I asked.

She read out the number, and my face fell. Brex and her mates had spent almost a thousand dollars.

'What do I do if I think there's some . . . incorrect charges to my credit card?' I asked.

'You'll have to lodge a dispute. You can do it online or I can grab a form.'

'Thanks. I'll take a look on the website later.' I smiled weakly, doing quick calculations in my mind. I had just enough balance to comply with my working visa requirements.

My next stop was the local mall. A bearded man in scruffy clothing sat cross-legged at the entrance, holding a cardboard sign: *Homeless, Anything would help, God bless you, Thank you!* I hurried past, feeling a storm of emotion. Pity, comradery, shame.

Shoppers passed him without a glance, clueless that homeless-ness might easily happen to any one of them.

I bought a SIM card. It meant breaking one of the hundred dollar bills. I returned to the homeless man and dropped a ten-dollar note in his cap. 'Sorry, mate, that's all I can do,' I mumbled.

Back at Sandy's, she answered my knock at her usual leisurely pace.

'Where's your old phone?' I asked.

'I put it on the kitchen table,' she said. 'You're welcome.'

The older model was there, tucked in its original box as promised. I inserted the SIM and used the contact details on Sandy's phone to add entries for her, Georgia, Dad and Erika. I texted them all: *New number x.* They were the only people that mattered right now. Next, I downloaded the flight app, checked my details and texted Georgia with the confirmed arrival information.

I was tired again, too tired to function. Told Sandy I was taking a nap.

She smirked. 'Getting into the London time zone?'

When I woke, the curtains were still open and the sun had gone down. I reached for my replacement phone. Georgia had messaged: *Not long now! x*

I messaged Erika – *how ru feeling?* – then dragged myself from bed. I followed the prattle of the TV into the lounge, where Sandy had her feet tucked beneath her on the sofa.

'Feeling better?' she said.

'A little.' I sank into a chair.

'They found that prisoner,' Sandy said.

'Who?'

'Curtis Burbank. The murderer police have been searching for.'

'Where was he? Did he make it across the border?'

'No, he's dead. They found him at some derelict building by the beach.'

61

ERIKA

I sank to my bedroom floor, clutching my bloodstone crystal between my palms, trying to leach calm from its sleek coolness.

The dead man Mac saw on the roof was an escaped prisoner called Curtis Timothy Burbank. Apparently he'd been all over the media, the police were hunting for him, but it was the first time I'd heard his name. I researched him online with growing horror. While we'd been hanging out at the resort, relaxing and getting high, Theo and I sleeping together, Burbank was hiding nearby. Had he seen us, was he watching us?

I read a decades-old article published when Burbank was arrested and facing trial:

> *Two men have been charged over the kidnapping, assault and murder of South Australian man Damien Warlock. Opening her case on Monday, prosecutor Amanda Sabatino told the court the accused pair had lured the victim to the Pennington Marina, where they boarded a small boat, held Mr Warlock*

captive and assaulted him over a period of two hours after a dispute over a drug debt.

'This was a premeditated, sustained and brutal attack,' Sabatino said.

The two accused then returned to shore with their victim and drove to a Parkfield residence where the assault continued. The court heard that one of the accused, twenty-five-year-old Curtis Timothy Burbank, transported the dead Mr Warlock to bushland near Mansfield Estate where he buried him . . .

When the story broke, my phone wouldn't stop buzzing. Mac and Theo, trying to get through to me. I didn't blame them, it was an understatement to say the news was a shock. Mac and I had expected the dead man to be discovered eventually, but not the 'escaped murderer' wrinkle. I ignored all calls and texts. Needed to settle my nerves and straighten my story.

Mum noticed I wasn't eating or talking. She knocked on my bedroom door and I told her to go away. 'Are you sick?' she said.

'Yes. Leave me alone,' I said.

I wouldn't be able to fob Mac off for long; she'd arrive on the doorstep if I didn't respond. So I messaged her and Theo, and arranged to meet at a lookout not far from a hilly trail I occasionally walked. I wanted a quiet location.

———

I arrived before anyone else and parked in the shade of a eucalyptus tree. Adelaide shimmered in the heat below, the setting sun reflecting off the office and apartment blocks. As I waited, I opened my phone and read a fresh article:

BURBANK DEATH MYSTERY

SA Police are appealing for information following the discovery of absconded prisoner Curtis Timothy Burbank, found dead at a mothballed construction site at Barren Cape. Convicted murderer Burbank had been missing since Wednesday after fleeing during a prison work program. The cause of death has not yet been released. SA Police Detective Superintendent Francene Yung said a task force was being established to investigate the death, as well as Burbank's initial escape. 'We're asking members of the public, if they know something, to get in touch with SA Police or phone Crime Stoppers,' Det Supt Yung said. SA Police would not confirm whether they were interviewing Burbank's criminal associates.

On Facebook, I found a clip on Channel 7's page: *Burbank found at Barren Cape. Major Crimes investigating.*

There was a video. I saw the resort fence, the multi-storey buildings and the sandy carpark, now covered in emergency vehicles. People trudged around dressed in light blue disposable coveralls and face masks. The footage shifted to the beach, where the camera swept the seaweed on the shoreline before panning to the resort. It all appeared much more grey and foreboding than our fun beachside hang. I felt disconnected as I watched, the vision both familiar and alien.

I heard an engine. Mac's Fiesta was careening towards me. She'd barely parked alongside before she leaped out. Despite the heat, she was wearing a cap, pants and a long-sleeved shirt. In armour, ready for battle.

She climbed into the passenger seat, leaned across the console and stared. 'Are you all right, E?'

I shrank back, worried about what she'd see in me. 'Yeah.' I could barely croak the word. This was too intense.

'It was Curtis Burbank! It was fucking *Curtis Timothy Burbank*.'

'I'd never heard of him until last night,' I said. 'Had you?'

'I saw a few news stories, but I never made the connection with the body. He didn't look like a prisoner to me . . . I mean, I don't even know what they wear.'

'Well, if he was hiding out, the resort makes sense.'

'I should've checked all the buildings ages ago. Then again, I'm glad I didn't.'

'This might sound awful, but it feels better that it was a convicted murderer rather than some innocent person. Don't you think?'

Mac gave me an odd look. 'I guess so. But nobody deserves to be killed.'

'Do you think karma caught up with him?'

'Erika, you know I don't believe in that stuff.'

I shifted in my seat. 'Do you reckon those kids were involved? I never . . . met them. What do you think?'

'I think they're capable of anything.' She tucked her hands in her armpits. 'Hey, the media said that a security guard found the guy.'

I nodded.

'Erika, did you call Crime Stoppers or not?'

'Actually, I changed my mind—'

'You lied to me!'

'Please don't be mad. I knew the man would be found eventually, I didn't want us to be involved.'

Another engine sounded. We turned to see Kingy's ute nosing into the carpark.

'Oh no. I thought you were only inviting Theo,' Mac said.

'I did, he must've told the others.' I was disappointed, but if I had to answer questions, I may as well face everyone at once.

'How much does Theo know?'

'Nothing! Only that I was looking for you and that you were still at the resort. He assumed you shifted rooms and I didn't correct him. He doesn't know anything else, including what you saw on the roof. Don't tell them.'

'What's the harm in it? It's all over the news now.'

'If we start talking about Curtis Burbank's body, we'll be talking about me rescuing you. The entire story will unravel. Do you want them to know about the kids beating you up, forcing you into the basement?'

She shook her head. 'No, I don't. It's none of their business.'

There was no opportunity to talk further, because the guys had piled out of the ute. Theo came directly to my window, his eyes shiny with dread, the same as the morning we'd left the resort.

'Did you have to bring everyone?' I said.

'They wanna know what's going on too,' he said.

The rear doors opened and the car sagged with the additional passengers. I closed my window and switched on the air conditioning. The trio hadn't even settled before the questions began.

'How long do you reckon Burbank had been hiding there?'

'What should we do? Do we contact the police?'

'What's the point? We don't know anything.'

All three were leaning forwards. 'Woah, give me space!' I squished myself against the door.

'Do you reckon we'll be questioned?'

'We might get some kinda reward for information.'

Mac twisted to face them. 'Shut up for one second!' The car fell quiet. She touched my knee. 'Are you okay?'

I nodded.

'Mac's right, be cool,' Kingy said. 'One at a time.'

'We've been discussing it and we didn't see the guy,' Theo said.

'But remember when I saw someone from the balcony?' Kingy said. 'That could've been him.'

'Have they given an update?' AJ opened his phone. 'Maybe they know more, like how he died.'

'The cops are asking for people to come forward.'

'Well, we don't know anything, we didn't see anything.'

'How long do you think the body was there?'

'Whereabouts did they find him?'

'I wish we'd never gone there.'

Theo dragged two hands down his face. 'Oh, man, did we leave any stuff behind? The cops could trace us using DNA.'

'Mate, they haven't got our DNA,' Kingy said.

'The main thing is, we need to sort our story. This is *nothing* to do with us.'

AJ snickered with an eerie, high pitch. 'Yeah, we didn't kill him . . . unless one of you wants to confess? What happened during Night Hunt?'

'Grow up, mate, this is serious, we could go to jail.' Theo shouldered him. AJ shoved back, and the car shook.

'Stop it,' Mac growled.

Kingy opened his door and dragged AJ out. We all followed. It was a bad idea to hold the meeting in my cramped car. We assembled under the eucalyptuses, Theo and AJ glaring like boxers between rounds. I surveyed the weedy area, hoping no sightseers would arrive and disrupt us.

'Let's go to the cops before they come knocking,' Kingy said. 'If we leave it too long, it'll look suspicious.'

'And say what?' AJ said.

'That we were there, but we saw nothing.'

'That's dumb, it doesn't help anyone.'

'Yeah,' Theo said. 'They'll be looking for suspects, they'll try to force a confession out of us.'

'We didn't know the guy, didn't touch him, didn't even see him.'

'Doesn't matter, they'll paint us as young people getting high on the beach.'

'They can't blame us for something we didn't do.'

'Innocent people are framed all the time.'

'Plus, we'll be admitting to breaking and entering.'

They debated for a while longer, while Mac and I cast glances at each other.

'He couldn't have been there long,' AJ said. 'We roamed all over, we never spotted him.'

'I don't know about you, but I didn't go into every building,' Theo said. 'It wouldn't be hard to avoid us.'

'Especially when Burbank didn't want to be seen,' Kingy said.

Theo pointed at Mac. 'You said there was a girl there, you wanted help finding her. She could've seen something, she could be speaking to the police and might tell them we were there.'

'Nah, she's not the type,' Mac said.

'How would you know?'

'Maybe the kid *did it*.' AJ sniggered. 'Kid killer.'

Mac moved close to me, whispered: 'Should I tell them?'

'No, don't complicate things,' I whispered back.

AJ scowled. 'Hey, no secrets.'

Theo raised his hands like a preacher. 'Okay. I vote we say nothing, we stay out of this. If the police track us and ask questions, we admit: yes, we were at the resort. We were camping, that's it. We didn't see the dead guy. If we had, we would've reported it immediately. Got it?'

'That's all true,' Kingy said.

'I need everyone to agree, right here, right now,' Theo said.

One by one, we nodded.

Kingy was studying the ground. 'We're forgetting something, I know it. We'll get in the shit.'

'Just stick to the plan,' Theo said.

Kingy and AJ headed towards the ute.

Theo put an arm around me. 'You gonna be all right? This is pretty wild.'

'Yeah . . . I'm all right,' I said.

'Wanna hang out tonight?'

A few days ago, I would've jumped at the chance to be with Theo. Now, though, I didn't trust myself to be around anyone. 'Not tonight.'

'Okay, bub, I'll call you later.' We kissed, then he walked away.

AJ raised a hand goodbye and the ute rolled out of the carpark. Mac and I stood listening as they took the hillside's twisty road, then I walked to the brink of the lookout. My shins rested against the low timber guardrail. The sun had dipped and there was a blinding haze over the city.

Mac joined me. 'This is too messy. Details are going to leak. We can't stay quiet.'

'Yes, we can! He was an escaped prisoner, it's nothing to do with us.'

'But Brex must have been involved and we know about her and—'

I grabbed Mac so hard she winced. 'You're leaving the country, that's all you need to think about. This is not your fault – Burbank was hiding out, justice caught up with him. Shut it all out, Mac. Avoid the media. I'm going to ignore it for my own sanity, and you should do the same.'

62

MAC

As I drove the winding road from the lookout, I thought about what Erika had said, my biceps stinging from the pressure of her fingers. She was highly strung – and it was little wonder – but above all, she was looking out for me. Could I shut myself in a bubble and pretend I had nothing to do with what happened at Barren Cape? Or was Kingy right – would we be found out eventually?

I took a hairpin turn, wishing Erika had picked a safer spot to meet. I'd never been comfortable driving hills, and in the state I was in, it was downright hazardous. I focused on the curves, on staying within my tight lane, and when I reached the flat suburbs, I pulled over. My hands were shaking, I rubbed sweaty palms on my thighs.

Only two nights to go.

Back at Sandy's, I found my suitcase and swabbed away the dust.

She watched from the doorway. 'You all right? You look awful.'

'I'm fine,' I said.

'You don't want to be sick when you're travelling.'

'I said, *I'm fine!*'

'I don't know why I even try.' She walked away.

I combed through my winter gear, selecting jeans and jumpers. All the while, Sandy's old phone lay on the mattress, screaming at me to check the latest news. I resisted.

When the phone lit up, I flinched. What was I expecting, a call from the police?

It was a text from Erika. She'd sent three beautiful pictures of London's skyline.

Her message said: *Concentrate on this. You have so much to look forward to x*

She was right. I had to put the past nightmarish months behind me. Being homeless, being harassed by Anton. Finding a dead man. I wasn't responsible for any of it – why should I continue to suffer?

Sandy re-entered the room, carrying a mug. 'Here, thought you might need a cuppa.'

'Thank you.' I smiled tentatively.

'We haven't discussed what's happening with your car.'

'Can you sell it for me? You're a sales expert, after all. I trust you completely.'

'Pfft. *Now* you appreciate my sales nous.'

We shared a quiet laugh.

'Yes, I suppose I can list it online for you.' She blew on her hot drink. 'Would you like me to drive you to the airport?'

Normally I'd refuse, but it seemed important to let her in. 'That would be great. Thank you.'

'What time's the flight?'

'Eight pm. I need to be there a bit earlier.'

She sat beside me on the bed. I was surprised, both at her closeness, and the comfort it gave. Like me, Sandy wore no rings on her fingers – she said it interfered with her typing. Unlike me, her nails were always colourfully painted. Today, it was alternating shades of fuchsia and mango.

'Found everything you need?' she said.

'Yeah, so far.'

'I reckon you should wait until you're in London to buy a winter coat. They have better quality ones over there – our Aussie coats are pathetic, really.'

'Ha, you're probably right.'

'Don't pack anything sharp in your carry-on luggage.'

'I know, I know . . .' I sipped the tea and braced for more pesky advice.

'I haven't been to England, though I always thought I would,' Sandy said. 'The years fly by and before you know it, it's too late.'

'But it's not too late.'

'I'm too old and cranky for long haul flights.'

'You might enjoy it. You could read, watch movies on your iPad, do your puzzles. You have to visit me and Georgia. We'll do some touristy things together, like the flea markets. I bet you'd love that. Or how about Stonehenge?'

'I'm keen on one of those *Outlander* tours of Scotland.'

I laughed. 'Sure.'

'Oh – pack a hat and sunglasses, too. You might think they're unnecessary, Mackenzie, but they do have sunshine over there.'

'Good idea. Thanks for looking out for me.'

'Thanks for letting me. You don't, normally.' Sandy grinned, deepening all of her wrinkles, and rather than making her look older, it made her look younger.

'I don't?'

'You're very independent, you've never appreciated me offering to help. You've always seen it as me telling you what to do.'

'Really?' I frowned. Recalled all the moments when Sandy had left me to my own devices, the sports matches and the class excursions where she was the absent parent. I'd blamed it on her being busy or disinterested. Now, other memories were returning. Me, shoving school invitations in my locker rather than bringing them home. Me, asking other parents for a ride because I was keen to be in the car with my friends.

'It's fine, I'm used to it,' she said. 'And all that self-reliance will stand you in good stead when you're in the UK. You're going to thrive over there, I know it.'

'Thank you.' I buried my face in the mug, the steam creating a wetness in my eyes.

63

ERIKA

My stomach wouldn't stop roiling; whether from anxiety or hunger – or both – I couldn't tell. When the rest of the house had gone to bed, I went to the kitchen. Mum had left a dinner bowl in the fridge for me. I picked at the stir-fry, and couldn't taste a thing. Mum cared about me, everyone in the house cared and loved me, but that could change if they learned what I'd done.

I desperately wanted Mac to go to London and put this behind her. It would be the best outcome. Her leaving would draw a line under everything that had happened, and yet part of me wanted her to stay. So much revolved around her; if anyone could understand me now, it was her. Still, with distance, it'd be easier to keep her safe.

I went to my room, the door clicking softly behind me. Lay on my side on the bed, staring at nothing. Thinking about my final hours at Barren Cape.

The girl – it must've been Brex – she almost caught me. As we ran, I swear I felt fingertips brush my arm. Then I was teetering on the rim of the swimming pool, every sense electrified.

I sidestepped. She sailed past.

She was there. She was gone.

I remembered being unable to move. The ocean roared in the background, dry palm fronds clacked together. I licked my lips and edged forward. The pool gradually revealed itself: a dim, empty basin. Only it wasn't completely empty.

The top of Brex's head appeared first. She was facedown and completely motionless.

'Hey', I said.

She didn't stir.

'Can you hear me?'

Nothing.

I lowered myself in. Below ground level like this, I had a sense of being in a gladiators' arena. I'd vanquished my opponent, but hadn't expected this.

'You better not be pretending.' I toed one of her shoes with mine.

She was immobile as a sack of sand.

'Fuck, fuck, fuck.' I knelt by her, hands hovering, too terrified to touch.

She was shorter than me, hair falling messily over her face. She wore pastel shorts and sweater, the latest Nikes on her feet; the outfit of a sweet, happy tween. I couldn't see any signs of breathing. What had I done?

I got to my feet. 'Anyone there?'

An ambulance, I should call an ambulance and let them take over. I needed a phone for that.

I whimpered as I put a hand in her pocket, squeamish about touching her. I found my phone, the selfie of me and Mac shining back. My thumb hovered over the keypad. What exactly was I going to say? A dead girl lay at my feet.

I fought to keep a level head.

Brex had fallen because she was chasing me. She meant to hurt me. Her family would want answers; everyone would want answers. Was this manslaughter?

What did I know for sure?

Brex and her friends had kept Mac tied up.

Theo and the boys didn't intend to return to the resort ever again.

The security presence was practically non-existent.

There were no witnesses – even her friends had run.

My next steps would determine the rest of my life. And they'd impact others.

Mac! She was waiting for me. She was my priority.

I struggled from the pool, wiping my hands on my clothes. If there really was such a thing as hyperfocus, I slid into that state, thinking only of my friend cable tied underground. There was no time to run for help; I had no idea if Brex's mates were nearby and if they'd return for her. It was dangerous to leave Mac alone any longer.

I rushed back inside the building, rifling through Mac's gear under the stairs, until I found scissors. When I freed her, I was barely coherent, barely able to function. She put that down to our mutual traumatic experience.

So many lies.

Mac had told me about the dead man but when it came to Brex lying in the pool, I held back. The news could be too much for her. She'd been worried about the schoolgirl, seemed invested in her, and I wasn't sure of her reaction. Would she be horrified and want to go check on her? So I said nothing. Told myself I was protecting Mac, but in reality I was more selfish than that. I was protecting myself. I didn't initiate any of this.

Once I decided to keep it secret from Mac, everything else followed.

After leaving Mac at the layby, I sped back to Barren Cape, hoping she wouldn't be behind me, hoping she wouldn't wonder about my taillights going in the wrong direction. I parked close to the fence. Opened the boot and removed my sleeping bag. Tucked it under one arm and jogged, watching where I placed my shoes, steeped in tunnel vision.

My plan was to wrap Brex in the sleeping bag, then drag her from the pool and to my car. I'd drive a few kilometres away, find an area of isolated bushland and hide her before sunrise. The dead man on the roof? Well, that was none of my business.

But my plan fell to pieces.

Because when I returned to the pool, it was empty.

64

ERIKA

My legs wouldn't hold me up, I sank to the pool's edge and gaped into the grey void.

Was I going mad?

Brex had definitely fallen. I'd seen her, touched her – she was lifeless.

But there was no girl now.

I switched on my phone light and panned it around. Only a vacant concrete crater, with scattered dry leaves and twigs. I slipped in and began searching, taking only seconds to find blood. A few scarlet droplets; not a lot, but enough to tell me I hadn't been dreaming. A bit further on, a slick of vomit. Ugh. She'd been here, she was injured but she had survived. She must've woken up and left. I wept in relief, which turned into a cackle. What a fuck up, what a mess. I'd come here to remove her, drive away, get rid of the evidence. But of course that wasn't going to happen. I wasn't that person. Transporting a corpse wasn't fated for me!

Sore and losing steam, I hauled myself out. I craved the warmth and safety of my bedroom.

Waves murmured on the shore. The steel gates rattled.

Brex was alive.

So, where was she now?

I spun, skin prickling. She could be watching, madder than ever, waiting to attack. I'd been completely oblivious and unsuspecting. There'd been no need for me to come back at all, and I'd put myself in danger once more.

Then again, maybe she'd crawled from the pool and was lying somewhere wounded. How scary it must have been, to wake on the concrete, all alone in the dark. I should help her, I should finally call an ambulance. It wasn't too late after all.

'Are you there?' My voice was tentative. 'I'm not going to hurt you.'

The pool was between me and the buildings. Behind me, the fence and esplanade. I took a few steps, but wasn't sure which direction to choose.

'I'm here to help you,' I said. 'I mean it. I'll drive you to the hospital, or take you home, whatever you need.'

Then the air was pierced by a scream.

It was coming from the beach.

'Brex! Is that you?'

I ran. I followed the fence until I found AJ's opening. The sleeping bag fell; I ignored it. My feet thudded along the esplanade.

'Brex, where are you?'

What happened to her? After crashing into the pool, she'd be confused, concussed. She shouldn't be moving, I never should've left her, should've checked her properly, shaken her awake. I could have told Mac everything, and together we would have retrieved the girl and taken her to hospital. Despite everything she'd done, it would've been the right thing to do, and I was sure Mac would agree.

Much of the sand had been swallowed, the waves surging at full volume. What if the tide was dragging Brex out? I leapt onto the shore, shouting for her. The ocean lashed my legs and my clothes were quickly sodden.

Another scream, far behind me, near the cave.

It was abruptly cut off.

I ran to the rocks and scrambled over, hands steadying me on the uneven surface. Seawater streamed through the crevices, the breeze chilled my wet skin. The esplanade lights didn't reach this far, and I burrowed forward almost blindly.

Sounds. Voices. Fighting.

'Hey!' I yelled.

Two shadows appeared, struggling at the mouth of the cave. One tall, one short.

'Help me!' It was Brex, hair falling into her stricken eyes.

A man had hold of both of her arms.

'Stop!' I picked up a stone and threw it, as if it could stop a schoolyard fight. It rattled at their feet.

The man glanced at me. 'Fuck off!'

Brex's shorts were around her knees.

'Get away from her!' I shrieked.

She squirmed out of his hands. He leaned forward to grab her again, but she'd twisted out of reach. I threw another rock, sending it bouncing off his leg.

'I told you, fuck off!' he roared.

'You're hurting her, I'm calling the cops!' I felt for my phone.

'She's my kid, I'm bringing her home.'

'Bullshit. I saw you what you were trying to do, you fucking sicko.'

The man lumbered towards me. Brex hitched up her shorts and crawled over the rocks, wasting no time in creating distance.

'Stay back.' I unlocked my phone but the man was too close. I turned, moving as fast as I could without slipping. Not fast enough. He had me by the arm, was yanking hard. 'Ow! Brex!'

But the girl had disappeared. I'd rescued her and in turn, she deserted me.

'Give me the phone,' the man snapped. He was muscular, wore a dark tank top and jeans.

I pulled my arm but he wouldn't let go. 'No!'

He slapped me. 'I could drown you right now.'

My cheek was scalded and my eyes overflowed. But he'd dropped his hold.

I bolted over the rocks. My foot slipped, my knee striking the ledge. I cried out in pain. His fingers found my ankle, then his hands were all over me, clawing me towards him. I fought to grip the slimy boulders but was losing. I palmed a rock, heavier than a brick and jagged and hard. Twisted and swung my arm, putting all my force into it.

It slammed into his temple.

'Shit!' He wheeled away, crouching with a hand to his scalp. 'I'm gonna fucking kill you.'

Swollen with adrenalin and rage, I lashed out with both feet, connecting with his knees.

He tipped sideways onto the stone.

CRACK!

The rock fell from my hand.

The man was still, limbs spread like a starfish, head tilted towards the ocean.

'Hey,' I said. My body was shuddering so fiercely, I hugged the slab beneath me. Water lapped at my sodden shoes and licked the cuffs of his jeans.

Shakily, I got to my feet.

'Brex! Where are you?' I struggled past the cave and into the grass. 'You're okay now.'

I shone my phone light into the bush. She was gone. If I were her, I wouldn't have hung around either. First, I'd left her for dead in the pool. Then when she dragged herself out and was trying to get home, this psycho tried to rape her.

'Oh god.' I plonked onto the ground, head in my hands. My body was full-on shivering now, from the cold and from the terror. My nose was dripping. My face still stung from the slap.

What should I do what should I do what should I do?

A bird called out.

How long had I been sitting? I glanced around. The resort was well out of sight. Mac had said the sun rose behind the buildings.

I struggled to my feet and returned to the edge of the rocks. The sky was lighter and the man was lying where I'd left him. A bird soared over the water, its black outline gliding and wheeling. It was large-beaked, maybe a pelican. I tiptoed towards the sand, giving the man a wide berth, and fetched the sleeping bag from the footpath. I'd returned to Barren Cape to hide a body, and I'd come prepared. My face broke with bitter tears; relief, mania.

I focused on the smaller details. The lifting of the limbs, the tucking of the nylon. Body wrapped, I dragged it up the slippery slope as the sky grew lighter. *Slither, thud, slither, thud.* It was heavy, but I put my back into it, working my way closer to bushland bit by bit. I took a moment to rest at the cave's entrance.

Just a few days ago, Theo had been singing here. Goofy, happy.

I reached the end of the inlet. What had Theo said, that first time we swam together? Carnaby was next door, or was it Mistle Beach?

I began working on the grave, recalling a pet rock I'd made in primary school. I'd painted it yellow and drawn long lashes above the eyes. Took it home and talked to it like an imaginary friend. I wondered where it was now. Rocks took millions of years to break down.

An hour later, when I parked outside my parents' house, the sun was peeking through the wattles and banksia. The street didn't stir. There was grime on my hands, wet sand under my nails. The bruise on my knee was the size and colour of my bloodstone.

My car door creaked as I opened it. If I moved fast, I could slip into the bathroom before my family woke.

65

BREX

The air conditioner in the wall whirred loudly as I lay watching TV from the sofa. Flynn had slipped a cushion under my head. The swelling had gone down, thanks to the ice packs he'd made. Since that night at the beach, I had a headache the size of a football, but I'd survive.

I'd woken up on dirty cement, aching all over, confused by the grey walls surrounding me and the stars overhead. That's when I realised I'd fallen into the crater. My head spun when I pulled myself into a sitting position. I leaned to one side and puked like I'd just come off a roller coaster. Then the real agony began. My head felt like it'd been hit by a hammer. I cried aloud, didn't care about hiding, chasing or hunting anymore. I fucking hurt and I wanted someone to come help me. Now.

'Flynn? Cindi?'

I'd swayed to the nearest wall and dragged myself up. A trickle escaped my nose; I brushed it with my hand. Sticky blood. There was more on my chin. Goosebumps covered my bare legs and I shivered like an old woman. I didn't know how long I was unconscious or where Star's friend had gone. What sort of a low-life leaves a kid unconscious at the bottom of a hole?

I had to hurry; she could've called the cops for real. They'd find Burbank dead on the roof. Plus, she might've freed Star, who would come gunning for me.

'Guys! Where are you?'

Flynn and Cindi had gone. I couldn't believe they'd left me and I had to get home all by myself in the middle of the night.

'Fuckers!'

I shuffled towards the beach and when I reached the fence, I leaned on it to ease me along. The street light of the public toilet grew closer, then I was at the loose panel. Somebody had left it open, thank god, because I didn't have the strength to shift it. Probably Flynn and Cindi. I would've preferred if they hadn't abandoned me, but there was no point crying about it.

When I moved through the gap, a bit of wire snagged my top. I ripped away, growing madder by the second. What a shitshow. I didn't care if I never saw this beach again. My idea to burn down the buildings had been a great one; I would've done it there and then, if I wasn't so shattered.

I took my usual path to The Cave. I'd rest inside until morning, then decide what to do next with my fucked-up life.

Shithead was standing at the entrance.

'I knew you'd be here.'

My heart bashed at my chest. I couldn't form words. Seeing him was like seeing an alien: it didn't make sense. His bald head gleamed in the moonlight.

'It was me who told you about this place,' he said. 'You probably don't remember.' He grinned.

I stayed numb.

'I worked on that building site,' he said. 'Used to sit on these same rocks at smoko and admire the view. I had a cushy job, and then the project collapsed. Useless bastards, couldn't organise a piss-up in a brewery. I had to go to Melbourne to find work. But I missed your Mum. And I missed you, of course.'

'Wha—'

He pointed at The Cave. 'When I got back to town, I came here for drinks with my mates. Saw your little graffiti on the wall. They're your initials – and your toy boy Flynn, right?'

The aching in my head throbbed harder.

'Your mum's worried about you. Actually, she's fuming. She's gonna knock your block off, you've been so cheeky lately. I offered to find you and bring you home. Because I'm a good boyfriend.'

More blood trickled from my nose.

He stepped closer and grabbed my chin. 'What happened to you?'

'Nothing.' I tried to turn away, but he wouldn't loosen his hold. He reeked of beer.

'Did Loverboy hit you?'

'No!'

'Never mind. You're still pretty.'

He stroked my face. It was disgusting, and I whacked his hand away. His expression changed. He locked me between his arms and I felt my feet lift from the ground.

'Noo!' I found my lungs at last, letting out a long scream.

Grunting, he forced me towards The Cave's interior. I struggled and kicked and kept yelling. He spun me around, my spine tucked into him. Yanked my shorts from my waist.

'No!' I fought, threw my head backwards.

'Hey!'

The shout broke through my terror. I looked towards the water. It was Star's friend. She was still here.

'Help me!' I pleaded.

She shouted at Shithead, he shouted back. I kept squirming.

'I'm calling the cops!' She threw a rock.

Shithead's arms dropped and I was free. I pulled my shorts up and stumbled away. Fled past The Cave and into the scrub, pushing forward, not even feeling the branches shredding me. The other two were still arguing. The dumb bitch should be running, like me.

I found a track. Barely knew which direction to go, only that I should sprint.

The shouting faded. The dirt was soft under my feet and I stumbled a few times. Kept looking over my shoulder. Pulled my shorts higher, gripping them at my waist. Fuck! Shithead. I was right to feel icky about him, of course I was. And if that chick hadn't turned up . . .

My face was a mess of blood and tears. I coughed and wheezed and cried. It was ages before I reached the proper road. There was no traffic and I walked the centre line, head pounding, skin stinging from all the branch cuts. Everything was heavy. I spat blood onto the ground, a nasty taste in my mouth. I didn't know where I was headed, only that I had to put distance between me and Shithead.

'Brex!'

Flynn was running towards me. Behind him, Cindi climbed out of the scrub.

I started crying again. Flynn held me upright when he reached me because I'd collapsed like I was boneless. 'You waited,' I said.

'Of course we did.'

Cindi put her arm around me. 'We've been watching for the cop cars, but they haven't shown yet.'

'She didn't phone the cops, she was lying.'

'You're bleeding . . .'

'Shithead was there.'

'What? Where?'

'At The Cave. He came looking for me.'

Flynn stared. 'What happened?'

Tears were streaming. I pushed my mates away, grabbed a tree branch and bent it, wanting to break things, but Flynn stepped in my way.

'You're okay now.'

'Tell us what happened,' Cindi said.

I wiped my face. 'He tried it on, but that chick interrupted. Star's friend.'

'The one we were chasing? *She's still there?* We thought they left ages ago.'

'Yeah, well, she was screaming at him when I left . . .'

'What about Star, is she still in the basement?'

'I don't know.'

Flynn pulled up a corner of his T-shirt and used it to dab my nose. 'Let's get out of here.'

'Where to?' I said. 'I lost the credit card, I lost everything.'

'We'll go to my place. You can stay as long as you want, I don't care what my parents say.'

My lids closed. 'I don't think I can walk any further.'

'Here.' Flynn bent his back. 'I'll piggyback you.'

Cindi helped me up as I flopped across Flynn, my face in his shoulder. We had a long walk ahead.

***

'How much spaghetti do you want?' Flynn called out.

'Heaps!' I said.

I picked up the TV remote and flicked between channels. Burbank's body had been found, it was all over the news, but so far nobody had mentioned a woman tied up in a basement room, nor any high school kids.

Knock, knock.

Flynn and I stared at each other. He put a finger to his mouth – *ssh* – and crept to the window to check. 'It's your mum.'

'Fuck's sake.'

I opened the main door, but stayed behind the screen.

Mum was wearing shorts and a denim shirt, her hands on her hips. 'Come on, get in the car.'

'No.' I could see my brothers squirming in the back seat. The engine was running, the air conditioner chugging.

'Excuse me?'

'I'm not coming.'

She blew out an angry breath. 'Have you seen Michael? He went looking for you the other night, he was worried.'

I snorted. 'Worried? Right.'

'I haven't seen him since then.'

'Hopefully we never see him again.'

The car horn blasted.

'Stop that!' Mum shrieked. My brothers laughed as they scrambled to their seats.

She turned back to me. 'I'm not mucking around, get in the car now, or don't bother coming home.'

I closed the door on her.

She pounded on the screen again. 'Brex! You can't stay here forever.'

I waited until she'd stormed off. Sat on the sofa again, picking at the scratches on my arm. It was true, I couldn't stay here forever. Flynn's parents were complaining again, and whenever they were home, I stuck to his bedroom. That couldn't go on.

He walked from the kitchen with our dinner bowls. 'Budge over.' He sat beside me, our thighs resting together. 'Where do you reckon he is?'

'Shithead? Dunno, but he could rock up any time, and I'm not going home while he's around.' I had a flashback to The Cave. Him tugging my shorts. His beery breath. My heart started beating fast again and I squeezed my eyes shut.

Flynn nudged me. 'Okay?'

I nodded.

'We can leave Adelaide this weekend,' he said. 'My brother's back on Saturday and we'll take his car.'

'He won't let you.'

'I won't ask.'

I began eating. 'Cindi too?'

Cindi was grounded, we hadn't seen her for a while.

'She won't want to leave,' Flynn said. 'Doesn't matter, as long as she keeps her mouth shut.'

'She will.' I stirred the pasta. 'Where would we go, what would we do for money?'

'Like I said, let's try Melbourne. There's heaps of jobs there. I could apply at another supermarket.'

'And where would we sleep at night?'

He shrugged. 'We'll figure it out when we get there. I just don't want to be here anymore.'

'Me neither.'

'All right, it's a deal.'

We looked at each other and smiled.

66

MAC

Sandy drove me to the airport, holding the steering wheel in that strange little way of hers – hands looping the lower half, fingertips curled towards her waist. She spoke most of the way, slipping into her usual jibes, but I realised it was nerves, not nagging.

'Don't get in the way of Georgia and her housemates,' she said. 'It's very nice of them to accommodate you.'

'I'm not a puppy, I'm not gonna poo on the rug.' I laughed.

'Mackenzie, that's gross! Now, when you arrive, make sure to buy a thank you present. Actually, you could grab a bottle of South Aussie wine at the airport.'

I stared out of the window at the dark streets and began silently saying goodbye to things. Goodbye, Clover's café. Goodbye, gym. Goodbye, Anton the stalker. Goodbye, real estate listings.

Goodbye – and fuck you – Brex.

As we neared the terminal, I asked to be left at the drop-off zone.

Sandy looked at me. 'You don't want me to come in and wait with you?'

'There's no need and anyway, parking's so expensive.'

'All right, if you're sure.'

We stopped at the kerb and Sandy supervised as I retrieved my bags from the boot. Other vehicles crawled past, a plane engine roared. The terminal shone brightly, crowds surging behind the vast windows.

'Come here.' Sandy held me, her chin digging into my shoulder. She held me for longer than usual, and I leaned into her more than usual. Waited until she let go first.

Blinking fast, she dashed to the driver door. 'Message me as soon as you get there!'

'I will. Bye.'

Inside the terminal, I checked in my luggage and passed through security. It was ages until boarding. I strolled past stores selling expensive perfume and watches, killing time and stretching my legs before the long flight. My phone vibrated – Dad was calling.

I walked to a quiet corner while we chatted. 'Say g'day to Big Ben for me,' he said. 'Send lots of photos.'

After our goodbye, I remembered Sandy's gift suggestion, and scanned the bottles of Barossa shiraz and cab merlot. A cheery voice interrupted my browsing.

'Found ya.'

'Erika!'

She wore baggy jeans and the Afends T-shirt I bought for her birthday. 'I couldn't let you leave without saying goodbye,' she said.

'Aw, thank you.'

We beamed like we hadn't seen each other in years. Still, she looked tired. Perhaps it was the unusual lack of makeup. 'Are you okay?'

'Absolutely,' she said. 'How about you – excited?'

'I still can't believe it's happening.'

We ambled past storefronts, then perched on a padded bench. I wanted to unpack what had happened at Barren Cape but couldn't find the words. It had started out as a private, illicit adventure. My unfinished room, the sea view; it was all so innocent. I never would've dug under the fence if I'd had an inkling about Brex or Curtis Burbank.

'I've been avoiding the news . . .' I said. 'Have there been any updates, any arrests?'

'No.'

'Is that normal? Surely the police have made progress by now.'

'They think it's related to organised crime, because of Burbank. He was in a gang before he went to jail. I don't know if they'll ever work it out.'

'So there's no traces of us? Or the kids?'

'I don't think so.' Erika was staring at a gigantic winery photo on the opposite wall, one leg jiggling. 'I should've been a better friend. I'm sorry for what happened.'

'God, it's not your fault.'

'It is! I started it, I brought Theo to Barren Cape. Everything went to crap after that.'

'You *rescued me*. Nobody knew where I was and nobody cared. You were amazing. You searched the resort all alone even though you were terrified. You're my hero.'

A pair of young women sat opposite us, both wearing headphones, travel pillows coiled around their necks. I wondered where they lived; did they have their own place or were they still at home with their parents?

'You know, it's not too late to talk to the police,' I said. 'I can change my flight, stay here for a while longer, we can go to the station together—'

'Mac, no!'

'Or we could call Crime Stoppers and drop Brex's name? She must be responsible for his death – her and her friends. There's no other explanation. We can call right now on one of the airport phones.'

Erika turned to me, our knees touching. 'Stop. We've been through all this. We're not saying a word, hear me?'

Travellers passed by in all directions, rolling suitcases, pausing to read the departure boards. The world moved on. I would, too. 'Fine,' I said.

An airport announcement blared. Although it wasn't for my flight, we took that as our mutual cue. 'I should go to the international terminal now.'

'I'll walk with you.'

We crossed the shining tiles without speaking, focused on navigating the crowds, and stopped at the escalators.

'I'll leave you here, then.' Erika took my hands. She looked serious. I hoped she wasn't about to cry. 'I'm gonna miss you.'

'Same,' I said.

'Promise me you'll enjoy yourself. Promise me you won't chuck it in after a couple of weeks. Stay in London, stay in Europe, make the most of things, no matter what.'

I nodded. 'Okay, sure. I'll try.'

We hugged. Her hair smelled freshly washed, squeaky clean. Then I stepped onto the escalator and was ferried away from her.

I joined the security queue and kept my gaze forward. Stared into the passport face scanner, glad I didn't have to look into a real person's eyes. I couldn't handle a stranger's inquiring stare; might crumble under the scrutiny, unable to keep a lid on my emotions.

In the international lounge, I stood facing the enormous windows even though they only reflected the bustling airport behind me. I stayed flexing my feet and pacing until boarding was announced. The moon shone behind a wisp of cloud as we trickled down the gangway and into the belly of the plane. I exchanged a brief smile with the aisle passenger who moved aside so I could reach my window seat.

In the air, I gazed down on the glittering city. The long, orange-lit laneways of the major roads, an occasional glowing sports oval or shopping centre. Vehicles trawled slowly. Then the lights were gone, replaced by tranches of opaque land and sea. We banked right and I leaned into the view. Even though it didn't make sense to our route, I fancied I could see the waves of Barren Cape below. Rolling, thrashing, icy in the night, and nobody to hear them. Nobody to greet them in the pink morning.

67

ERIKA

I hurried across the airport forecourt, past the water feature and sculptures, chin tucked, trying to hide my tears. Took the carpark stairs to the third floor rather than sharing an elevator with strangers. Locking myself in, I gripped the steering wheel like it was tethering me to sanity. Travellers passed by my rear window with their wheeled luggage. A child sang out, car boots slammed.

That was it, Mac was gone. I'd successfully convinced her not to contact the police, and she was on her way to a new life. Shielding her was the final piece of my apology for ruining the resort.

I started the engine and drove. Cruised through a roundabout without giving way and didn't flinch when an irritated car horn blasted. Left, right, along wide avenues, and into Port Adelaide. I parked and walked past bustling restaurants until I reached the calm wharf. Sat alone on a bench alongside the red lighthouse for more than an hour, watching the reflection of the Birkenhead

Bridge lights on the river. Groups of chatting diners ambled behind me.

I opened the flight tracker app and typed in Mac's flight number.

She was in the air, en route to Doha, a 13-hour non-stop flight. I zoomed in, watching the minuscule yellow aircraft as it jerked across the screen, moving like a wounded bee. Soon, Mac would be thousands of kilometres away.

If she knew what had really happened at Barren Cape, she would've never boarded that flight. She would've insisted on staying and supporting me.

I thought about the man in his rocky grave. Had thought about him most of my waking hours. He was going to rape that girl, it was clear. Then he'd attacked me. He wasn't a good person, he had a black heart. But his family could be wondering where he was. They hadn't done anything wrong, they didn't deserve to live in limbo. And I didn't deserve to carry his weight with me forever.

I shut the flight tracker app and walked past the rowdy restaurants again.

Turned a corner and climbed the wide steps of the police station.

AUTHOR NOTE AND ACKNOWLEDGEMENTS

I began writing this book when I was on holiday at a rented beach house during the tail end of Covid-19. I thought: *if the world collapsed, this would be a perfect place to bunker down.* Back then, the story had a very dystopian flavour and I eventually reworked it into modern thriller. Some would say, however, that Australia's current housing and rental crisis is indeed dystopian.

I grew up in a South Australian Housing Trust maisonette. These were government-built dwellings of two connected brick homes which were a mirror image of each other. At its height, the Trust (now Housing SA) had an estimated stock of 60,000 houses. I always considered government housing to be a reliable safety net; sadly, that's no longer the case.

Today, although the population has significantly increased, the estimated number of Housing SA homes is around 33,000. Although I've never been homeless, my childhood contained many nights of displacement, and the challenges faced by Brex and Mac are quite real to me. If you're concerned about the housing issues explored in *Barren Cape*, you may want to support the work of Mission Australia. Please see www.missionaustralia.com.au

Now, I have important thanks to share.

Thank you to my agent Melanie Ostell; once again I'm so grateful to have you in my corner. Thank you to Ben Ball and Dan Ruffino at Simon & Schuster Australia for believing in my second book; and thank you especially to Cass Di Bello and Rosie Outred – *Barren Cape* has benefited immensely from the incredible amount of thoughtful feedback you provided. It was a pleasure (and a reassurance) to work with Kylie Mason again too.

Thank you to my fellow authors who took the time to read and endorse this novel, I truly appreciate it. Thank you to the hard-working and talented booksellers, librarians, Bookstagrammers and book reviewers for continuing to champion Australian fiction. Writers don't take any of it for granted.

Finally, thank you to the A Team: David, Sam, Able, Kalyn and Janny. Life's good, thanks to you.

BOOKCLUB QUESTIONS

1. *Barren Cape* is written from three perspectives: Mac, Erika and Brex. All three do a lot of growing up over a short space of time, but who do you think learns the most?

2. Michelle Prak creates a terrifying scenario out of Australia's housing crisis. Did it change your mind about homelessness? How would you define homelessness before and after reading?

3. What other social issues and themes does the book explore?

4. What would you have done in Mac's situation? Who would you turn to for help?

5. How did you feel when Erika brought Theo to the resort?

6. What are your thoughts on the relationship between Mac and her mother, Sandy?

7. How does the setting of Barren Cape and the abandoned resort impact the novel?

8. What do you think will happen to Brex?

9. Do you think Mac will find stability in London? How long do you imagine she'll stay there?

10. Who do you think are the real villains of the story and why?

ABOUT THE AUTHOR

Michelle Prak is a professional communicator with a thirty-year career in PR, social media, politics and journalism. Her short stories have been shortlisted in several competitions, and she was runner-up in the Furphy Literary Award 2021. Her debut thriller *The Rush* was published in 2023. She lives in Adelaide and teaches communication subjects at the University of South Australia.

Enjoyed *Barren Cape*?

Discover *The Rush* – another gripping read by Michelle Prak. Chilling, tense and twisted, this compulsive thriller will send adrenaline coursing through your veins . . .

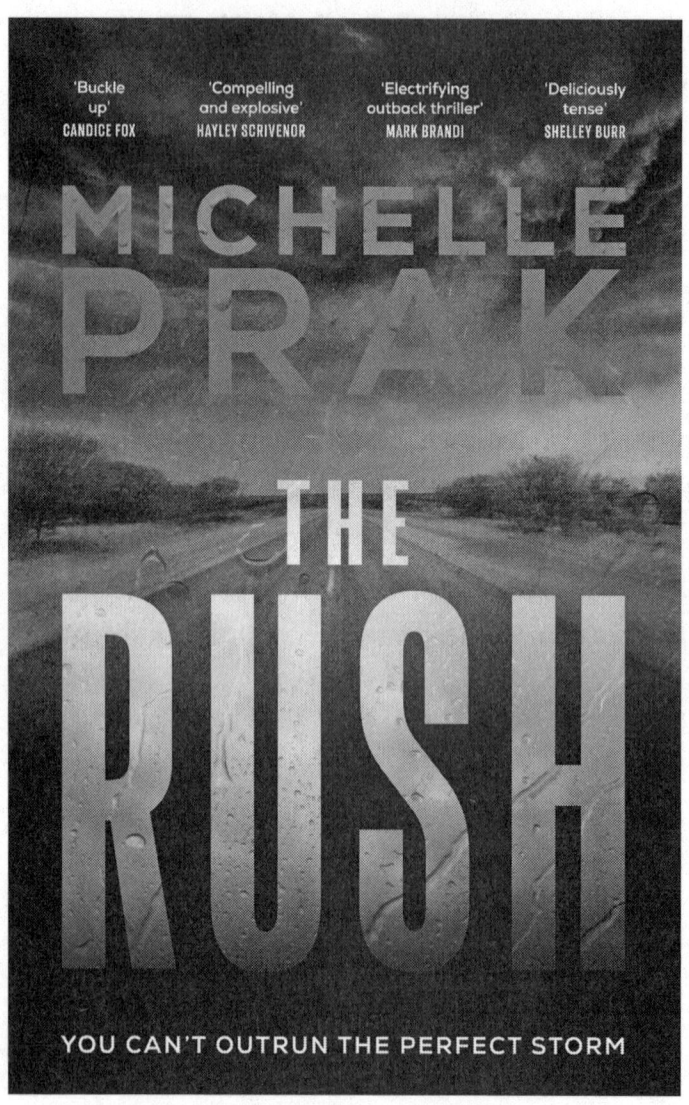

Available in paperback, audio and ebook